Wicked Brute
The Wicked Trilogy
Book 1

M. James

PNK Publishing

Natalia

I never really thought I'd look good as a brunette.

The cheaply dyed sheen of it in the mirror does nothing to convince me. It's no artfully layered and balayage salon job, that's for sure. I manage well enough with my own two hands and a box from the store that it doesn't look *entirely* flat and fake. Still, it's a far cry from my days as a natural version of what I hear they're calling *expensive blonde* these days.

Of course, dyed hair—even the cheaply done kind—isn't strange in this place. Which is part of why I'm here. It's easier to blend in.

Even if a few months ago, I'd never have been caught dead in a place like this.

"Athena! I didn't know you were dancing tonight!"

Ruby's sharp, crowing voice—not her real name—reaches me from all the way on the other side of the room as she bursts in, dressed in shorts so short that they'd almost count as stage lingerie and a crop top that barely covers her breasts. She's curvier than I am, and the clothes cling to her like a second skin, accentuating every swell and curve of her bust and hip. Combined with a narrow waist, huge blue eyes, and dyed red hair, she drives all the men who come to the club absolutely wild.

We all have our strengths. Mine is being an actual, *trained* dancer, once upon a time. In a place that prioritizes lewd gyrating over real skill, I bring something to the table that the customers here rarely see.

They're not exactly the types to hold season tickets to the Moscow ballet.

"I picked up a shift." I lean forward, brushing eyeshadow over one closed lid. My look is always the same, and I don't deviate from it. The most important part is that it looks nothing like what I used to do with my makeup. Before, I was a devotee of a bare lid, a clean face, a sharp wing, and a red lip. Now, I've learned the art of a smoky eye, thick liner, and faux lashes to make my blue eyes look wider than normal and how to apply contour and blush to accentuate my sharp cheekbones and delicate features.

The red lip, though, stayed. I've learned that men—the type of men who frequent this club especially—like brightly colored lipstick on the dancers. It encourages them to spend more, to take us back to the inaptly named champagne room, where they can more intimately imagine us leaving traces of that same lipstick on their cocks.

It's not something I'd ever entertain the idea of, but plenty of the girls do, and I can't fault them for it. Tips aren't the best in a place like this, and a girl's got to get by.

"You need to take a day off." Ruby plops into the chair next to mine, unzipping her clear makeup pouch as she pulls it out of the huge tote bag that she always carries with her. There are more things in there than I'd ever dared guess at—I've seen her pull all sorts of items out over the span of time I've worked here. Lingerie, tampons, makeup, a curling iron, a dildo, a lunchbox full of snacks, water bottles of vodka—I'm pretty sure it's less a purse and more a bag of wish fulfillment, as if Ruby is some kind of particularly benevolent genie. "I don't think there's been a night that you haven't been here in *weeks*."

I shrug, peering in the mirror as I carefully apply lash glue just above my actual lashes. I hate wearing falsies–they feel thick and heavy and as if I have a creature glued to my eyes–but they're a must. I made it precisely one shift at the club before Ruby whipped out a spare set and showed me how to apply them, lecturing me thoroughly on why I could *never* go out on stage without them ever again.

She's been the closest thing I have to a friend ever since.

"Gotta pay rent," I say casually, tapping my nail against the lash as I let it dry. "It's criminal, what they're charging for that shithole I'm living in."

"That's why you need to take me up on my offer and move in to my place." Ruby glares at me playfully. "I have a spare bedroom and everything. We could split the rent and have girls' night every night. It's not the Ritz, but it's a hell of a lot better than where you're at now, from the sound of it.'"

"And you know I'm never going to take you up on it, as much as I appreciate the offer." I grin at her as I glue on my other lash, trying to soften my words. "I like my quiet time."

I can't tell her the truth, of course, which is that I lay awake some nights wishing that I *could* take her up on her offer. As much as I really had enjoyed my personal space and quiet in my old life, I crave company now, to not be alone with my thoughts, especially in the dark. I'd give anything not to live alone.

But I can't. It would put her in too much danger, and Ruby doesn't deserve that. She's been nothing but a good friend to me, even if she is loud and abrasive at times.

Ruby rolls her eyes playfully. "Well, you can at least come over after our shifts next Saturday. I'm throwing a party."

"*After* we get off work?" On Saturday nights, closing the club means staying until two in the morning, even later sometimes if there are enough paying customers still spending. The thought of partying after a long night of dancing at that hour makes me feel exhausted before *this* night has even begun—which makes me feel much, much older than my twenty-five years.

Ruby wrinkles her nose at me. "We'll sleep when we're dead," she declares, getting up and shimmying out of her shorts as she starts to change into her lingerie for the night.

It's just a turn of phrase, but a shiver runs down my spine anyway, an echo of the one I felt earlier tonight as I walked to the club. The neighborhoods that I live and work in aren't really ones that a young woman wants to be on foot in, but I hadn't been lying when I said that I picked up a shift because money is tight. Getting a cab is a luxury I can't afford.

I nearly did tonight, though. The letter I found shoved under my door this morning when I padded out to my tiny, cramped kitchen to brew coffee is buried deep in my garbage can now, under potato peels and coffee grounds, but it doesn't matter. I can still see the words stuck to it, cut out and glued to the standard-issue sheet of printer paper.

It should have been laughable. It was something straight out of an early 2000s serial killer movie. Hardly original—the nondescript paper, the mismatched words from magazines and newspapers, as if the person who wrote it and left it had done so after reading a copy of **Terrifying Young Women for Dummies**. I should have crumpled it up and thrown it away without a thought instead of standing frozen, staring down at it for long, ticking seconds with my blood turning to ice in my veins before I finally shoved it down into my trash can and dumped the old contents of my coffee filter over it.

But it wasn't funny. Not just because of my present situation, but because I've known the kind of men who do these things. I grew up around them.

I can't help feeling that whoever left it *wanted* me to think they were stupid. That they're just some obsessed customer from the club who's watched too many Netflix documentaries and thought it would be funny to scare a stripper into thinking she was being targeted.

They want me to let down my guard and assume it's just some idiot. To not take it seriously.

The alternative, of course, *is* to take it seriously. Which is bad in its own way.

There's no going to the cops. The Russian police are a joke anyway, as terrifying to an ordinary citizen as to an actual criminal. Even if I thought they could or would help me, all I'd be doing is turning myself in. The *politsiya* would love to get their hands on me.

I walked to work anyway. When faced with a stalker or giving up precious rubles… I opted to take my chances.

I distinctly felt as if there were eyes on me the entire way, crawling over me, making me pick up my pace more than normal. Usually, I try to walk slowly, casually, as if I belong here, and no one should think twice about it. Hurrying, rushing, in neighborhoods like these indicates that you're not supposed to be there.

That you're afraid.

I haven't often felt afraid in my life. It's possible, actually, that I've experienced too *little* fear, and that's what landed me in my present situation. But tonight, as with many nights since I came back to Moscow, I felt that stinging chill of fright.

Even now, ensconced in the brightly lit dressing room of the club, I can't shake that feeling of being watched.

Of being *followed*.

You're just being paranoid, I tell myself as I swipe my red lipstick on, picking up Ruby's curling iron to add some wave to my hair. *You've done an excellent job of covering your tracks.*

No one would expect you, the daughter of a once-powerful Bratva leader, a former prima ballerina of ever being within a dozen blocks of this place.

I picked this club for that reason precisely. The *Cat's Meow* is one of the seediest strip clubs on a street of seedy clubs, lit up on the exterior with neon lights and figures of naked women, guarded by bouncers so muscled and huge that they span two of me. Anyone looking for me–the *me* I used to be–wouldn't come here. They'd assume I'd die before ever stepping foot into this place as a bystander, let alone as a dancer.

The same goes for my apartment, a tiny, leaky studio in another rundown neighborhood with broken stairs, broken furniture, broken faucets–and sturdy locks. I rented it precisely because it's the kind of place that would have made me gag before, back when I was accustomed to thousand-thread-count sheets, caviar for breakfast, and designer clothes shipped to my door.

The letter has to have been from some infatuated customer. Who else would know you dance here? Who else would look for you here? It makes more sense that someone followed you home from the club.

The alternative–that someone linked to my father in some way has found me–is far more terrifying. I'd rather deal with an entitled, horny incel from the club any day over the Russian Bratva.

Ruby wiggles her hips next to me, reaching for the curling iron. "Hand it over," she demands playfully. "Besides, you're the first one out tonight anyway."

I wince at that as I stand up, moving away a few steps to trade out my tattered sneakers for heels. It's hard to hide ballerinas' feet in the type of shoes that a dancer here wears, but I try to avoid drawing attention to them all the same. I keep my toenails painted now, at the owner's request, after he was horrified by the lingering bruising on my toes from years of being crammed into pointe shoes. Nothing can change the way they look beyond that, but the polish helps, and I always choose heels with wide straps over the toes.

If Ruby or any of the other dancers have ever noticed, they haven't said anything. There's a code here, it seems, that no one asks *too* many questions. I'm certain I'm not the only one hiding something. Even Ruby, as outwardly verbose as she can be, sometimes has a secretive look in her eyes, as if she's holding something back too.

It's a generalization to say that no one ends up working at a place like this by choice, but it's one I'm willing to stick to.

"What are you wearing tonight—*ooh*, that one! I love that." Ruby flutters her eyelashes to me as I wiggle into the gold lace bra I brought for the stage tonight. Gold or silver lingerie has become something of a staple for me, building on the stage name I'd chosen—Athena. It stands out in a sea of jewel and sweets-themed stripper names, but I don't mind.

For the first time in my life, I'm afraid more often than not. Having a goddess' name with me on stage, especially the goddess of war, feels like the sort of shield I need.

"You're going to kill it." Ruby flashes me a thumbs up as I hear the cues for my stage music start to come up, and I stride towards the door, feeling my heart somersault in my chest.

In all my years as a ballerina, I can't ever recall being nervous. I danced from a young age with a confidence that had catapulted me to the heights of the Moscow ballet, earning me fame and accolades—and a reprieve from the unwanted marriage that would have ensnared me much earlier if I hadn't brought my father so much prestige from my position. I stepped out on stage every time as if I belonged there—because I unequivocally believed that I had.

This stage doesn't particularly feel like one I belong on. Though I've conquered it every time, I always feel nervous when I step out. Tonight is no different.

The club is crowded. I see throngs of men around my stage—three, four, five deep in places, all watching and cat-calling as I stride out, swaying to the music. I feel a momentary flash of fear that I've never had before on stage, a chill down my spine as I remember the letter.

What if whoever pushed that under my door is here tonight? What if he's looking at me right now? Watching me, imagining…

I remind myself that it doesn't matter—as my heel hits the slick, hard surface of the stage. There are more terrifying things out there than men who clip words out of magazines and glue them to paper to scare a woman who won't sleep with them. There are bigger things that go bump in the night. Worse things that can happen than a scary letter.

I know because I've seen them, heard them. My father was one of those terrifying things.

If I can conquer that, I can conquer anything.

I can feel my softly curled dark hair brushing against my shoulders, swinging back and forth, the scrape of the cheap lace of my lingerie against my skin. I let the music wash over me, calling back the old immersion techniques of my days in ballet.

Hear. Touch. Smell. Feel. Become.

I focus on the sound of the music, the slick surface of the pole beneath my hands, the feel of the cool metal against my body, and the rigid texture of the stage. I desperately try *not* to smell my surroundings. I've become mostly numb to the miasma of alcohol, sweat, perfume, and cologne that fills the room, but it's still unpleasant.

I become something else. *Someone* else, someone I've never been.

I give myself over to the alter ego I've created, to Athena, and I dance.

The music fills me, twisting my body, spreading me open, turning me into a thing of lust and desire, created only to please the men surrounding the stage waving bills at me. I forget who I was, who I am, and focus on this.

The thing that might save me, if only because no one who knew me before would ever dream that I would be here, doing this.

That I would have fallen so far.

I spin down the pole, landing in a split on the stage. The crowd approvingly shouts as I push my ass up in the air, legs still spread as I bounce on the hard surface, my back arched deeply as I slide upwards, sinuous and graceful, onto my hands and knees. I grab the pole, throwing one leg out as I spin to my feet, and just as I rise up again, I see him.

A man in the very front row, directly in front of me. I freeze for a split second, startled.

Sandy blond hair falls into a sharp, chiseled masculine face, the faintest of stubble on his strong jaw. He's wearing a black shirt open at the chest with the sleeves rolled up, showing muscled forearms covered in tattoos—including one of an eagle at his wrist.

He's *handsome*. Gorgeously, inordinately so.

So few men who come here are. They're portly, unkempt, balding, unhygienic, or some combination of all of those, more often than not. But this man is none of those things.

He doesn't look like the kind of man who would leave a letter like that under someone's door.

But then again, he doesn't look like he belongs here, either. He looks too clean, too polished, too *expensive*. Like the kind of man whose credit card doesn't have a limit. The type of man who drinks better liquor than even the best served at this place.

The kind of man who would never set foot in a club like this without reason.

His eyes are ice-blue—and they're fixed on me with an intensity that none of the other customers here can claim. It sends another of those cold shivers down my spine, because the way he's looking at me is more than attraction, more than lust, more than desire.

He's looking at me as if he knows me.

As if he's here for me, specifically.

Mikhail

Years ago, Moscow felt like home.

Not anymore.

I glance at the cracked clock on my side table as I run my hand through my hair, looking in the mirror. The bar I'm going to isn't the dingiest of places, so I don't want to look like a slob, but I also don't want to stand out too much. Once upon a time, the stark white-blond of my hair would have made me stand out anywhere, but I've long since given up the color it used to be. At least, since I've been in Moscow to hide instead of the reason I used to come here–to work for one of the most powerful Russian *pakhans* to ever lead a Bratva.

The *Ussuri*, the Bear.

Once my boss, now my enemy. My own personal Baba Yaga, the boogeyman I've run from for a year now, is trying to find the key to returning to his good graces.

To the life I used to live.

I reach for my wallet, opening it to check that my cards and cash are still there. As I open the slim pocket, I see the edge of the picture I carry there, and I hesitate.

You could do with a reminder.

Slowly, I tug the picture out from its hiding place, unfolding its deeply creased edges. I open it up, holding it to the weak light, and feel my heart twist inside my chest.

The woman in it is young, beautiful, with a laughing smile and shining blue eyes, sitting cross-legged in the grass with her long platinum blonde hair thrown over one shoulder in a thick braid. In her lap is a child of three or four, with that same white-blonde hair, laughing blue eyes, and a gap-toothed smile. She's pointing at the camera, urging the child to look.

Just holding the picture in my hand, I can hear the laughter, *feel* the joy emanating from it. It's a joy I haven't felt in a long time, a sound I've nearly forgotten. I can feel the cracks of my heart start to bleed all over again as I look down at the woman and child, my other hand clenching into a fist at my side.

Viktor Andreyev isn't the only reason you're here. You're here for your revenge, too. You're here to make sure their blood doesn't cry out for vengeance for all the rest of your days.

You're here to make his *family suffer the way yours has.*

The clock ticks, reminding me I have somewhere I need to be. Carefully, I refold the picture, sliding it back into my wallet.

Tonight, if I'm lucky, will yield another clue.

When I leave the apartment, it's raining out, so I hail a cab. I slide into the warm, musty space, trying not to breathe too deeply as I give the driver directions to the bar, leaning back against the seat as he pulls into traffic. If not for the contact I'm meeting tonight, I might not have gone out at all, but the prospect of a stiff drink sounds better and better the closer we get to my destination.

Another man in my position might have hesitated to go out often at all, but it's long been my belief that the best place to hide is in plain sight. As far as Viktor Andreyev knows, I'm likely dead, but nonetheless, I doubt he'd look for me here first. Moscow is the site of a hundred jobs I'd done for him, two hundred—more, even. We'd traveled here together, drank together, picked out women to fuck together—and then taken them back to our rooms separately. We'd killed together. For more years than I like to count, I'd been his trusted brigadier, his hand of violence.

His left hand, while Levin Volkov stood on the right.

I have no idea who his left is now. I don't have the same contacts I used to, nor can I trust the same people. But I don't fear Viktor Andreyev finding me in a Moscow bar.

Especially not this one.

I know the man I'm meant to meet by description. I see him as soon as I walk in and shake off the rain, sitting at a table far back, lit only by one dim lamp attached to the wall. Without hesitation, I stride through the crowd, walking towards him with purpose. He catches sight of me halfway, and I see his eyes widen slightly with fear, as if he didn't entirely expect me to show up.

Fool.

I pause at the bar, mostly because I want a drink before I go any further and somewhat to throw him off. I enjoy the look of confusion that flits across his face as he watches me as I order a vodka neat from the bartender.

"Make it two, actually," I tell the wiry-looking man, who shrugs and grabs a second glass. I enjoy keeping others on their toes, and I can guarantee that my contact isn't expecting me to buy him a drink.

His main concern is likely whether or not he'll end the night with my knife in his throat.

I haven't entirely discounted the possibility.

"T-thank you," the man stammers when I sit down, pushing one of the glasses of vodka toward him.

"Consider it an incentive to loosen your lips, beyond the payment I've promised you." I lean closer, pitching my voice low. "What do you have for me? You said it was good, Yuri, don't disappoint me."

The man smiles, a toothy, half-rotten smile that makes me want to flinch back, but I don't. "It's about Konstantin Obelensky," he says, the gleam in his eyes clearly saying he's proud of himself. "Good stuff, *da*?"

A flush of cold rage washes through me as I sit back, stiff and angry. "Fuck your information," I snarl, my voice still low. "What can you tell me that I don't already know? Konstantin Obelensky is dead."

There are a number of rumors swirling around the city about how exactly that came to pass. One of them is that he had his bastard daughter–another rumor that no one is exactly sure of the truth about–locked up in his compound, before a rescue squad came in guns blazing and killed Obelensky. There are other rumors, including ones involving poison, mutiny, his legitimate daughter poisoning him, that same daughter shooting him, and a particularly disgusting one involving an affair with that daughter, which climaxes–no pun intended–with her stabbing him in the throat mid-coitus.

My suspicion is that none of them are true. One thing remains the same, however, throughout all the stories. His daughter, the *legitimate* one, played some part in it.

Beyond the rumors, one thing is true beyond a shadow of a doubt–Obelensky is dead.

And I'm fucking furious about it.

I wanted to be the one to kill him. Now, without that to lean on, I've been at a loss as to how to move forward–what to do next in my quest for revenge and redemption rolled into one.

Yuri had been meant to help me. Instead, he's given me nothing of value.

I consider the option of my knife in his throat, throwing the vodka I purchased him in his face, and weighing them as Yuri looks at me dumbly.

"This is good information," he insists. "Listen."

"I don't want to hear about Obelensky," I hiss through gritted teeth. "I know all I need to know about him. I asked you for *new* information."

"This *is*," Yuri insists, reaching into his pocket. "Look."

He unfolds a photo, pushing it across the table towards me. It's a poor copy of one, actually, but in color, so I can see more details of what's in front of me.

What's in front of me, however, makes no fucking sense.

It's a picture of a woman—a stunningly gorgeous one—in silver lingerie with her back against a stripper pole in the middle of a stage, her hands stretched above her head to grasp it. Her dark hair is wild around her face, her eyes wide as if with stunned pleasure, her back arched deeply, her lips parted. She's a statue of lust, a work of lewd art cast in poorly taken photographic form, and the moment I see her, I feel a deep bolt of arousal that I haven't felt in some time.

My cock twitches in my jeans, hardening instantly at the sight of the dark-haired woman. I do my best to ignore it, although it's difficult. I haven't been with a woman in a while, too caught up in my search for information and my reticence to bring anyone back to my apartment—hardly the kind of place I've been accustomed to bringing dates in the past—and the perfect figure of the woman in front of me arouses every slumbering primal instinct I have all at once.

In fact, I can't recall having been this turned on by *anyone*. Certainly not a grainy photo.

"Who the fuck is this?" I ask irritably. "I ask for information, and you bring me an ad for an escort?"

"A stripper - at a club in another part of town," Yuri corrects me blandly. "And she's Obelensky's daughter."

He lets that last bit of info land on the table like a mic drop, reaching for his vodka with the barest hint of a victorious smile. "I told you it was good information."

I stare at him as if he's lost his mind, which he absolutely fucking has. "That's not fucking *Konstantin Obelensky's* daughter," I tell him flatly, laughing. "You're out of your goddamned mind. Natalia Obelensky disappeared right after the break-in at Obelensky's compound. Besides, that woman isn't her."

"It is," Yuri insists. "I wouldn't have brought it to you otherwise. Knowing your…temper."

I shove the photo back towards him, grimacing irritably. "This isn't her. Natalia Obelensky was a blonde, and notoriously vain. And even if she did decide to dye her hair and masquerade as someone else, she'd never set foot in a place like that."

Yuri frowns. "Take a closer look," he insists, pushing the picture back towards me. "*Look*. It's her. My information is good; I'm sure of it."

I lean forward, peering closer at it in the dim light, trying to keep an open mind. "This is ridiculous," I mutter, but I try to see what someone else might have noticed—if there could be a grain of truth.

Natalia Obelensky is—or was—the only legitimate heiress to a massive Bratva fortune, the daughter of a vicious and powerful man, and a woman who lived her life surrounded by luxury. A prima ballerina with multiple accolades—classically trained, beautiful, accomplished, desired.

The idea that she would so much as set foot in a club like the one I see in the picture is insane, let alone that she might *dance* at one.

But as I look closer, I can see a hint of possibility. *Very slender, small-breasted, not your typical exotic dancer. Lithe, muscled legs, though that could be from the pole. Classic features, except for the dark hair.*

What stands out to me the most, though, is her bearing. I've been to many strip clubs, from seedy to the most expensive and luxurious, the kind where only a thousand men hold exclusive memberships for themselves and a guest. In all that time, all those clubs, all those dancers, I've never seen a stripper with the kind of bearing this woman has.

She looks like a goddess, a statue, poised and perfectly posed, her entire body holding the most graceful of movements in the instant the photo was taken. She looks like nothing I've ever seen.

She looks like a ballerina.

At that moment, a hint of doubt enters my mind.

I need to find out for myself.

I glance up at Yuri, narrowing my eyes. "Where was this taken?"

He grins, holding his glass of vodka towards me in a mock toast. "See! Yuri's information is good, *da*?"

I grit my teeth. "The name of the club?"

"The *Cat's Meow*. Kind of a shithole, to be honest. I was surprised a girl like that would work there. But then again, that makes sense, right? No one would expect to find her there."

I don't want to let Yuri know that I had similar thoughts. No sense in letting his ego get too big. "I'll look into it."

I push his envelope of cash discreetly across the table, sweeping the photo off of it. Yuri pulls a distressed face as he watches me fold it up.

"Aww, no," he complains, even as he reaches for the money. "I was going to take that with me."

"I don't want to know what you'd planned to do with it." I tuck the photo away, and as I do, I think of another folded photo, another woman with lighter hair and a sweeter smile.

You'd better hope I don't believe you're Natalia Obelensky, whoever you are.

Because when I get my hands on her, Natalia Obelensky is fucking dead.

Natalia

The way the man is looking at me, his ice-blue eyes and the intensity of his stare, throws me off for a moment. It feels as if he's not just looking at me, but *through* me.

As if he sees something that no one else in here can, or does.

Get a grip, I snap at myself, spinning away from the man so that I can't be pinned by his gaze any longer, like a butterfly to a corkboard. *It's not unusual for men here to fixate. It means nothing.* He *means nothing.*

The letter wasn't from him. Not a man like that.

I can still feel his eyes boring into my back, cutting through me, and I grit my teeth, forcing a smile as I throw myself into the performance. The music picks up, the beat shuddering through the stage, vibrating in my bones, and I let it wash over me again and carry me away. I let it wash *him* away, the lingering stickiness of his eyes on me, and I tell myself to forget about it.

He's hardly the first customer to develop an obsession, and he'll hardly be the last.

Every man who comes in here has a type. I, unsurprisingly, tend to appeal to the ones who have a "princess" fetish, who like women who seem unobtainable, aloof, even disparaging of them. I've never been able to fawn over the men here or pretend to love and adore them the way some of the women do. Still, it's drawn my own little group of loyal customers over the brief time I've worked here.

Some of them have moved on, but they're always replaced by others. *This man is just a new one,* I tell myself, arching against the pole as I raise my hands over my head, undulating for the eyes on the opposite side of the stage. *A new admirer. A new source of tips. He'll be fascinated for a while, and then he'll move on, too.*

That shiver runs down my spine again as I think of the letter. One of them hasn't moved on. One of them is going too far.

I see you, bitch.

A bullet is too quick for you.

You'll pay.

All in cutout, tacked-on words. A caricature of a threat.

The music rises and falls, and I go with it. I've danced so many times to this track that it's second nature by now, and this is my favorite part of it. I change up the routine a little every time, keeping it fresh, and the regulars fucking love it. They love to think it's a special show all for them, that I'm so into it that I'm giving them something new and different out of the pure, unadulterated lust flowing through me.

They'd be horrified if they knew the truth—that while I often throw myself into the music, I know this dance and the variations I've spun on it so well that I could write a grocery list in my head and still not miss a mark. I don't normally, not wanting to risk fucking up when I *need* this job, but I do it now, trying to calm my racing heart with the most mundane things as I hook my leg around the slender pole.

Peanut butter. Eggs. Cheap bread. Noodles. Sauce. I visualize a piece of paper, my hand on a stubby pencil, scratching it all down. Writing by hand, since what I have now could barely be called a phone. Just a flip burner to satisfy the club's requirement that they have a way to reach me. No touchscreen, no apps, no quick access to anything.

There was a time when I would have been utterly horrified by the idea of being unchained from my iPhone. When I was raised on caviar and crustless sandwiches and wagyu, I couldn't have told you what a peanut butter sandwich tasted like. When the thought of *needing* a job would have been something so foreign I couldn't have comprehended it.

I never thought of dancing for the ballet as a job. It was a passion, an accomplishment, an *escape*. It was everything I wanted, and clung to, to keep me from disappearing into the life my father had planned for me.

"Athena!" A short, stocky man waves a fistful of bills in my direction, his face pleading as I dance toward the edge of the stage. "Oh god, I–"

He's red-faced, sweating, staring at my tits. His hand holding the bills shakes. As I bend down, hair falling forward, shaking those tits for him, his eyes widen until I'm worried they might bug out of his head. When I gracefully fall to my knees, hips arched and thrusting as I throw my head back and undulate in front of him, giving him a chance to stuff those bills into the thin rhinestone-encrusted strap of my g-string, he looks as if he might pass out.

For a moment, I forget about the letter. I forget about the man with piercing blue eyes. For a moment, I forget that this isn't me, that this place is somewhere to hide, to pretend, and I let the music sweep over me.

My first few nights at the club, I was disgusted by all of it—the smells, the cheap lingerie, the ludicrously high and shiny heels, the pounding music, the cheap liquor masquerading as top-shelf booze, purchased at wholesale and poured into bottles that don't reflect the actual contents. I was disgusted by the men and the sex pervading everything, the game that every dancer played in their own way to eke tips out of desperate customers. It had felt like hell.

I, quite dramatically, declared to myself on my way home that first night that I'd rather die than go back.

But my decision was that. Risk trying for something better, something less unlike my former self, and risk my life in the bargain–or stick with the plan and the shitty apartment and the bottom-of-the-barrel club. It had felt like a fall from grace, like having my wings clipped, and in many ways, it had been.

After a few weeks, I discovered something.

The dancers that I pitied held power over these men. They doled out attention and favors as they pleased, dangling their fruits over the open mouths of men who wanted to be their begging and willing slaves. Not every girl wanted to be here, but the majority of them didn't seem to hate it. They weren't forced or trafficked into it like I suspected–although I'm *very* certain that isn't true for every club on the street. The owner, Igor Vaslev, turned out to be a lewd and leering man, but a fair one, and one who didn't force his dancers to do anything they didn't want to. He also didn't stand in the way of them breaking laws to do more than the club rules allowed–as long as he got a cut.

It was a two-way street, and I was traveling down it. I had a choice to go along for the ride or get off on the next exit, and I made it.

Though men like the red-faced one shoving bills in my panties still revolt me, there's an inevitable rush to it that I would have never thought I'd feel. As I slide forward on my knees, the money securely in the thin strap, and crawl close to his face as I arch my back and bounce on the stage again, I feel that thrill of power.

I could tell this man to do *anything* in exchange for a small sexual favor, a glimpse of flesh, and he would.

I rock back on my heels, sensually rising back up on my feet as I twist in front of him, turning back towards the other side of the stage. As I do, I immediately see *him* again.

The sharp face. The piercing ice-blue eyes. The small smirk at the corner of his full mouth as his eyes rake down me, assessing me. He takes his time doing it as I gyrate - his eyes pausing at my throat, my small breasts, my flat, firm belly, and my long legs. A dancer's body, every inch of it, toned and trained, and I see the appreciation in his eyes.

The *lust*. It darkens them briefly, gives them a glimmer of heat in all that ice that nearly takes my breath away. I feel a thrill rush through me as I see his eyes flick back up to my face, looking at me as if he's trying to *see* me. As if he's captivated by me–but not in the way the others are.

His tattooed, muscled arms cross over his chest, flexing. His expression is curious but hard. This isn't a man who would beg or grovel for anything. This isn't the kind of man I could wield power over.

He looks like the kind of man who wields it himself. Who makes *others* beg. In my present situation especially, I should find it terrifying. The shivers running over my skin, prickling it and raising the hairs, should be ones of fear, not arousal.

After this morning, especially, I should be afraid.

But all I feel is a slow, dazed heat spreading through me as he watches me, his eyes never leaving me for even a second. He doesn't have money in his hands. No offers of tips for a more personal experience.

I shouldn't pay attention to him. Shouldn't give him the time of day. *The arrogance - to stand there watching me so intently, without even a single ruble to offer.*

He looks as if he can afford to tip, and tip well. Unless the well-pressed, quality clothing, the watch on his wrist, and the styled hair is all a farce. A facade to make the girls fawn over him without having to pay to take them back to the champagne room—because he can't.

Which is it? Despite myself, I'm fascinated…and even more so, I'm curious. I've always loved a good mystery.

The last beats of the song hit, and automatically, without thinking, I finish the dance. My feet propel me forward even though my mind is elsewhere, towards the steps off the stage, down into the throng of horny, eager men. It's the routine every night for every dancer.

A solo number, then mingling, until you get the signals from someone that they might want more. The cheaper option of an on-the-main-floor lapdance, or, if you're lucky, they'll ask to take you back to the champagne room. It's another part of the night that I could go through on autopilot if need be at this point. Still, I feel as if I'm buzzing under my skin, anxious and overly aware of everything around me.

The man's gaze left me unsettled, prickly. *Surely he wouldn't be so brazen as to leave me that letter this morning and then show up tonight? And I've never seen him here before. I would have noticed. So it* can't *be him.*

I hear the beat of the music picking up, intro-ing Ruby's dance. I feel some of the crowd around me part and move away, drifting towards the stage to see her come out, but one man with thin dark hair sprawls onto the chair nearest me, motioning for me to come closer.

"Come wiggle that fine ass for me, *lyubov*," he slurs. I move towards him, already swaying as I turn to face away from him and back towards the stage as Ruby comes out in her signature red.

Without meaning to, I look for the man with the blue eyes. I want to see if he looks at Ruby in the same way, if he gives her the same intense stare, the same assessing gaze—or if it was reserved for me.

I should want him to look at all the dancers like that. It's less creepy if it's not solely directed at me.

I can't help the small flare of jealousy in my stomach as I look for him, though, as illogical as it is. I haven't felt special or noticed, for what feels like a long time now. Not since Adrian–and even then, not for long.

But it doesn't matter. I scan the crowd, but I don't see him. The space where he stood is filled in now by more of the same clientele that comes in every night, and no matter where I look, there's no sign of him that I can see.

He's vanished.

Mikhail

It's beginning to rain again as I step outside. I stay close to the overhang at the back of the building, watching the rain drip down in front of me as I fumble in my pocket for my pack of cigarettes.

Three days. It's been three days since Yuri passed me that photo of the woman he claimed was Natalia Obelensky. There was no real reason to wait; he said she'd been seen there most nights of the week. In fact, it seemed as if she rarely took a night off. I could have gone the next night–hell, I could have probably gone the *same* night and seen her.

But I waited.

It's possible to conjecture any number of reasons as to why, but deep down, I know that a large part of it is that I didn't want to be disappointed. The idea that Natalia Obelensky might have fallen into my lap seemed too good to be true, but the idea that it might be because of a lap *dance*, that the Bratva princess might have fallen so far from grace as to be turning tricks at a cheap strip club, seemed absolutely ludicrous.

Now, I'm not so sure.

I'm unsettled by all of it—by the prospect that it might be her, by the simplicity of it all, and most of all, by my reaction to her.

If this woman is Natalia Obelensky, then she's no different than any other job, even if this is more personal. I've come across plenty of beautiful women in the course of doing my job, particularly when working for Viktor Andreyev—none of them have left me with this unsettled desire, the urge to forget why I'm really here and become just another customer salivating over a nice pair of tits and perfect body.

And *goddamn,* is it perfect.

The purpose of coming here was to determine if she really is Natalia, I remind myself as I slide the cigarette into my mouth, the orange flame of my lighter standing out against the wet darkness. *You don't have an answer to that yet.*

I've seen pictures of Natalia before, of course. Pictures of her with her hair slicked back into a tight ballerina's bun, her even thinner figure in a leotard, tulle frilling out at her hips, and her perfectly arched feet crammed into those torture devices dancers call shoes.

I've seen pictures of her at events for the Moscow ballet, at galas she was required to attend because of her father's station, her honey-blonde hair cascading over her shoulder in a froth of waves or pinned up elegantly, that perfect body poured into an expensive designer gown, those imperfect feet propped up in high heels.

None of that makes it easy to determine if *this* might be her—if the dark-haired, lustful beauty on stage a few minutes ago with a dancer's body and a sinner's face might be the same woman I'm hunting.

What's more unsettling is that I no longer feel sure if I want to keep pursuing this lead at all.

What if it's not her? I take a drag of my cigarette, blowing the smoke out into the rain. *Or what if I decide that it is, and I'm wrong?*

Nothing like that has ever bothered me before. I've never been the kind of man who scruples at violence or at doing what needs to be done. I was Viktor Andreyev's brigadier at Viktor's most violent–the left hand who dealt out consequences, pain, and death. When he gave me orders, I was his loyal dog, willing to bite and devour where he told me to.

Now, look what's become of me.

I take another angry drag of my cigarette, frustrated with myself. *What makes her different than the rest of them?* She's no different than Sofia Ferretti, whom I kidnapped out of a New York basement club when Viktor decided he wanted her for himself. She's not any different from any of the girls I picked up off of streets like the one I'm standing next to now, shipping them back to New York for Viktor to sell off to the highest bidder.

The only thing that could make her stand out is if she were the woman I'm looking for–in which case, her fate would be much worse than what eventually befell any of those women.

I snort, flicking the ash into the rain. Sofia Ferretti is now Sofia *Romano*, queen of the New York Italian mafia. The women Viktor sold are living like queens of a sort now, the concubines of billionaires, princes, and sheiks. As for Sasha Federova, who I remember most clearly of all–well, I can't exactly say what her fate was. But it, too, was tied up with Natalia Obelensky.

I grit my teeth before taking another drag. *A year.* It's been over a fucking year since Viktor took his blushing new bride to Moscow to parade her in front of his peers, and Konstantin Obelensky saw a chance to cut him off at the knees. Over a year since Konstantin, fucking snake that he was, managed to get Alexei Egorov to betray Viktor and stage a coup that nearly shattered Viktor's Bratva entirely. Over a year since I barely escaped Alexei's rampage with my own life, only to find out that Viktor thought I had been complicit.

Fifteen years of being his loyal dog, biting on command, and that was the thanks I got. He'd been angry and paranoid, ready to wipe the board clean of anyone who might have been on Alexei's side, and since I hadn't come straight to Viktor's, he'd believed me to be a part of it. I'd been lucky to have heard that through the grapevine, or else I might have come back of my own accord and gotten a bullet through the temple for my troubles.

All the while, I'd been looking for the source of the coup, knowing that Alexei would never have had the balls to pull off something like that himself. I'd been fucking right.

Obelensky had been pulling the strings, something Viktor was unaware of. He'd been so goddamn focused on reconnecting with his family, nurturing his newfound romance with his wife, and protecting her and his children, so eager to blow up the business we'd spent years building on to turn his empire into something more palatable for the Rossi woman, that he'd overlooked entirely finding who the head of the viper was. It hadn't been Alexei, that's for fucking certain.

I'm going to bring him that fucking information. I'm going to tell Viktor who it was who really put his wife and children through that hell, whose cock Alexei was sucking to cause him to make such a stupid fucking decision. I'm going to find Natalia Obelensky–if she can be found–and once I finish asking my questions and taking my revenge out on her, I'll deliver what's left to Viktor to question or kill as he chooses.

I'll be the one who brings all of it to him. The man he threw away. And then, when Viktor thanks me, when he begs for my forgiveness, when the *Ussuri* himself pleads with me to return to the fold, it will be *my* choice as to whether or not to take my place again within Viktor's Bratva.

I'll be able to ask for what I want. Money, power, favors. And I'll buy it all with information and Natalia Obelensky's blood.

Which is why I have to make *very* certain that this woman is the right one.

I can't hesitate. I can't scruple at what needs to be done.

Most of all, I can't allow myself to be distracted.

I blow out the last of the smoke from my cigarette, thinking of the woman on stage. She's unlike any woman I've known in a very long time. Beautiful, graceful, with the hallmarks of a classically trained dancer–I'm sure of that, at least. And her bearing...

She hadn't flinched from my gaze. If anything, it had seemed to empower her–until she'd realized I had no intention of stuffing any rubles into those cheap panties of hers. Her attitude had changed instantly–haughty, dismissive, and it had sent a jolt through me that I forgot the feeling of.

My cock throbs at the memory, swelling uncomfortably against my fly as I shift and stub my cigarette out against the wall. Breaking a woman like that would be exquisite. The struggle, the fight–I let out a hiss of air between my teeth as my pulse picks up, thinking of how she might react if I stripped away that cheap gold lingerie, baring the bits of skin she managed to keep hidden to my gaze.

She wouldn't flinch away, cover herself, or scream and cry. She'd fight back, bite and claw, and when she did eventually lose, it would be so much sweeter.

Fuck. I reach down to adjust my rigid cock, unable to resist rubbing my palm against the hard line of it for a moment, feeling the pleasure fizz in my veins. I haven't been this aroused in a long time, aching with need and craving the feeling of a slender soft body pinned beneath mine, delicate wrists caught in the circle of my fingers as I drive into tight, wet heat.

I doubt she offers extras, but in this kind of club, someone does. I could go back in, find a dancer who would suck my cock for a few rubles, and get the release that I so desperately need so that I can focus again. But even as I picture it, the dark-haired woman on the stage, the one they announced as *Athena*, swims into my head again.

Anything else suddenly seems cheap, a faded facsimile of what I really want. Natalia or not, the woman has captivated me—and that's a problem.

I've never been *captivated* by any woman. All my life, I've practiced detachment. Sex for perfunctory pleasure, nothing more. When I have craved something darker - more violent, more consuming, I paid for it….and there was never any question of obsession.

None of them ever made me feel like *this*.

Stubbornly shoving my erection down, I fumble in my pocket, pulling out my wallet and the photo it contains. I unfold it, looking down at the pretty, smiling face of the woman there, and a calm resolve fills me and deflates my arousal. Nothing about the picture could ever make me feel lust. Looking at it has the desired result, replacing the burning heat in my veins from watching Athena dance with a cold and renewed anger.

If she is Natalia, I want my revenge. If not, I'll enjoy finding out, and then I'll look elsewhere. I can't leave Moscow until I've discovered proof that I can bring back to Viktor—and I refuse to spend the rest of my life like a rat in an alley, scurrying from place to place to avoid being caught.

The rain is coming down harder now, the red neon from the street glowing through it eerily, and I clench my teeth as I reach for the door that will lead me back inside the club.

I doubt there's any actual champagne served in the champagne room of this place. Still, it will give me private time with the woman who calls herself Athena; right now, that's what I need more than anything else.

I need answers—and she's going to give them to me.

Natalia

Their faces have started to blur.

They always do, by this point in the night. As the solo dancers have come out on stage, I've given lap dance after lap dance to customers on the main floor, teasing their arousal even higher as they watch the women on stage gyrating and bouncing and swaying for their pleasure. I've made trips back and forth to the bar, garnering a few extra tips for bringing the men their drinks myself instead of delegating it to one of the cocktail waitresses.

They always love that–the pretense that they have me to themselves for a little while, at their beck and call, delivering drinks and dancing for them and them alone while they toss the drinks back… until their attention is caught by another dancer.

I've been here a very brief time, admittedly, but I can't seem to get the hang of the *fawning* that so many of the girls are masters of. I can't ever entirely shake the hint of disdain that I know drifts around me, the impression I give off that I think I'm better than these men, that I belong somewhere better than *this*. Some men like it and seek me out specifically for that haughty disdain, but most of them end up preferring to spend their champagne room rubles on the dancers like Ruby, who are capable of putting on an act like no other. They want big eyes and breathy whispers, gratitude, and desire that seems genuine, and it's hard for me to fake that.

I would never have been good at the girlfriend experience.

"Athena!" A voice from a few feet away, carrying over the music and conversation, calls out my name. It's deep and rough, and I know it immediately—it's Davik, one of the staff who doubles between taking champagne room bookings and guarding the rooms themselves. He's a man as wide with muscle as he is tall, with buzzed white hair and a stern expression. I've never known a single dancer to get in trouble with a customer taking things too far when he's outside her room. I tip him well after shifts, even though I can't really afford it, because I know he'll keep me safe.

"What is it?" I step away from my last customer, whose attention is already wandering to a tall, lithe blonde dancer coming down after her turn on the main stage. "Please tell me someone's bought private time with me."

The night is still young, but even so, it's been longer than I would have liked without someone asking to take me back to the champagne room. The money from floor lap dances doesn't go far, especially after tip-outs at the end of the night. Though I got a decent amount from my solo dance, it wasn't as much as I normally have gotten.

I was too distracted by that man. They could tell. They're like fucking sharks; they can always smell it.

"Good news then." He gives me a grin that changes his stern face altogether, making him look younger and more jovial. I like Davik—in some other world where I could have friends, *real* friends, we might have been that. "Fella just asked for time with you. An hour. If you want to go back, I'll bring him in."

I frown. "Shouldn't I go say hello, offer to escort him back?" That's how it usually goes if a girl isn't already back there entertaining someone else—just another way to make the men feel special and pampered.

Davik shakes his head firmly. "Not this one. I got a feeling from him, little lady. I want to make sure he understands the rules *real* thoroughly, before I let him back there with you." He pats my arm, giving me what I think is meant to be a reassuring look. "Just go on back and get ready, and I'll bring him to you."

A small, cold shiver goes through me at that. Davik has worked at places like this for a long time, and if he gets a sense about a customer, I trust him.

What if you've got this all wrong? What if that letter wasn't from someone who saw you at the club at all?

I swallow hard, forcing the feeling down as I nod and stride towards the velvet curtains that separate the main floor from the rooms in the back, to go and find an empty one. *You're overreacting*, I tell myself with every step. *The letter was just some random sicko who gets his kicks out of scaring women he thinks are beneath him. It wasn't that man. And you should be happy about this. Seems he does have money after all—and you're about to earn some of it. A decent amount, if you shake this off and do your job well.*

The one open room is the smallest of them, which gives me a twinge of nerves at how close I'll be to him without the space that some of the other rooms might have provided. The metal and white-lacquer-topped stage is in the center with its sleek silver pole, a white leather couch curved around it, and cool blue light fills the room when I switch them on. I pick a slow, sultry beat for the music, hoping it will help calm me down.

I don't know why this man unsettles me so much. I've encountered customers of all types in the short time I've worked here—eager, aloof, creepy, and on rare occasions, respectful. More often, they're eager and borderline obsessive, looking at me like hungry dogs faced with rare meat. It's not something I'm entirely unfamiliar with—a young woman in any station of life gets used to being appraised by men who look at her as if she were a meal—but there's an added desperation to it here that made me deeply uncomfortable at first.

I wouldn't have thought I could get used to it, but in many ways, I have. I barely notice most of them now, and by the time I'm finished performing, I've more often than not forgotten about them.

This man is different.

It's probably only a few minutes before the door opens, although it feels much longer as I wait, poised against the stage. I hear the rough, low tones of Davik's voice saying something to the man, and then he steps inside.

The moment the door shuts behind him and we're alone together, I feel that same chill down my spine. When he'd been standing next to the stage, there had been tension in him, a calculating appraisal of me, but now he seems looser, more relaxed. *A few drinks in him, probably.* I let my gaze slide over him as if I'm appraising him in turn, but I'm not prepared for the warmth that pools in my belly at the sight of what's standing in front of me.

That sharply handsome face, all chiseled cheekbones and jaw, and those startling ice-blue eyes, sandy blond hair falling to one side, artfully styled and tousled. A dark teal button-down, unbuttoned enough to show the hint of a muscled chest, smooth-skinned and inked with tattoos, just like the forearms visible where his shirt sleeves are rolled up. The chain bracelet on one wrist, the watch on the other, the shirt clinging to a flat stomach and disappearing into tailored trousers.

He sticks out in this place like a sore thumb—but then again, so do I.

That must be why he was so interested in you, I tell myself, to try and calm the riot of butterflies I feel in my stomach. He's watching me now as he steps into the room, those blue eyes giving nothing away, the slightest smirk on his full mouth.

Unbidden, I feel that thrill of attraction again, and something else too—excitement at the idea that I'll be the one arousing this man, making him want me, hunger for me, *crave* me. I'm usually disgusted by the carnal urges of the men around me, but suddenly the idea of him sitting on the couch, hard and wanting while I flaunt myself just out of reach, has my thong clinging to my intimate flesh with a sudden and unwanted arousal.

Get yourself under control, Athena, I tell myself flatly. *This is your job. Don't forget that.*

Which, of course, is why I'm so thrown off by it all. I've never, not even once, been sexually aroused by a customer before. In fact, the idea of them coming in here, and purchasing our services like items on a menu, has always been repulsive to me.

He's no different. It makes no difference that he's handsome. He's the same as all the rest.

"Athena?" He says my name, the word clinging to his lips like sticky caramel, and I feel something inside of me go soft and warm.

Christ, Natalia. It's not even been that long since you had good dick. Several weeks, sure, but you've gone that long before. Control yourself.

"You found me." I push myself away from the stage, swaying towards him on my impossibly high heels, stopping a little less than arm's length away as I reach out and touch his chest with just the tip of one manicured–thanks to Ruby–nail. We're all suffering under the same financial constraints, so the girls look out for each other where they can.

Gone are the days of bi-monthly visits to my home from my favorite nail tech.

"I had a little help." His hands stay by his sides–points to him for that, at least. A lot of men try for a grope at this point, with a door closed behind them and the privacy of the room. Still, it won't hurt to remind him of the rules.

"Davik is good at giving directions." I scrape the tip of my nail a little lower, across that tattooed flesh. "And you should know he's never that far away. So it's important that you're a good boy and stick to the rules. No touching—on your part, at least." My nail slides a little further down, my fingertip pressing against warm flesh. "No threats. No—"

"He told me the rules." The man laughs, his blue eyes crinkling ever so slightly at the corners. "Twice, in fact. He must like you a lot."

There's a hint of possessiveness to his voice, almost a flicker of jealousy that makes me step back. "He's in charge of our well-being." It's all I can do to keep my voice low and sultry instead of letting it go cold. *I might belong to you for the next hour, but that's all—and that's with limitations. Don't go getting any ideas.*

"You're lucky, then. I haven't noticed that many clubs of this… caliber are all too concerned with the well-being of their girls." There's a hint of disdain in his voice, and for all that I feel the same way about the *Cat's Meow*, it makes me prickle to hear someone else speak about it—and by association, me—in that tone.

"If you find this place so repulsive, why don't you go somewhere else?" I rake my gaze down him again, letting my own mouth curl into a haughty expression, the one that makes a certain kind of man lose his mind. Whether this man is that type or not remains to be seen. "You look wealthy enough to not need to go slumming on this street."

He fully smirks at that, his mouth twisting with amusement as his eyes flick down to my breasts and back up again. "I think the reason is self-explanatory," he says smoothly. "It's standing in front of me. Otherwise, I wouldn't have paid such a pretty amount to be in here."

"Well, I'd hate for you to feel you overpaid." I tip my chin up, giving him a challenging glare.

"With you in front of me? Never." He steps forward, closer to me, and I unwittingly take a step back before I can stop myself. It's never a good idea to look put off by a customer, but now I've done it, and I think frantically of how to make up for my literal misstep.

I double down on it, stepping back again, closer to the stage, and I throw him a seductive, playful look that says *chase me if you want me*. I turn my mistake into a game, and it seems to work, because his icy gaze takes on an almost predatory look as he follows me toward the stage. I step back, and back again, until the cool edge touches the back of my thighs and the man is a hands-breadth away from me.

He's so close, close enough that I can feel the heat of his skin, the warm puff of his breath between us. He's not touching me, not yet, at least, but somehow that's almost worse. If he tried to touch me, I could push him away, reprimand him—even call Davik, if it was bad enough. But this—he's not doing anything wrong, and yet he's doing *everything* wrong.

His mouth curls upwards into a smile, full-lipped and inviting, and his eyes twinkle for a moment with wicked amusement as he looks down at me. "You know," he says slowly, his voice low and rich, "usually by now, I know a girl's name once I'm this close to her."

It takes everything in me not to give away how he affects me. I've never had to try before. The effort has always been in pretending to *want* their attention, not the other way around. I can feel my throat closing, wanting to swallow convulsively, my fingers itching to grab the edge of the stage; my body draws toward him like a magnet. I have a sudden, erotic vision of him holding my hands above my head and pinning them against the pole, my body pressed back against it, all of that hard, muscled heat pushed against me—

"You know my name," I breathe. "You were watching me during my stage routine. It's Athena."

He smirks, and I feel his hand flex close to me as if he's struggling not to touch me. I wish, desperately, that I didn't *want* him to. I caught a glimpse of his hands earlier, broad and long-fingered. I can easily imagine one of those hands wrapping around my breast, cupping and squeezing.

"Your *real* name, *lyubov*," he murmurs, and something about the roughly-whispered endearment sends a bolt of lust straight between my thighs.

I should want to slap him for being so forward, for calling me something so intimate, but instead, I find myself wanting him to say it again, only this time next to my ear, his lips brushing against it.

I have to get away from him, and in a way that's not so off-putting that he leaves in a huff, demanding his money back and getting me into trouble.

Quickly, I stiffen, twisting to reach for the pole and vault myself elegantly onto the stage. Now I'm the one over *him*, looking down as I turn and arch against the pole, sliding my hands down it as I circle it slowly in a preview of what's to come. I feel a momentary flash of victory, the power back in my hands, but I see amusement flicker in his eyes, and it's like a cold dash of water.

He knows what I'm up to, and if there's one thing I detest–in my old life or in this one–it's a man who thinks he's always two steps ahead of me.

"I thought Davik told you the rules. *Twice*, you said. Maybe you should consider spending some of the money that bought your time in here on a doctor, instead. To check your hearing." I arch into the pole, sliding my hands upwards as I press it between my breasts, slowly pushing my body along the length of it. He might be making my job difficult, but no one is going to accuse me of not doing it.

"Oh?" He raises an eyebrow. "I think I've been very careful to follow those *rules*." His voice lowers, darkening, taking on a heat that seems to skitter over my skin like sparks. "For instance, a moment ago, it was all I could do not to touch you. But I didn't–like a good boy. Just as you said."

"You asked my real name." My belly presses against the pole, and I grip it in both hands, sliding them downwards again. "That's against the rules. I gave you the only name I use within these four walls."

"Athena." There it is again, sticky sweet, as if he enjoys the taste of my name on his tongue. "It'll have to do for now, since I don't want to end our time together so quickly." He circles around the stage as he speaks, and I can feel his eyes on me, dragging over my body with an exquisite slowness that makes me feel tense and shivery. "Do you want my name?"

"No." The word is more clipped than it should be. In fact, it's not what I should have said at all. I should have turned towards him, breathed *yes* as I squirmed on the pole, and made him think that I'm dying to know more about him, that, at this moment, all my thoughts are for him.

Instead, I'm so focused on not letting him know how he affects me that it's hurting my performance.

"Shame." He sinks back onto the couch, reclining. "All the money I paid to be in here, and you don't have the slightest interest?"

"You paid for a dance." I arch my back, still looking away from him as I slide my hands further up the pole, preparing to pull myself onto it. "Nothing more than that. If you want something specific for your entertainment, let me know. I am here to *please*, after all."

I leap up at that, hooking my leg around the pole as I arch against it, swinging towards him and holding myself there. I see the heat in his gaze as he watches me, the growing need, and it sends an unwanted flush through me as well.

"What if I want more than a dance?" His voice is low and husky, and as he shifts on the couch, I catch a glimpse of the ridge of his cock pressing against his fly, already hard for me.

Is it long? Thick? How would it feel–

The actual words hit me a second after he says them, and I stiffen, sliding down the pole and landing on my feet as I glare at him from the stage.

"I'm a dancer, not an escort." The words come out as clipped as the *no* had earlier, and I can feel the tension radiating through my body.

"Some of the girls offer…*extras*, but I don't. So maybe you should find one of them instead."

"I'm here for you." His voice is smooth, silky, and it sends a chill through me that chases away any last lingering heat of arousal. *I'm here for you.*

Those four words, strung together in that order, are some of the last I want to hear anyone say to me now.

"Or maybe you should tell me your name after all," I snap, struggling to keep the rising fear out of my voice. "So I can tell Davik to make sure you don't come in here again."

The man sits up a little, leaning forward with that same smirk lingering on his lips. "It's Mikhail," he says smoothly. "But I'm telling you that for your own sake, not Davik's. I'd love to hear you say it sometime."

Mikhail. The name strikes a chord as if I've heard it somewhere before. But in all likelihood I have–it's a common name. Nothing particularly remarkable about it. And I'm sure as hell not going to say it now.

"You paid for a dance," I say smoothly. "One that you're wasting, with all this back-and-forth. Now I can leave, and you can see if you want to go toe-to-toe with Igor for half your money back, or you can relax and enjoy what you paid for–and *only* what you paid for."

He looks far too pleased for a man who has just lost an argument. He leans back against the white couch again, his hands at his sides. I catch a glimpse again in the shifting lights of the ridge of his cock pressing against the fabric of his pants, thicker than before.

"By all means, *Athena*," he says smoothly, his voice still low and rough. "Dance for me."

Natalia

I leave the club at the end of my shift more unsettled than when I arrived.

Mikhail. I have a name, now, for the man with the icy eyes.

He behaved himself for the rest of the dance. In fact, his behavior had been more exemplary than a lot of men who pay for private time, as much as I hate to admit it. He hadn't tried to touch me, not even when I came off the stage for the last part of the dance that was meant to be more up close and personal. He hadn't tried to touch himself, either, not so much as a flick of the wrist or a furtive rub against the erection that I noticed had become more and more prominent as the hour went on.

He did look thick. And long. *Huge,* in fact, possibly bigger than any man I've been with so far. The thought had done nothing for my steadily growing arousal as I danced. It had been only by pure skill borne out of long practice that I managed to pull off the performance at all, hoping that he hadn't noticed how much it had turned me on.

The flush on my skin could be chalked up to exertion. But every time I bent over, spreading my legs, I prayed that he couldn't see how wet I was, my thong clinging to my pussy folds as I'd gone through the motions of my routine.

I was fucking *drenched*. And none of it made sense.

Now, walking back to my apartment with the familiar pit of dread in my stomach that comes from walking down shady streets with an envelope of cash tucked in my waistband, between my shirt and jeans and my skin, even that feeling can't completely shake the lingering arousal.

He shouldn't have turned me on at all. He was arrogant. Insulting. Over-confident. Entitled, even. The kind of man I encountered far too often in my previous life.

The kind of man who really shouldn't have been at my sort of club at all, I remind myself.

Similarly to earlier in the evening, I walk as quickly as possible without making my hurry too obvious. The last thing I want is to attract attention—*more* attention, anyway, than I usually attract walking this late at night—when I have what had turned out to be a decent night's worth of tips on me. My first instinct about Mikhail had turned out to be right—he did seem to have money.

He tipped me a generous portion of it at the end of the night. That, combined with my other earnings from the week, will be enough to pay my bills that are due while possibly getting some groceries that don't involve either peanut butter or cheap noodles. I should feel grateful, but all I really feel is annoyed and anxious.

The letter this morning had been bad enough. My apartment has never felt like a particularly safe haven, but that delivery made it feel even less so. The thought of it sends a creeping sensation over my skin. I wonder if I'll find anything strange waiting for me when I get back tonight—or *anyone*.

But no amount of unease can completely chase away the itchy, frustrated feeling that clings to me like an unwanted perfume. Not even Mikhail's high-handed attitude was able to.

Am I really that deprived? It's been weeks since I've been with anyone, since Santorini, and I tell myself it's just that. In my past life, I wouldn't have gone so long without getting laid. I had my own secret apartment—or at least I told myself it was secret—away from my family's home where I technically lived and away from prying eyes. I paid for it with money sequestered away from my ballet salary, and I used it not only for my own escapes, but also for taking men home with me.

As my father's daughter, the *only* daughter and heiress to the Obelensky fortune, I'd been expected to remain innocent and virginal, clinging to my maidenhood in order to gift it to the husband of my father's choosing one day. As old-fashioned as my father was, I think he'd expected to go through the entire archaic rigmarole, bloody sheets and all.

Fuck that, had been my silent response. Sheets could be faked, and I had no intention of forgoing pleasure in order to stay pure for some future unwanted marriage, especially when my ballet career meant that marriage was delayed. No, if I was going to eventually be handed over like a broodmare to some man—whether I liked it or not—I was going to get *copious* amounts of dick of my own choosing before that.

And I had. I cut a swath through Moscow, enjoying the favors of men as I pleased, choosing the ones I wanted and high-handedly rejecting the rest. It was easy to play the demure heiress when need be, pleading innocence and the need for marriage if I wasn't interested, and easier still to lure them in if I was. Most of them were average at best—both their cocks and their skills in bed—but it wasn't so much the physical pleasure of sex that I was after. That could be achieved with the myriad of sex toys I kept at that same apartment—all long gone now, much to my dismay. My absence meant the apartment was no longer mine, and by the time I came back to Moscow, everything I owned that was in it was gone as well.

The thrill of those men lay in the middle finger that I gave my father every time I took one of them to bed. I might eventually have to give in to the cage of marriage in order to keep my inheritance, I reasoned, but I was going to make sure that I was as far from virginal as possible. In fact, there'd only ever been one thing I hadn't done, more out of lack of interest than anything else.

So, yes. It's been a while. And you always did like men with a bit of an edge to them. I tell myself that as I walk up the stairs to my apartment door, keeping my head on a swivel as I fumble for my keys, looking for anything out of the ordinary. *It's just horniness and nothing else. He might not even come back, and then you won't have anything to worry about.*

I lock the door behind me—all four locks—and drop my keys and the cash on the nightstand by my bed, stripping out of my jeans and t-shirt as quickly as I can and tossing them in the basket next to it. I always want a shower first thing after coming back from the club, but tonight I want one even more so than usual. I want to wash off the way Mikhail made me feel, that clinging, sticky sensation of *wanting*.

Turning up the water as hot as I can stand it, I look at myself in the mirror, still unused to how strange the reflection is. My face looks starkly pale with the dark hair framing it, and I find myself missing the softness of my old blonde, the natural sheen of it.

No use wasting time wishing for something you can't change. Maybe one day, when I've earned enough to get out of Moscow and far away from my past, I'll be able to go back to myself. Maybe I'll even dance again for something other than the pleasure of leering men. *I could teach ballet,* I think to myself as I step beneath the steaming water, losing myself briefly in a fantasy of an unknown future. *I could have a small apartment of my own, nicer than this. A neighborhood where I feel safe walking around. A job I enjoy.*

It's astonishing how much a person's priorities can change after such a drastic shift in circumstances. There was a time when I would have been horrified at the thought of teaching children, being satisfied with a small and simple place to live, or finding such relief at the thought of having a place to live where I feel safe. But I've now seen how far it's possible for a person to fall.

Even just this, standing in a hot shower and scrubbing myself clean with drugstore products, feels like a treat after the day I've had. The steamy air is full of the bubble-gum, synthetic scent of fake strawberry, the water swirling around my feet is tinged with the run-off from my hair dye, and I've never felt less like myself. But the heat loosens my tense muscles, and the soap sloughs off the lingering scents of sweat, other's cologne, and the tang of alcohol. I feel myself relaxing by degrees.

With that comes the sensation of arousal again, sliding over my skin as I wash, heating my body from the inside out. I don't miss Adrian himself, not after our last fight, but *god*, do I miss being in bed with him. He had a sizeable cock and knew how to use it, along with everything else, and I've felt a lingering craving for that pleasure ever since I left. Not for the man, but for the way he made me come.

Tonight's encounter with Mikhail only intensified it.

As I get out of the shower and dry off, even the rough fabric of the towel feels too much on my over-sensitive skin. I let out a low, frustrated groan as I toss it aside and walk naked into my bedroom.

I've been too exhausted lately to do much other than fall into bed and pass out after shifts at the club, but tonight I don't think I'll be able to sleep unless I do something about this. I stretch out atop my bed, letting my hands drift lazily down my bare breasts.

My entire body thrills to the touch, even just mine. I'm so keyed up that even my own fingertips trailing down my skin, circling my tightening nipples, leaves me twitching and breathless, my hips arching up and wanting my fingers elsewhere.

As much as I hate to let him back into my brain, I try to think of Adrian. I focus on black hair falling into my face and green eyes glinting wickedly down at me, of olive-skinned hands sliding over my breasts, cupping them, sliding down my waist as he maneuvered between my legs, his tongue wetting his lips in anticipation of tasting me.

"Ohh—" I moan softly, letting my legs fall open as my hand slides down my belly, brushing over the bare, shaven skin just above my pussy. I can feel how wet I am without touching, the inside of my thighs sticky with it, my clit throbbing with anticipation. Gently, I dip a finger between my folds, sliding it down to capture some of that wetness, and drag it back up to my clit, trying to simulate the soft wet heat of a man's tongue licking me there.

What I wouldn't fucking do for even one or two of my old drawer full of toys. In my old apartment, I would have already had something meant to do exactly that pressed against my clit, lapping at it with faint vibrations that would have me hurtling towards my first orgasm, and a thick dildo ready to push into myself after to give me a second. Instead, I'm left with only my fingertips swirling around my clit as I imagine strong, long-fingered hands spreading my thighs apart as icy-blue eyes look up at me from between them—

A jolt goes through me, shuddering down my spine. *Green. Green eyes.* I'm imagining Adrian, remembering that last good fuck before we'd fought for the last time…

My fingers move more quickly, sliding over my swollen clit, as I try to force my fantasies into submission. But the eyes remain stubbornly blue, the face pressed between my thighs the smirking one I saw tonight in the club, as he groans low and rasping in his throat, his tongue flicking over my clit.

I'm so close. I'm already on the verge of coming. My thighs start to tremble, and I can't bring myself to chase the fantasy away. My mouth drops open as my hips arch upwards, my fingers rapidly rolling over my clit as I come closer and closer to the edge, and all I can see is Mikhail's arrogant face as I imagine a hot tongue licking me, stroking me, sending me over the cliff into the release I so desperately need–

I let out a shriek of pleasure as I come, my clit throbbing beneath my fingertips as I buck my hips upwards, rubbing hard and fast. "Oh, *god*, oh–" I come just short of moaning his name, the spasms wracking me as I throw my head back, my fingers still moving throughout the entire climax, and I already know before they even start to fade that I'm not done.

I almost always come twice alone before I'm satisfied, and tonight is no different. My fevered imagination conjures Mikhail moving up between my thighs as I arch into him, that thick cock that I saw beneath his pants, freed, hard and dripping pre-cum for me. I reach down, spreading my folds with my fingers as I imagine the blunt head pressing against my entrance.

"*Fuck, fuck–*" I gasp, pushing two of my fingers inside of myself as I keep circling my clit, brushing against the outside of it now to give myself a moment to recover. My own fingers aren't enough, nothing close to the thick toys I had before, but it has to be. I need to come again. Once is never enough.

I want more. I want the thick heat of a cock, *Mikhail's* cock filling me up, and I'm lost in the fantasy now. Those full lips are on mine, those tattooed hands pinning me down by my wrists while he thrusts into me, long and slow at first and then faster, stretching me, forcing me to take every inch of his monstrous dick. I push a third finger into myself, scissoring them together, thrusting in a poor mimicry of what it would feel like to be getting fucked as hard as I want to be right now.

My body is buzzing with it, vibrating with the need. I roll over onto my stomach, face pressed down into the pillow as I imagine a hand at the back of my neck, holding me down. My fingers find my clit again, rubbing, my pussy so drenched that I can hear the wet slapping sounds of my own fingers as if there really is a cock pounding me right now.

If only. I imagine Mikhail kneeling behind me, forcing that thick cock into me from behind, one hand on my ass as the other pins me down by my neck. *Rub that clit for me, lyubov,* I hear him murmur in my ear. *Come on my cock the way you came on my tongue.*

"Oh god—" Another sobbing moan slips out of me, muffled by the pillow as I arch backward onto my hand, needing to come more than anything now, more than I need to breathe. "Oh *fuck*—"

I shove my fingers inside of myself as deeply as they can go, pushing back onto the imaginary cock, rubbing frantically at my clit as I curl them, sending myself that final step towards bliss as I come, clenching and moaning, legs spread wide for the cock that I so desperately wish I were coming on right now.

That feeling of desperate, satisfied bliss only lasts until I've pulled my hands from between my legs, lying on my stomach, trying to catch my breath, and then a rush of shame washes over me.

That, too, is unfamiliar. I've never felt shame about any of my sexual exploits. Even raised as I was to believe that sex for pleasure was the province of men, and that women of my status were only expected to lie back and turn those encounters into heirs, I wholeheartedly rejected that. But for the first time, I feel embarrassed about my fantasies.

Mikhail is exactly the sort of man I frequently encountered in my old life. He's the kind of man I probably would have fucked and never called again—or maybe called once or twice if he was especially good in bed and then discarded him. Back then, I would have been of equal status with him—maybe even more so.

Now, the balance of power is different. I don't want to feel attracted to him—*especially* because he's a customer at my job, but also because he's now the kind of man who could have power over me. In my present situation, nothing about that is good.

I *definitely* shouldn't be fantasizing about getting fucked by him, a few hours after meeting him for the first time.

But *god*, did it feel good.

The soft afterglow of the dual orgasms is still spreading through me, making me feel heavy-eyed and sleepy. I reach behind myself, fumbling for the blanket as I close my eyes, giving in to the embrace of sleep. At least there, so long as I don't dream about Mikhail, I won't have to think about my inappropriate desires.

Luckily, I fall into a deep and heavy sleep that I don't even come close to dreaming.

Mikhail

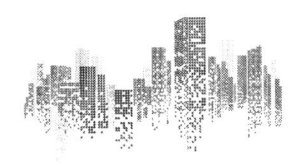

The screams are coming from very far away.

They're the unmistakable screams of a woman being hurt. High-pitched, frantic screams. Begging, pleading. "No, no, please don't, please—"

More shrieks, and then the muffled sound of crying behind a gag, a thick and choked coughing. The slap of flesh on flesh, and then another sound, that of a child crying. None of it should be able to be heard outside the thick windowless walls of cement, but he hears it all anyway, every pleading cry, every childish sob. He hears, but he can't move. His feet are mired down, held by some unseen force, and no matter how much he strains, he can't escape.

He can only listen, and know.

It goes on for a long time. The wet slapping sounds, man after man, as if she's been given to the whole compound's worth of guards. Through it all, the crying. It never stops. He knows he'll hear it in his dreams. And then, a voice.

A rough voice, cold and demanding, a voice used to getting its way. "Have you had enough yet, suka*? Will you tell us where he is?"*

A grunt, and then sobbing pleas. The gag must have been removed. "No, please. I don't know anything. I haven't spoken to him. Please, my son—"

"You know enough. Tell me, and I won't let my men have another round with you. I won't take part, of course, I don't enjoy well-worn cunt. But you can save yourself more pain if you give in. Think of your son."

A pause, punctuated by tears. "I'll even shoot you first, so you won't have to watch your son die. Would that help? I can't save him, I'm afraid. But I can make it easier on you both."

More crying. More pleading. A grunt of frustration and more of the fleshy sounds. More and more, until he feels he'll go mad with hearing it. Until the gunshot, followed by the reedy cry of a grieving mother, and then a second, feels almost like a relief.

At least for them, it's over. For him, the pain is just beginning.

He's led to their bloated bodies, fished out of the river a week later. He's taken there by a defector, a man who decided what happened that night was too much for even him. Unfortunately for that man, he decided that after taking part.

He makes sure the man's death is slow, until every torturous part of that conversation is extracted. Until he's convinced the man has nothing left to give. He makes the man stare at the bodies as he's taken apart piece by piece. Only when the first of his revenge is taken does he straighten, bloodied and sweating, and set about a proper funeral for them.

Not the man. He goes into the river.

Every last broken piece of him.

I wake with a start, sweating, my heart hammering in my chest. The rain is still beating down outside my window, the moon casting a pale, weak glow through it, and for a moment, I'm still half in the dream.

The pain and horror of remembering it, even dreamlike, is unmatched by anything I've felt since that day. The nightmares often come, and I know I won't sleep well afterward.

I wasn't there the night they were killed. But the man I tortured had spilled enough of the details to paint a thorough picture for my mind to taunt me with, night after night. Enough for me to dream of listening, helpless, as all that I had left to love had been destroyed.

My fault.

Cold fury spills through me, the blood in my veins freezing to ice and turning the sweat prickling over my skin cold, too. *I'll avenge you.*

The promise is as determined as ever, but the means of doing so is still lacking. With Obelensky dead, the most direct target is gone, stolen from me. *When I find out who killed him, I might choose to have words with them as well.*

There's no amount of need for bloodshed that will stop me. I've spilled enough blood to drown in a river of it, and I see no reason to start looking for absolution now. I'll do what I have to in order to see that they're avenged and that Viktor is made aware of who the real enemy is.

And what does that mean for the woman at the club?

Athena.

I grit my teeth, running my hand through my damp hair. I don't want to make a mistake. As violent a man as I can be, as little as I scruple at bloodshed, I have no desire to torture an innocent woman for information she doesn't have. *That would make me no better than him.* I have to be sure.

And would you be more sure if you weren't so fucking turned on by her?

I let out a low growl of frustration, swinging my legs out of the bed and stalking towards the far window in my boxers. The night is cool, made even more so by the rain, and I feel my flesh prickling slightly with cold.

Not because you're thinking of her?

Stubbornly, my cock twitches in my boxers, and I shove it down with my hand. I was terribly, painfully aroused while she danced for me earlier in the champagne room. I had questions for her, banter that might have given me more information about who she was and how a woman like her had come to dance in a place like that, but they all died on my tongue.

I was right about her. There had been no intimidating her. She fired back at every remark I had, even being willing to lose out on her tips for the night in order to have me thrown out for pushing boundaries. Her reaction had only made me more suspicious that Yuri, idiot that he is, might be right in his information.

Clubs like *Cat's Meow* are notorious for girls who offer extras. I bet any number of rubles that if I went into a private room with any of the other dancers there and asked that same question, they'd have been down on their knees for me before I could finish getting the words out. But *Athena* not only had refused but she had also been offended.

It was just another reason to believe that maybe the woman who called herself Athena hadn't been doing this all that long. Perhaps the club is a hiding place for her. A place where she thought she wouldn't be found.

But how to be sure? I need more to go on than just conjecture. I only have a photo of her and a concept of what she looked like before from other photos I've seen to go on.

The answer seems clear to me as I stand there looking out at the falling rain. I have jobs to do here in Moscow, underground work that keeps me from having to tap into any of my savings from my years working for Viktor, but they only take up so much of my day. I have time–time to watch her, to follow her, and to see what I can uncover about who this woman truly is.

It will mean going back to the club, too. My groin tightens uncomfortably at the thought, my cock stiffening, and I bite back a groan. Under any other circumstances, I would have stroked myself to a much-needed climax before bed, but I knew I'd think about her. The way she makes me feel already disturbs me, and the fact that I can't trust myself to touch my own cock without fantasizing about burying it deep inside of her only makes things worse. It's been tormenting me all night—since I saw the photo of her, even—fed by my need for revenge and how long it's been since I've come inside a woman. I know I need to get control of it before I lose myself to something more dangerous.

Obsession.

The morning finds me groggy and exhausted, feeling even worse from the fractured sleep than if I hadn't slept at all. I make myself something to eat in a daze, black coffee and buttered toast, and sit down on the couch with the laptop I acquired from a pawn shop.

In this line of work, a man goes through laptops like burner phones, destroying the drives and discarding them when they start to have too much sensitive information on them. This one is new—for my purposes, anyway—wiped clean from the previous owner and ready to be used until it's time to move on.

Right now, the purpose that I want to use it for is finding out more about Natalia Obelensky—as she was, not as she might be now.

The first results that come up are, unsurprisingly, mostly focused around the ballet. Natalia was something of a prodigy, showing exceptional talent at a very young age, which quickly propelled her into a promising, burgeoning career. Her father's influence likely could have gotten her into those schools regardless—but it was her talent and skill that got her there— and kept her there.

She was the youngest *prima* on record for the Moscow ballet and the recipient of numerous accolades. I flick through article after article on her, not just pieces about the shows themselves that she danced in but articles with paparazzi photos, articles dissecting her fashion, discussing what event she'd been seen at or hadn't. The combination of her dancing ability and her father's name and wealth had turned Natalia Obelensky into a minor celebrity, and she wore it well.

In all of the photos, she never has a hair out of place, never anything except a smile on her face. No matter how candid or unexpectedly taken, there are no photos of Natalia frowning, sweaty from class or the gym, or tousled and unkempt. She must have known she was the object of so much attention because she's always carefully prepared for it.

I come across several of the pictures I'd seen in the past, ones taken before a show or at some gala or another. Those I expect utter perfection in, but I pore over the others, the candid ones, looking for any hint of the woman I saw last night.

They could be sisters; I can admit that. But even that's not enough to go on. There could be a dozen or more women out there with the same fine, delicate features. The dark hair has changed her look considerably–if it is Natalia. Appearance alone isn't enough. I sift through the photos again and again, forgetting my coffee and letting it go cold as I look for a picture that reminds me of what captivated me when *Athena* walked out on stage.

There's no hint of it. Natalia Obelensky is always cool and calculated, her face a bland smile, her eyes expressionless. There are no photos that I can find of her dancing, only ones taken before and after shows, and nowhere do I find even the slightest sign of the lustful, seductive woman that made me so hard that it hurt last night.

Natalia Obelensky, in these photos, is not a woman I could become obsessed with. She's a woman I would enjoy breaking, enjoy watching as her pale skin slowly grew stained with blood, as she lived some of the horrors that the woman I want so badly to avenge did. She is a woman of wealth and privilege who deserves none of it, who condoned her father's cruelties to keep it, and who deserves to pay for it.

But Athena–

I feel a cold finger down my spine as I think of the dangers of assuming too quickly. I've never before come across the possibility of doing something that I couldn't live with. Still, at the thought of hurting the woman last night, I feel a sick knot in my stomach. *If I'm wrong. If she's not Natalia. And if she is—*

Regardless, I slowly realize as I flick through the photos again, *she's a solution. If she is Natalia, then you can move forward as planned. And if she's not, then you can let her go. You'll know that Natalia Obelensky is not someone who can be found just now, and you'll look for the next possibility.*

I'll need to follow her. Find where she lives. In the end, I might frighten her—but better that than tortured or dead—if she's not Natalia. And if she isn't, I'll simply disappear from her life. She'll get over it—in time.

At the thought of not seeing her again, of discovering that she's not Natalia and disappearing, I feel an unfamiliar knot in my gut. A frustrated, rebellious feeling.

What if I want her for myself?

The memory of last night comes flooding back, of being so close to her at the edge of the stage. All I would have had to do is reach out and touch her. It was so terribly hard not to. All that had kept me from it was the knowledge that I'd been thrown out of the club with Davik's heavy hand on my shoulder if I did. I'd lose my chance to find out more.

But *god*, I'd wanted to touch her. To *grab* her. To strip away the flimsy, cheap lingerie and run my hands over her bare skin. She had barely been wearing any scent, unlike the other dancers who doused themselves in perfume, but she smelled intoxicating all the same. I wanted to devour her. I wanted to lay her back on the hard lacquered stage and feast on her pussy until she screamed, then tease her with my cock until she begged for my name so she could scream it when she came again. I wanted to fuck her, hard and deep, and find out how much she could take.

If I thought I could get away with it, I would have.

"*Bladya!*" I grit my teeth, slamming the laptop closed. There hasn't been a woman in years who could hold my attention into the next day, and yet I lost myself in fantasies of the one from the club last night, until several minutes passed, and I'm left with nothing but a hard cock and a thorough frustration with myself.

I have a job to do. I set the laptop aside, doing my best to refocus my thoughts on the day ahead. I have a meeting with Valeria Belyaevna, and if I know what's good for me, I won't be thinking about any woman other than her.

An afternoon spent talking to the Widow Maker can be a deadly one.

Mikhail

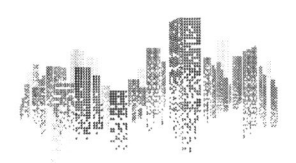

Meeting Valeria means taking the train out to Novogrod and a night spent at a hotel there before taking the train back. It also means too many hours spent sitting with my thoughts, which continuously drift back to Athena. My sleep was fractured last night, and I find myself drifting off as the train sways on the tracks. This time, my dreams are punctuated by pale flesh and gold lingerie, blue eyes staring hotly into mine.

In the dream, there are no rules about touching. I can grab her chin in my fingers and run the pad of my thumb over her full lower lip. I can press down, the edge of my fingernail sinking into soft flesh, warning her of the bite of pain that comes with talking back to me.

In the dream, she is mine to do with as I please.

I wake when the train comes to a halt, hard and aching. I adjust myself surreptitiously, my frustration mounting. There should be no woman on Earth who distracts me this much.

Focus on the job at hand, Kasilov.

I know the way to Valeria's loft, though no man with an ounce of self-preservation instinct would go there unless expressly invited.

Fortunately for me—so long as I'm successful—I've been subcontracted to help her with a job. That also means that, as long as she remains happy with me, I might be able to get some information from her.

It's a pleasant day out, and the walk from the train station to the part of town where her old, but well-kept building is located does wonders for my state of mind. I push Athena as far from my thoughts as I can, though I have no doubt she'll come back when it's time to ask Valeria the questions that I need answers to.

I take the stairs up to Valeria's floor two at a time, eager to finish this meeting as soon as possible. I won't be back in Moscow until tomorrow, no matter what. Still, every moment spent in the vicinity of Valeria Belyaevna is a moment at risk. The woman is a born killer.

Quickly, I rap on the door—three times in quick succession and then, after a moment, a fourth—as instructed. Seconds tick by, and then I hear footsteps padding softly towards the door, so quietly that someone without my long years of experience likely wouldn't have heard them at all.

The footsteps go still and silent. I knew this would happen too, per her instructions, and I repeat the pattern of knocking on the door. Even knowing I'm supposed to be here today, with her invitation, I feel a cold ball of ice in my gut as I wait for the door to open. There are few people in the world that I fear—Valeria Belyaevna is one of them.

A second passes, and then I hear the sound of locks flipping open. The door cracks, then swings wide, and the woman herself is standing there, green eyes narrowed at me.

"Good," she says sharply. "It's you."

She pivots on her heel, walking away from me with a crisp, purposeful stride, her long black braid swinging behind her as she walks further into the loft and leaves me to close and lock the door.

Objectively, she's a beautiful woman. She's built like an athlete, all lithe lines and muscle, a body honed as a weapon. For some—stupider men—that disciplined danger would be erotic. It would tempt them to make a foolish decision, and try to seduce her.

I'd sooner go to bed with a poisonous viper than Valeria, even if she asked. I'd have a better shot at making it out alive.

She perches on the edge of a wide ottoman in the center of her living room, a Bowie knife in her hand. She turns it over in her palm, glancing up at me as I take a seat. "You're here about the job."

It's not a question; she already knows why I'm here. If anything, it's a challenge, to see if there's something else I want. I'm not about to rise to the bait just yet.

"Who would turn down the chance to work with the Widow Maker?" I lean back on the couch, trying to look more casual than I feel. "No one who's heard of you, that's for sure."

Valeria snorts. "You won't be working *with* me. You'll be working *for* me. Doing my dirty work, so I can concentrate on more important things."

"Like what?" The question comes out before I can think better of it, and she looks sharply up at me, her green eyes narrowing as she reaches for the stone to sharpen her knife.

"I think that's my business and none of yours." Her lips press together, thinning. "Are you taking the job or not?"

"Would I be here if I weren't?"

Valeria shrugs. "Fair enough. It should be an easy enough job, for a man of your…skill." She waves a hand towards me, glancing up from sharpening again. "A man named Yuri Korov. He gave me bad information and led me to a dead end. So now I want him dead."

It takes every measure of self-control I possess not to let what I'm thinking show on my face, keeping my expression carefully blank.

"Yuri Korov," I repeat, feeling a pit in my stomach. Not for the sake of the man himself, but for the information he gave *me*. I'd been leaning towards believing that "Athena" really is Natalia Obelensky, that he'd been correct, but now my doubts surface again, making me waver.

Nothing slips past Valeria. She looks up, going still as her gaze searches my face. "You know this man already," she says finally, and it's not a question.

There's no point in lying to her, and no good could come of trying. I nod. "I've used him for information myself," I say carefully. "I'm familiar with him."

"Good. Then you'll have no difficulty finding him. I prefer if you draw it out a little. Make him feel some regret. And bring me a piece of him, so I know the job is done. I don't care what piece." She returns to her sharpening as casually as if she'd asked me to run out for butter and eggs, but it's not *that* that's bothering me.

I've been just as callous when it comes to carrying out jobs. I'll mourn the loss of a source of information, but if it's true that source has gone bad and Yuri has led me astray as well, I'll make his death even slower. I have no love for the man and no feeling about dispatching him from this earth.

"Should be an easy enough job. Even if he gets a whiff that he's in danger and tries to go underground, I'll dig him out. No problem."

"Good." Valeria sets the knife aside, leaning forward with her elbows on her spandex-clad knees. "Now for the rest of it. I know you have questions for me that have nothing to do with the job, Kasilov. So spit it out while I'm in a good mood."

I can expect no better invitation from her. "Natalia Obelensky," I say bluntly.

Valeria raises an eyebrow. "What about her?"

"I'm looking for her. Her father's dead, so I can't get to him. She's all that's left of the family now."

Valeria laughs, leaning back. "The Obelenskys are a hot topic these days, it seems. Are you looking to avenge her father? Some blood debt owed to them?" Her eyebrow lifts, and I know that how I answer the question will matter for what comes next.

"I wanted her father dead. Someone else has done that, so now I want the daughter."

There's a flicker of curiosity in her eyes. "For what purposes?"

"My own." *You're not the only one who can keep secrets. You might be a deadly snake, but I was the* Ussuri's *wolf.*

My heart beats hard in my chest, once, because a statement like that to a woman like Valeria is a dangerous one. Depending on her mood, she might take offense, or not.

To my surprise and pleasure, she chooses not to. She nods, picking up the knife again as she flicks it contemplatively against her fingertips. "Interesting," she says finally, "how many have come to my doorstep with Obelensky's blood on their mind. You are the third, but that's three more than I've had in recent memory. Although," she adds, twirling the knife, "that's not to say there haven't been many more who have wanted it. They just haven't had the balls to come to me."

"Who else?" It's my turn to lean forward, my eagerness forgotten in my need for information. "Who else came here looking for Obelensky?"

Valeria shrugs. "It's not for me to give names. An old friend–and someone he was helping. Obelensky had his woman."

"Your friend's?"

She shakes her head. "No. The one he was helping. He wanted to get to her, get her free of him. The interesting thing is–"

Valeria pauses, drawing out the word, her eyes glittering as she looks at me. She knows she has me on the hook, wondering what she'll say next, and she's enjoying every second of it.

"The woman they wanted back," she says finally, "was Obelensky's bastard daughter. I heard his other daughter, the legitimate one, had some play in all this. What it was, I don't know precisely. It's hard to separate rumor from fact, especially with something like this."

I struggle to keep my composure, seeing the beginnings of the truth unfold in front of me. "And you helped them? You helped them get to him?"

Valeria shrugs. "I gave some information in exchange for information of my own. A fair trade, when I had no love for Obelensky either. No reason to protect him. Business, that's all. You can't fault me for that." Her gaze chills a little, warning me off from a train of thought in which she's responsible for the loss of my first target. "He wasn't yours to kill. Someone else got to him first, that's all. We all lose sometimes."

"Well, now I have a new target." I don't look away, holding her gaze. "I'd like to know what happened to Obelensky. Who, precisely, killed him, and what Natalia's part was in all that."

Valeria shrugs. "I can't tell you much more. Natalia Obelensky is gone, as far as I know. I've largely stayed out of digging into the details surrounding Konstantin's demise. It's a clusterfuck and a power shift that I want no part of."

"That's where you might be wrong." I let a small smile creep onto my mouth, enjoying the novel feeling of the possibility that I might have information she doesn't. "Natalia might be here, in Moscow."

I pull the photo of her at the club that Yuri gave me out of my pocket, holding it out to her. After a moment's hesitation, Valeria takes it, unfolding the sheet of paper. She peers at it, frowning.

"You think this is Natalia?"

I shrug. "It was suggested to me that she might be. I've seen her in person, and–it's possible."

Valeria makes a face. "I've met Natalia, once. This woman isn't her." She scans the picture again, shaking her head. "She would never–"

She pauses, looking at the photo once more. "But then again–"

"What?"

Valeria blows out a long breath through her nose, scanning the picture and then handing it back to me. "Natalia isn't stupid enough to hide in plain sight. Too many people know her. Dyed hair and a different wardrobe aren't enough to change that. But hiding just out of sight, in a place no one would think she'd deign to go to…it's a risky gamble, but one that she might take–if she were desperate enough."

"What do you mean, *desperate*?"

"She likely has no way out. Of Russia, I mean." Valeria steeples her fingers in front of her. "Trying to get out on her own passport would be dangerous. Her accounts will have been seized by her father's friends or his enemies, her house is being watched, and her connections cut off. If she wants to get out, she'll need money to escape. Fake papers are expensive, and the price is only going up." She frowns. "Who gave you the photo?"

Once again, there's no point in trying to lie. "Yuri."

Valeria laughs. "Shit. Well, either he gave you bad information as well, or he fears you more than he does me. For your sake, you ought to hope it's not the latter. I wouldn't like that."

There's a predatory gleam in her eyes as she says that last, but I do my best to ignore it. "For his sake, I hope he did give me good information. But either way, he's a dead man. *I* fear you more than I care about him."

She smirks. "Good answer. For that, I'll give you something else, Kasilov. Something that will help you."

Adrenaline spikes in my veins, and it's all I can do not to seem too eager. "Anything would be appreciated, of course."

"I still have the Syndicate's ear. *Vladimir's* ear, when he's in a decent mood. I'll mention you. If you can get an audience with him, he might be interested in helping you–even compensating you–for cleaning up those loose ends if this woman really is Natalia."

"You think the Syndicate has an interest in this?"

"Having her floating around, unaccounted for, with the power vacuum left after her father's death? Not a good thing. They'd rather wipe the name out and start fresh, even install someone of their own in the space left behind. I'm certain of it." She smiles. "Play your cards right, and you might walk out of this with more allies than when you began."

I imagine that–the possibility of going back to Viktor not only with Natalia to deliver to him, but with stronger ties of my own to the Russian underworld. It sends a thrill through me, the idea of that kind of victory. But it also feels almost too good to be true.

"Why aren't you going to them yourself?" I ask carefully, raising an eyebrow. "With that kind of information, why not ask for their support, and collect her for them along with their goodwill and reward?"

Valeria pauses, and I can see in that pause that she's deciding how much, exactly, she wants to share with me. "I've gotten too tied up in it already," she says finally. "I want my distance from the Syndicate, a distance *I* choose, not more involvement." Her eyes narrow shrewdly. "The information doesn't come for free. I'll help you in what ways I can–so long as you cut me in on what the Syndicate pays you. Thirty percent. The rest is yours."

It's a good deal. The worst part is that it keeps me working closely with Valeria, who no one wants closer than arm's length. As long as I can keep her there, though, I should be safe. As long as I can deliver Yuri.

"It's a deal," I tell her flatly. "Thirty percent. And I'll bring you proof when Yuri is dead. He won't be delivering any more bad information."

"Take the piece off of him while he's still alive," she says with a cold smile. "Come back when he's dead, and not before. I don't care when you meet with the Syndicate, but don't return here until you've finished *my* job."

"Understood." I stand up as she does, knowing instinctively that the meeting is over, and I'm glad for it. I follow her to the door, adrenaline thumping through my veins at how close I am to being out of this death box of an apartment.

I can't entirely breathe again until I'm out on the landing, the door shut and locked behind me, but once I can, I'm glad I took the meeting.

Yuri.

The Syndicate.

Natalia.

It's all coming together. The next step is to determine if Yuri gave me the right information.

If he didn't, not even God will be able to help him.

Natalia

Another letter.

I stand in my kitchen, holding it in my shaking hands. It's dark out, which makes the fact that I walked out to find it just as I was about to leave even more terrifying.

What if whoever left it is still out there? Waiting?

Licking my dry lips, I look down at the piece of paper. It's in the same style as before—cut-out, glued-on words.

Pizda. We will find you. You will bleed.

"Well, you've already technically found me, haven't you, you bastard?" I ball up the paper in an angry fist, stalking across the kitchen to throw it into the garbage to join the first. My hands are still shaking, and I try to steel myself for the walk ahead of me.

It's a long way to the club, and for a moment, I can't make myself head for the door. It feels like an impossible task—to walk those blocks knowing that there's someone out there in the shadows who, just minutes ago, slipped something threatening under my door.

You could call off sick. Girls do it all the time. But even as I think it, I know I can't. I need the money. Every night, every shift, is one day closer to my escape from this place. From threatening letters and handsy men and cheap store-bought hair dye. Out there somewhere, in a smaller town in France, London, Amsterdam, or one of a dozen places, there's a version of myself living happy and free, my hair blonde again, my days spent without worrying that someone is in the shadows, waiting for me.

Somewhere, a version of myself has put the past so far behind her that she doesn't have to fear it catching up with her any longer. The thought is enough to propel me towards the door, out onto the landing, and down to the street, towards the job that will give me that chance.

If I can't make the money to get out of here, it won't matter anyway. I might as well be dead.

I can only live like this for so long. I can only hide for so long. I'll be caught eventually, and then–

I swallow hard, keeping to my quick but steady pace as I walk down the street. It's a little too warm out for a hoodie, but I threw on an oversized one anyway, hoping the bagginess will help hide the fact that I'm a woman walking alone. I'm slender and small-breasted enough that the combination of my loose jeans and the hoodie should make a difference, and I keep my head lowered, looking down and slightly ahead as I walk.

It's something I've honed and practiced since coming back, but tonight it feels more necessary than ever. I want to look around to see if anyone is following me, but I don't dare.

And then I hear footsteps behind me.

They're quiet at first as if they're much further away, and then louder. Steady, keeping behind me at a regular pace, my heart leaps into my throat. I suddenly feel cold despite the hoodie and the mild early summer night air, blood chilling in my veins, and I have to fight back panicked tears.

Another block, and the footsteps are closer still, but still at a steady pace. I can't pretend that it's not something strange. I can feel a warning prickle at the back of my neck, and as I see the light of a cab coming down the street, I make a snap decision.

Without looking to see who's following me, I step out into the street and hail the cab, praying to whoever might be listening that they'll stop. That I can get away from whoever is now much, much closer.

I steel myself for a hand on my arm, grabbing me or an arm around my waist, hauling me backward towards an alley. I brace myself to fight.

The cab stops, and I fling myself forward, snatching the door open and tumbling inside. As I do, the footsteps pass by me, continuing down the street.

"The Cat's Meow," I say breathlessly, craning my head over my shoulder to see who was walking behind me. All I see is the shape of a person, average height and somewhat broad shoulders, walking at a steady clip away from the cab that's now pulling out in the opposite direction. There are no defining features, no way to know if it's someone threatening, man or woman, if I've just wasted some of my precious money for nothing.

I lean back against the seat, feeling tears well in my eyes all over again. I wipe viciously at my eyes, not wanting to let them fall, but a few do anyway. I can't afford this cab ride, but what else was I supposed to do? Let myself be followed all the way to the club, just in case the person following me didn't already know where I worked? Risk whether or not it was someone after me or just another person out on the street?

I don't have answers to any of it, but it doesn't matter anyway. I made my choice, and I pay the driver when I get out of the cab at the back door of the club, steeling myself to go inside.

What I really want is to get back into the cab and flee back to the dubious safety of my apartment, but that would be even more of a waste. Instead, I shoulder my bag and walk inside, heading straight for the dressing room.

Ruby is already there, curling her hair. "Athena!" She practically squeals my 'name,' twisting so that the edge of the hot curling iron briefly brushes against her neck. "Ow!"

She shakes it free of her hair, frowning as she peers in the mirror at the light pink mark. "Dammit. Well, it just looks like a little hickey. It's fine." She flashes me a bright smile, which quickly fades as she gets a good look at me. "What the hell are you wearing? And why do you look like you've seen a ghost?"

"Just someone else walking down the same street as me, near my apartment." I shrug, giving my best impression of someone who knows she's overreacted, when in fact, I'm fairly certain that the *last* thing I did was overreact. The more time that passes since I hopped in the cab, the more sure I am that I probably averted disaster. "And I was cold."

Ruby gives me a look that says she doesn't entirely believe me, but she turns back to curling her hair as I drag the hoodie over my head and deposit it on the floor next to my chair. "Sooo," she says slowly, dragging out the word as if it's something delicious. "I heard someone bought time in the champagne room with you the other night. Someone *new*. Davik was talking about him with one of the other guys. I guess he got a bad vibe from him?" She wrinkles her nose, glancing sideways at me as she spirals another lock of her hair around the iron. "What about you? Was something off?"

"He was an asshole." I shrug, forcing back the quick flicker of desire that flares up at the mention of Mikhail. "Arrogant and entitled. You know, practically the first thing he did after he got me in the room was to ask if I did more than just dance and how much it would cost him?"

"And how much did you tell him it would cost?" Ruby's eyes twinkle with mischief. She knows good and well that I don't do anything more than lap dances, and she enjoys giving me shit about it.

"Please tell me you didn't turn him down flat. Davik said he looked out of place. Like he has money."

"If he wanted an escort, he could go two blocks over," I say stiffly as I get my makeup pouch out of my bag. "This is a strip club."

Ruby lets out a low whistle. "You know that's just what it says on the sign. A man like that—" she shakes her head, tugging loose the last curl and setting the iron aside, close to my mirror so that I can use it. "You could clean up. He'd probably pay any price you set, if he wants you that badly."

"I told him no. I don't do that. I don't want to." The words come out flat, staccato, probably harsher than necessary, but I can't help it. Mikhail's assumption that it was even a possibility had angered me more than I realized. "Men like that need to realize they can't just have anything they fucking want."

"You don't *have* to." Ruby's eyes widen a little at my outburst. "I'm just saying, men like that pay a lot of money to feel like they're powerful enough to convince a woman to service them." She grins. "If you're not down for it, maybe next time he comes around, I'll see if I can get him to go back with *me*. I'd happily take some of his money."

"Go for it." I shrug, but a small, hot, irrational burst of jealousy flashes through me at the thought of Ruby on her knees for Mikhail, one that I don't want and don't understand.

Get a fucking grip. You don't even like *him. What does it fucking matter if he's hot? He's an asshole, like you said. Let Ruby deal with him.*

I steel myself to see him again when I walk out onto the stage, the lights coming up as my newest track starts playing, one I don't know as well as the others. There's the usual crowd of faceless men around the stage, ones I don't remember and never will. Still, as I start moving through the steps and running my hands over the pole, I don't see Mikhail.

I scan the crowd for him, but there's no sight of the ice-blue eyes that I think I'd be able to easily pick out, or his domineering presence. He stands out here, a man among boys, a lord among peasants, and I know within seconds that he's not in the room.

Disappointment flashes through me, the same bolt as the jealousy earlier, except this makes me feel chilled and flat. I miss a step, sliding down an inch on the pole gracelessly before finding my footing. For the first time since I started working here, I hear a tittering of laughter.

Shame and anger sweep over me, hot and burning, and I clench my teeth. *You're not even here, and you're distracting me, you fucking asshole.*

I can't afford to fuck this up. One wrong step, one second of letting them see me as a source of humor instead of arousal, and I can see my tips for the night dwindling. Tips that I *need*. I haven't worked the last two nights—weekday shifts have been slimmed down, and as one of the newer girls, I don't have the same seniority that some of the others do, to hang onto those shifts. I've picked up unwanted days and nights from other dancers where I can, but there's only so much to go around.

After a moment, I manage to settle into my routine, but I still feel off. I can't seem to stop glancing around, looking to see if he's come in the door or is making his way through the crowd toward the stage. It makes me angrier that I can't shake the distraction.

You've never let any man get to you like this. Why are you starting now?

Focus. Out of everything that could distract you, it shouldn't be this.

I try to slip back into that place where everything is on autopilot, but this song is too new for me to do it effectively. I don't make any more mistakes as bad as that first one, but I feel *off*, like I'm a beat behind the entire time. I miss customer cues, too caught up in the inward argument with myself, and I know by the time my solo comes to an end that I haven't done this poorly since my first night—maybe not even then. There's only a smattering of tips, and then as if to rub salt in the wound, when I look up, I see Igor standing by the bar, his arms crossed over his chest.

Shit. He doesn't always come out and watch the dancers, but it seems like tonight he'd decided to do a scan of the floor. *Just my fucking luck.* As I descend the stage, I can tell that he's not happy.

No one flocks towards me for the chance at a floor dance, and I see Igor–a tall, imposing man greying at the temples–crook his finger towards me in a clear indication for me to head his way. I wince, but I have no choice but to obey.

Something else that pisses me off.

"You're not yourself tonight," he says flatly, without preamble, as soon as I'm close. "My customers don't appear to be happy. And when they're not happy–"

"--you're not happy." It's an easy sentence to finish. "I'm sorry–"

"You're a talented dancer." He huffs out a breath as if it displeases him to admit it. "But no one here is here for ballet. They want to be titillated. *Aroused.* Your skill matters less to me than your ability to seduce. That is your job here. To seduce and tease and toe the line of giving them what they want, so that they continue spending money in the hopes of having it. Do you understand?"

I feel my heart flip in my chest. Igor's eyes are narrowed and dark, his expression unhappy. *I don't want to lose this job.* I know I could go to half a dozen clubs on this street and find work–more, probably–but I'd come here because I heard Igor didn't allow his girls to be mistreated. I know that won't be true of every club.

"I'm sorry," I say with as much humility as I can manage. "I'm just not feeling well, that's all. It won't happen again."

"Call off if you're sick," Igor says bluntly. "Another girl will be more than happy to take your spot. One who will make me money."

"I'm sorry–" I start to repeat, but he cuts me off.

"Go home. You can return when you feel well enough to focus on your work again."

There's no arguing with him. I can hear the cold finality in his voice, and even in the brief time that I've been here, I know Igor well enough to know when he can't be reasoned with–which is most of the time. I just nod, turning and walking quickly back towards the dressing room, my face downcast to hide the well of tears in my eyes.

What a fucking waste. I should have just called off from the start. I barely made enough on stage to make up for what I'd spent on the cab ride here, and I'll have to tip the house out of that, which means tonight is a loss. And I have no one to blame but myself for letting myself be so distracted.

Even the letter hadn't thrown me off as much as Mikhail had.

One of the other girls, a gorgeous platinum blonde who calls herself Taffy, is the only one left in the dressing room when I swoop back in, my teeth sunken into my lower lip to try to keep from crying. She looks up, startled, and then her face relaxes as she sees that it's me.

"Athena–are you okay?" She cocks her head, looking concerned. "Did that man come back? The one from the other night? I heard Davik didn't like him–"

"Word really spreads fast around here, doesn't it?" The words come out sharper than I intended, and Taffy flinches back. "I just don't feel good. I'm going home."

"What if he comes in tonight? You don't want to miss out–"

"Then one of you can enjoy. He's a customer, not my fucking boyfriend." I can hear the acid in my voice, made worse by the fact that I feel another of those hot, instantaneous flashes of jealousy at the thought of Taffy straddling him.

I strip out of my lingerie, pulling the loose jeans and hoodie back on for the walk back. I feel tense and pissed off, all my muscles sore, and I'm suddenly longing for a hot shower and to fall back into my own bed. *I'll just sleep it off. Reset my brain. Tomorrow will be better.* I have a feeling Igor won't be happy if I come back to work tomorrow—I think I'm on some kind of temporary hiatus until he feels like I've had enough time to think about what I've done—but I can't afford to not risk it. The worst-case scenario is that he fires me, and then I'll go to another club. I can't go days without working a shift.

"I hope you feel better!" Taffy calls after me, and I wave at her, doing my best to acknowledge it with the current mood I'm in. I rub the back of my neck as I walk down the steps leading out of the back door of the club and to the street, trying to work some of the soreness out. It doesn't help much.

Bag slung over one shoulder, I make my way past the puddles and cigarette butts, out to the sidewalk. I desperately want to call a cab again but resist the urge, thinking of the meager cash in my pocket tonight.

There are no footsteps following me this time as I head back to my apartment. However, I still have that uncomfortable, prickling sensation that I'm being watched. For all I know, I *am*, and after the second letter, it's hard not to imagine someone skulking in the shadows, watching me walk home, thinking of what they'll do next to try to frighten me into—what, exactly?

What do they want? To catch me? Hurt me? Just to scare me? That particular not-knowing makes it worse. I have no idea what this person's goal is, and though in my past life, I tended towards realism, if not optimism, now it's hard not to jump to the worst-case scenario. I want out of this nightmare, away from this feeling of being trapped, like I'm caged without any ability to see who's on the other side of my bars watching me.

The only way to accomplish that is money.

Money will buy me a fake passport. A new name. A new start.

There's no getting out of Russia, no starting over without that.

The second I'm in my apartment, I slam the door behind me, locking all four of the locks tightly. I stride into the bedroom, stripping off my clothes, and I glance at the large windows on the left side of my room. They're bare and facing the street, and I find myself wishing that I'd spent the money to replace the blinds or buy curtains—something my landlord will absolutely never do.

I feel exposed, but a tiny thought slips into my head, startling me.

What if it's Mikhail following you? What if he's outside right now, watching you through those open windows?

I think of those ice-blue eyes dragging over my body, taking in my exposed flesh, and my arms drop away from my breasts without my meaning for them to. My skin prickles, suddenly chilled, but a thrill washes over me at the same time.

A small part of me, one that shocks and horrifies me, feels *aroused* at the thought. I squeeze my thighs together, feeling the dampness there, and a knot forms in my belly.

I shouldn't want this. I shouldn't. I've never been an exhibitionist. Never thrilled at the idea of a man I hardly knew watching me, lusting after me.

What is wrong with me?

I tell myself he's not there. That *no one* at all is following me, much less the wealthy, arrogant asshole with the cold blue stare who had managed to insult me within five minutes of meeting me. I tell myself that all of this is in my head.

It doesn't change the fact that a part of me is excited at the possibility that it might not be.

Mikhail

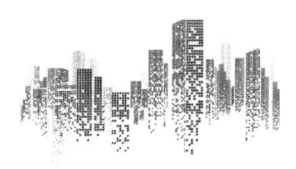

I didn't mean to follow her all the way back to her apartment.

I talked myself out of going to the club tonight. I wanted to see her outside of it—when she's not putting on a show. To see how she walked, how she behaved, how she carried herself. *It might give me a better idea as to what the truth is,* I reasoned.

It was easy to follow her. Easier than I imagined it would be. It took me a moment to realize it was her when she came out, dressed in that loose clothing that was clearly meant to make her look less feminine. Less of a target for men who might want to hurt her. She came out too early, long before her shift should have been over. If I hadn't arrived earlier than I expected to, I might have missed her.

She was upset, clearly. It was clear from the way she walked, hands shoved in her jean pockets, chin tucked in, shoulders slouched. *What happened in there?* I thought when I saw her. I felt a quick, unexpected flash of anger that someone might have hurt her in some way.

It brought me up short. I have no reason to care if she's upset. No reason to give a shit if someone hurt her feelings. It shouldn't matter to me.

Only I'm allowed to hurt her, I reasoned with myself as I started down the sidewalk after her. *Her pain is all mine.*

I expected her to pick up on the fact that she was being followed at some point—to have to duck into a nearby alley to keep from being caught. I hadn't thought I'd make it all the way back to her apartment or that I'd walk along the sidewalk adjacent to it only to come face to face with the windows facing directly into her bedroom.

I know it's hers because I see her standing there. She looks forlorn, exhausted, and I half expect her to fall into bed clothed and for that to be the end of it.

She reaches down, pulling the oversized hoodie she's wearing up and over her head. I'm treated to the sight of her slender form in a tight grey tank top, her small breasts outlined, braless, against the soft fabric.

For a moment, I forget I'm standing in the middle of the sidewalk, transfixed.

Her hands go to the button of her jeans, and my cock twitches as I realize she's about to start undressing. It shouldn't be as erotic as it is, watching her undo it, watching her push the loose denim down her hips. I've seen her in nothing but scraps of gold fabric, yet watching her undress like this, entirely unaware that I'm standing outside, is rapidly hardening my cock to the point of pain.

I've never been a voyeur. It's never been my kink; if I were asked, I'd still say it isn't. But this—*her*—

It has nothing to do with the job or with my goals. This gives me nothing, tells me nothing. It can be for nothing except my own personal pleasure, and yet, I can't tear myself away.

My cock throbs, aching, and I dart backward, climbing over the low iron fence surrounding the bushes at the edge of the sidewalk. I crouch down, mostly hidden, and watch as she reaches for the tank top.

I wonder if she's going to take it off, or if she's just stripping down to sleep. My pulse beats hard in my throat, what blood that's left in my head that hasn't rushed down to my cock pounding in my ears as she tugs the fabric upwards, revealing the pale, flat expanse of her belly. Higher, and I see the slight curve beneath her breasts, then tight, hard, rosy nipples as her arms rise upwards. Her body goes taut, her hipbones sharp above the edge of her panties, and my mouth goes dry with the hot wave of lust that tears through me.

I've never been this hard in my entire life. When she hooks her thumbs into the edge of her panties, pushing them down, I feel as if I'm going to burst. The throbbing, aching desire is too much to bear, and as she turns, her perfect ass framed in the window, I swallow hard with no saliva left in my mouth.

She disappears into the room just beyond, and I'm left with a choice to make.

I can leave now, go back home and take care of my now-painful arousal, and get some sleep before I decide what to do next.

Or—I can wait for her to come out again.

From the location of the room and the wisps of steam I can see faintly from beneath the door, I'm sure it's her bathroom. My cock strains at the front of my jeans at the thought of her under a hot spray of water, soap sliding down gleaming wet flesh, her hands spreading soap over her breasts. I know I *should* leave, that watching a naked woman outside of her window isn't part of the plan, but I can't tear myself away.

I want to see her again—naked and vulnerable, bared only to me.

I've never been a man who concerned himself very much with what's right and wrong. I can't find the will to start now.

It feels like an eternity before she comes out again. The door opens, and I feel myself tense. Every muscle in my body feels rigid, not just my throbbing cock, as I see her walk back into her bedroom with a towel wrapped tightly around her slim body, tucked neatly into the space between her breasts. Her black hair falls down her back in a wet curtain, clinging to her skin, and my palms itch with the desire to wrap it around my hand, pulling her head back for my teeth to bite at her long, swanlike throat.

Her hand goes to the towel, and I feel my chest tighten. I want to see her again, all that pale flesh, and it feels as if my vision narrows down to just her, the world around me going silent. There's only the sharp line of her collarbone, the slight swells of her breasts above the nubby fabric, her long fingers tugging it loose and letting it fall away so I can see every inch.

Her skin is still damp, glistening in the low light. I feel my breath hitch in my throat as she climbs onto the bed, and I half expect her to reach over to the lamp and switch it off, ending this. But instead, as I watch, her hand presses against her chest, sliding downwards.

Is she—

It's hard to believe what I'm seeing. I watch, my lust beating in my veins like a second heartbeat, as her fingers cup beneath her breast, sliding over and up the soft flesh to pluck at her hardening nipple. I see the slight arch of her hips, the way her thighs part, and I know what I'd feel if I were next to her now—the quick indrawn breath, the twitching shudder of her skin as she's slowly aroused. Even out here, with brick and glass between us, I can feel the steady, slow burn of her desire as it heightens.

Her other hand comes up, both of them squeezing her breasts, pushing them slightly together as she rolls her nipples between forefingers and thumbs, tweaking and pulling. Her hips shift from side to side, her head tilting back, and I can see her full lips part.

I can almost hear her breathing quicken in my imagination.

When one of her hands begins the slow slide down her belly, down towards the soft folds that I know must be drenched by now, I can't stand it any longer. My hand falls to my fly, thumbing open the button with a sharp, jerky motion, yanking down my zipper. My cock spills free into my hand, hard and aching with a need beyond my ability to stop myself, and I close my fist around it, eager to watch her.

Her back arches as her hand finds its way between her thighs, and I know her fingers are on her clit. I can imagine how slick she must feel, how hot, and my fingers circle my own swollen cockhead, gathering my leaking pre-cum onto my fingertips. I slide it down my shaft, squeezing, stroking, trying to match the quick movements of her hand.

She looks beautiful, exquisite, beyond anything I could have imagined. Her legs fall open, knees spread wide as her hips arch up, and my mouth aches for a taste of her. I want her tied to a bed, spread-eagled and unable to move, my lips and tongue torturing her pussy until she'd give me anything in order to let her come. I want my bed drenched with her, the scent of her on my fingers, and my hand moves faster, my throbbing cock eager for release.

Not yet. I want to come with her. I can see her hand moving more quickly, too, rubbing more frantically now, and I slow my own strokes, feeling my balls tighten dangerously. I can hear nothing, but I can imagine her moans as I see her mouth open, knowing she must be close.

I know I've crossed a line that I never imagined I would. I've never done anything like this before–but something about her arouses me beyond the point of sanity, makes me feel as if I'm losing my mind with desire. Something in the back of my mind goes off like a warning bell, reminding me that no woman has ever done this to me, that I'm hovering on the edge of something dangerous–but at this moment, I'm too far gone to care.

I see her other hand drop down between her legs, and my cock throbs in my hand, fresh pre-cum trickling down my shaft, very close to being my release instead. I know she must be sliding two fingers into herself, feeling the sweet hot clench of her pussy around them as she pulls them deeper, hungry for cock, hungry to be filled.

My hips jerk forward, fucking my fist as I imagine sinking into those hot depths, fucking her so hard and fast that I'd hear nothing but her screams of mingled pleasure and pain, my cock filling her beyond anything she's ever felt.

Fuck, fuck–I squeeze my cock hard, feeling the first swelling of my climax, desperate to hold it back until I can come at the same time as her. *I'd have made you come already, malen'kaya balerina.* She twists on the bed, her hips snapping upwards, and I know she's on the edge.

I can't hear her cry of pleasure, but I know when she comes. I see the hard arch of her back, the way her thighs suddenly snap closed, clenching around her hands as she keeps fingering herself, riding the waves of pleasure. My hand becomes a blur on my cock, my left hand gripping the edge of the fence to stay upright as my hips jerk wildly, my cock erupting with a hot wave of dizzying pleasure as I spill my cum into the dirt and shrubbery beneath me, watching the woman I've become obsessed with orgasm inside her bedroom just beyond.

I'm still coming when I see her roll onto her stomach, ass arched upwards as she drives her fingers into herself harder. My cock throbs with new lust even as my cum is still spilling out. I keep stroking, my slick shaft still hard as I watch in stunned arousal.

I want to fuck her so badly it hurts. I've never felt anything like the blind lust that overtakes me, never stayed hard after an orgasm. Still, I keep stroking, my hips jerking in time with hers as I watch her fuck herself back onto her own hand, her face buried in her pillow.

It's all too easy to imagine wrapping my hand around that wet, dark hair, pulling her head back as I fucked her from behind, making her come like that until she was so drenched that all I'd have to do is nudge my cock upwards a little in order to sink into her tight asshole–

You're clearly not a virgin, Athena–or is it, Natalia? But have you ever been fucked in the ass?

"Oh god—" The words spill out of my lips in a harsh grunt, heedless of anyone who might hear, but the world has dissolved around me anyway. There's nothing but her, nothing but the sight of her other hand coming up to rub her clit again, her legs splaying wide as she pushes herself into the mattress, ass still arched back as I see her start to come again, grinding against her hand as she drives herself to a second orgasm.

To my utter shock, I feel a bolt of pure pleasure tear through me as my balls tighten and my cock erupts for a second time, jetting more hot cum against the bushes. My entire body shudders, my teeth clenched around a moan, as I come twice without a break in between for the first time in my life.

I watch her slump against the bed as my cock finally starts to soften in my hand, and I feel as if my entire body is pulsing. The awareness of where I am and what I've just engaged in starts to come back to me, and I quickly fix my clothing, tucking myself back into my jeans and zipping them up.

This is turning into an obsession. This has nothing to do with revenge. She'll never even know you were here. This is on you, and nothing else.

I watch her fumble for a blanket, dragging it up over herself as she snuggles down into her pillow, her other hand reaching for the light switch. I feel my heart drop a little in my chest with sudden disappointment as her body disappears under the blanket—and then everything else fades into darkness—and I know I'm dancing very close to the edge of something I don't want to cross over into.

It was just tonight, I tell myself, looking around to see if I'm clear to come out of my hiding place. *She got me worked up at the club, and I hadn't had a release since then. I just needed to let off some steam. Tomorrow, I'll get back to the real purpose of this.*

As I slip out of the bushes and start back down the sidewalk away from her apartment, I tell myself that I won't push the envelope with her again. I won't toe the line so closely between what actually matters to my plan, and what's just my own desire.

But as I walk down the dimly lit street, hands shoved in my pockets, my thoughts are still full of the sight of her, face buried in her pillow as she shuddered and came on her fingers…and I know that tonight, my dreams will be better than the ones I've had before.

They'll be full of what I imagine to be the sweet sounds of her moans.

Natalia

There's someone outside my window.

I can't see who it is, exactly. I can see them out of the corner of my eye, a shadow, a person, but when I try to look, they slip away, like trying to catch a ghost.

I can hear their breathing. Panting. A desperate, clawing need to find me, to catch me, like prey. I'm being hunted; I can feel it.

I should be afraid. I should be quivering in terror, running for my life. But instead, I feel a strange thrill, prickling my skin and rippling down my spine.

Catch me. Hurt me. Do your worst.

I don't know who it is. I sit in front of my mirror, brushing out my hair, wincing at the stark blackness of it. I hate it.

"This isn't you, Natalia."

A voice echoes behind me, as amorphous and shadowy as the figure following me. I look down at the brush in my hand and see thick chunks of dark hair tangled in it. More scatters across my vanity, blowing away in an unseen and unfelt breeze, and when I look up, my hair is honey-blonde again.

I reach up to touch it.

"That's so much better, isn't it, lyubov*?"*

The voice is familiar. I feel hands on my shoulders, clutching, clamping down. And there, above my head, I see them floating, looking at me.

A pair of ice-blue eyes.

I wake up, gasping into my pillow. The room around me is bright, flooded with sunlight–yet another reason I wish I had coverings for the windows. I wince at it, blinking and squeezing my eyes shut before opening them again and pushing myself up on my elbows.

I look at the clock next to my bed. *11:00.*

"Fuck!" I squeeze my eyes shut again, burying my face in the pillow. I told Ruby I'd go shopping with her today, more as a means of getting her to stop badgering me about letting her come over to my place to hang out than anything else. As much as I enjoy her company, I'm not about to let anyone else into my space, especially after the threatening letters slipped under my door.

Under other circumstances, shopping might not be such a good idea, either. Fortunately, Ruby is in the same sort of financial straits that I am now, which means we won't frequent any place where I might run into someone from my old life. No one I'd ever met as Natalia Obelensky would darken the door of a shop in this part of town–or several blocks around it.

The only problem is, I'm supposed to meet her in fifteen minutes.

I fling the blanket back, dragging myself out of bed. I feel a faint soreness between my thighs, brought on by how hard I slammed my fingers into myself last night–wanting a rough and hard orgasm to push away the feelings left over from the awful night. What I really wanted was a cock pounding me into oblivion, wiping my thoughts bare, leaving me gasping and liquid at the end of it, but I made do.

It wasn't enough, though. It never is.

There's a worn dresser on the other end of the sparsely furnished bedroom, and I stumble over to it, fumbling in the top drawer for a pair of clean panties. I drag the black cotton boyshorts over my hips, yanking out a clean, loose black tank top with a small pocket above the breast, and throw it over my head. I'm small-breasted enough to not bother with a bra, and most days, I don't, opting for loose enough clothing that it doesn't matter.

A pair of straight-cut black jeans, worn combat boots from a charity shop, my hair loosely gathered at the back of my head, and I'm ready to meet Ruby. Looking in the mirror, I feel certain that even someone who knew me once would have a hard time recognizing me now.

It's not just the hair. It hasn't been all that long, but I look older. *Harder*. There was a lightness in my face before that I can see has been extinguished. I can see lingering bitterness there, instead.

I should be in Santorini, laying in a bikini on the beach while a handsome green-eyed Greek man feeds me grapes. Or in Paris, walking down cobblestoned streets. Browsing a museum in London. Sitting on the deck of his yacht.

What the fuck was wrong with you, Adrian?

I grit my teeth, shaking away the memories. They're no good now. I don't want to recall how good it was before the fight, either. I don't want to remember when I thought I had a chance at something beyond the life I resigned myself to. Now I've fallen into a pit of despair, and the only way out is to claw my way up and envision something entirely new.

It feels exhausting.

Please don't let there be anything new under my door today. I don't know if I can handle another threatening letter.

I let out a sigh of relief when I step into my kitchen and see that there's nothing by the door. "Thank *fuck*," I whisper as I open it, stepping outside, but as I reach behind myself to pull the front door shut, something swings against my hand.

I spin around sharply, reaching for it.

A thin gold chain, the length of a bracelet, hanging from the doorknob. On it dangles a tiny charm, and when I slip it off the doorknob and hold it up for inspection, my heart pounding in my chest, I see a small phoenix.

My heart stops in my chest.

Rebirth. Rising from the ashes. Something that disappears and returns.

It's a message, but not one I want. It means whoever left it knows too much about me. Too much about where I've been–and what I've done.

I clutch it in my fist, feeling a tremor ripple through me as I shove it into my pocket. My thoughts immediately go back to my father's compound, to the men I helped find their way down there, in search of my half-sister.

Sasha Federova. Maximilian Agosti. Levin Volkov.

What if I'm their loose end?

I can't imagine my sweet sister would have a hand in this. I've never been a trusting person by nature, but I also think I'm someone who's good at reading others. Sasha isn't cruel or vicious, and she isn't someone who would worry about loose ends. I also can't imagine what reason she would have for wanting me gone. She played a very small part in my father's death, and he was the only person she had left to fear, as far as I know.

As for Max and Levin–

I clench my jaw, trying to puzzle it out as I walk. *Would they have a real reason? To keep me silent about what I know? What I helped them do?*

I don't think so. Even if they wanted me dead, which I don't believe, neither man seemed the type to do *this*. Levin would look me in the eyes while putting a bullet through my brain. Max–well, I was honestly surprised that Max had that kind of violence in him, even when my father threatened the woman he loved.

It's not one of them. *But who is it?*

It's all I can think about as I walk. Even in the bright sunlight of the mid-morning, I feel like I'm being followed, watched. I feel shivery and uneasy, the fear of the footsteps behind me last night and the eeriness of my dream lingering around me. I have the same urge I had last night–to go home and crawl back into my bed.

But I can't stay there forever, and Ruby will take my mind off things.

She's at the small, shabby cafe that she asked me to meet her at, her hands wrapped around a steaming cup of tea, a china plate of a different pattern than the cup set in front of her with a small stack of breakfast bread. She sees me the second I step through the door, half-rising to wave me over, and the excitement on her face makes me glad that I crawled out of bed.

"You look like you just woke up," she says in a teasing, accusatory tone. "If Igor could see you now…."

"He'd probably think I'm actually sick." I look at the menu, suddenly eager for something hot and caffeinated. "I look like this because I *did* just roll out of bed."

"I did, too," Ruby confesses as the waitress brings me hazelnut coffee. "I actually thought I was going to be late. I worked–" she yawns, widely enough to pop her jaw, "–until the club closed last night."

"We could have taken a raincheck on this." The coffee tastes burnt, but I'm exhausted enough that I don't really care. The banana bread that I took off of the plate between us is good, sweet and nutty, and I take another bite of that to offset the taste of burnt coffee. "I could have used the extra rest, too."

"Don't be ridiculous!" Ruby smacks my hand lightly. "I've been trying to get you to spend the day with me forever. There's no way I was going to pass this up."

"Where do you want to go?" I, personally, have no plans to buy anything. Every little bit I make that doesn't go towards food or bills is tucked away, and even the coffee I'm drinking feels like a luxury I shouldn't have allowed myself–much like the cab last night.

Ruby shrugs. "Somewhere to look for clothes, maybe? And some new makeup? There's a customer who keeps taking me back to the champagne room, tipping a lot. I think he might want a different kind of arrangement soon, and if he does, well–" she shrugs. "I want to be ready."

"Different? How so?" I frown, not entirely comprehending what she means. I'm sure if the client is tipping well, Ruby's already found a way to expand the menu of services offered to him. I'm not sure where it goes after that.

"You know–" She wiggles her eyebrows at me, and when I still look at her uncomprehending, she sighs. "I forget you're new to all this sometimes. Companionship. An…arrangement."

"Like–dating a customer?" The thought makes me feel a little queasy. "I wouldn't want to date someone who treated me like I was an entree to order off a menu."

Precisely why I never wanted the kind of marriage I was meant to have. That's exactly how the type of man my father would have married me off to would have viewed me–something to appraise like a piece of art or jewelry–choose to keep or reject.

Ruby laughs. "I guess–but it's not really dating. It's just business. They get my time and my…services, and I get money. The perk is that they get to enjoy all of that outside of the club–on their own time. In an environment *they* choose. It's not unusual–I've done it before. It usually lasts a while, until they run out of money or get bored, or for the married ones who have wives that expect fidelity, until they get caught skimming the family savings to pay me. Things go dry for a while, and then inevitably, someone else comes along who wants the same thing or something similar. It's just another job."

Just another job. It sounds vaguely horrifying to me, the idea of having to continue to carry on with a customer outside of the club, but I just smile, taking another sip of my coffee. "I mean–if that makes you happy–"

"*Money* makes me happy," Ruby says with a laugh. "And one day, I'll have enough that I can go anywhere I want, fuck anyone I want, *do anything I want,* and tell all the rest to fuck off. But until then, I'd rather do this than–" she gestures broadly at the coffee shop as if to indicate working out in the regular business world in general. "I never had a passion for anything that would make me money, and all my talents seem to involve sex, so I might as well make use of it while I can."

"I can't argue with that." I really can't. *Go anywhere I want, fuck anyone I want, do anything I want–*Ruby echoed everything I've been striving for in just a handful of words. It makes me wish I could open up to her. I wish I could tell her what *I'm* trying to do, what I've been working so hard towards, about the escape that I dream of.

All it would do is put her in danger, too.

"Enough about work, though," Ruby says, popping the last of a piece of pumpkin bread into her mouth and standing up as she drinks the last of her tea. "Let's go enjoy the day."

We head out of the cafe onto the moderately busy street. I dressed to avoid eyes, but Ruby didn't–probably because it doesn't matter how she's dressed. She'd draw eyes no matter what. She's wearing a blue plaid skater-style skirt with a white button-down, the sleeves rolled up to her elbows, and blue flats, her red hair cascading everywhere. She looks like a schoolgirl who's grown out of her uniform, and I'm grateful for her flamboyant style, because it pushes me even further back into her shadow.

Which is exactly where I want to be.

We end up in a discount shop, sifting through racks of clothing. Ruby finds a short, tight green dress with a sweetheart neckline and capped sleeves, holding it up for me to inspect. "I could put my hair up, pretend to be a proper kind of lady. I bet he'd like that. He's older, and if he took me out in public, I think he'd want me to be a little more conservative—"

"The green would suit you." I shrug. "I don't think you could ever look *conservative*, though, not with that hair."

"True." Ruby laughs, flicking one of the curling pieces over her shoulder. "Alright, I'll look for more."

Once upon a time, I loved shopping. A wave of longing washes over me for afternoons spent with friends, browsing through department stores, swiping credit cards without bothering to look at the tags. A life that feels so far away now that I'm sometimes not entirely sure it happened.

Were any of them ever really your friends, though?

None of them would speak to me now if they saw me. Even if they recognized me—probably, *especially* if they recognized me. They'd be too afraid that my fall from grace was catching. That the loss of what my name had once meant would tarnish theirs.

They'd only ever been my friends because I had the same power, status, and money. They *envied* me back then, because they'd all been married or engaged, shoehorned into arranged partnerships with men chosen by their families. I'd still been free. They asked me over brunches, dinners, and drinks to tell all the wild stories of the men I slept with, the escapades I had, and what it was like to have my own apartment. They all promised to keep my secrets.

They were jealous of me.

Now, they'd treat me like dirt on their shoes.

I glance over at Ruby and her armful of dresses. Back then, I probably wouldn't have spoken to her, either, and it makes me feel guilty. In a very short time, she's been a better friend to me than any friend I ever had before. It makes me wish I could be a better friend to her.

You are being a good friend by not telling her things that would put her in danger.

"What about your guy?" She raises an eyebrow as she joins me, pawing through the other side of the rack. "The handsome one."

"I told you—"

"Yeah, I know. He's an asshole. Taffy said you got super annoyed with her, snapped that he's not your boyfriend." Ruby grins at me. "Don't worry; none of us will touch him."

"I don't care if any of you do," I retort, feeling myself flush with irritation. "And anyway, yes, you would. Any of you would. He has money."

"Well, I guess I can't speak for the others, but *I* won't step on your toes. I've got my own whale, anyway." Ruby wiggles her eyebrows suggestively again.

"I told you, I don't care. He's a dick. Besides, he didn't come back the other night. He probably wanted to slum it once, and now he's good. He's over it."

"Davik didn't like him," Ruby says contemplatively. "Maybe it's better if he doesn't. Or maybe you should try to see if you can find anything out about him. See if someone else knows what he was doing at the club."

"I don't know anyone around here, remember? And I'm not going to go poke around in the *nice* part of the city, asking questions. That's borrowing trouble." I frown at her. "You know that as well as I do."

Ruby shrugs. "That's true. But—" she frowns, considering. "I could ask around if you want? I know girls at the other clubs on our street. I could see if he's been to any of them, if they know anything. You know—just in case he does come back. You should know if there's anything weird about him, since he clearly liked you in particular."

Don't be an idiot. Say yes. Ruby is offering me free information to find out things about Mikhail *for* me without me having to put myself in any kind of danger. I remember the thought I had last night, how I wondered if Mikhail might be the one following me.

If he *is*, if he's the one leaving things at my apartment, Ruby might be able to find me clues that would confirm that. Or, she might find nothing. Either way, it would be a step closer to solving the mystery of the man with the ice-blue eyes.

You might be putting her in danger, if he is the one leaving the letters. Which is exactly what you've been trying to avoid.

"That would be nice of you," I hear myself saying before I can stop the words from coming out. "You really don't have to—"

"It's no problem." Ruby waves her hand. "Honestly, we all do it. If someone new comes in who takes a liking to one of us, and anyone gets a bad vibe, we ask around. Sometimes we find out things that aren't good, and sometimes it's nothing. But we all have to look out for each other—it's not as if anyone else will."

We have to look out for each other.

Something tightens in my chest when I hear her say that, a longing for the kind of deep friendship and camaraderie she's referring to. We have something like it now, the beginnings of it, at least, but how long will that really last?

As soon as I'm able, I'll leave this place. I can't stay here.

But a part of me feels guilty about leaving my friend behind.

Natalia

The feeling of being watched doesn't leave me. I'm acutely aware all day of the gold chain and charm in my pocket, as if it weighed so much more than the mere ounces that it actually weighs. "Is there a gold shop anywhere around here?" I ask Ruby as we leave the cosmetics store, an idea springing into my mind.

She arches an eyebrow. "Why? Going to buy some jewelry?"

"No. I just found something on the ground outside my apartment. I thought it might be worth something."

I reach into my pocket, fishing out the gold chain and charm. I hold it out on my palm for Ruby to see, and she peers at it.

"Probably not much. But I do know a place. And every little bit counts, right?"

"It does." I couldn't agree more. *It's not as if I'm going to wear it.* Even a few rubles is better than throwing it in the trash, and the thought of turning my stalker's threat into something beneficial to me feels particularly satisfying.

The pawn shop Ruby takes me to is in a particularly shady part of town, near my apartment. There's an older man who looks nearly a hundred years old if he's a day behind the counter, peering at a thick chain with a loup. I feel suddenly embarrassed about the thing in my hand.

It's not even mine. It's just something that was left on my door. It's not like I'm begging him to take my valuables.

The man looks up as we approach the counter, giving Ruby a lewdly appraising look. She bats her eyes teasingly at him, and he grunts, grinning a toothless smile at her.

"Can I do something for you ladies?" he asks in a croaking voice, setting the loup aside.

"For me? Nothing that wouldn't give you a heart attack." Ruby flashes him the kind of smile that could, quite possibly, have that result anyway. "But my friend has something for you."

"It's not much." I step up to the counter, holding out the chain. "But I thought it might be worth something." I don't bother mentioning that I found it. This doesn't look like the type of place run by someone with principles about finders keepers, but I don't want to risk it.

"You're right that it's not much." He holds it up, turning the chain back and forth. "But it's fourteen-karat. So not worthless." He picks up the loup, giving it a closer look. "Let me think."

Ruby leans forward, her elbows on the counter as she gives him a brilliant display of her cleavage. "The charm is really pretty, I think. Very nice craftsmanship."

I could have hugged her for the way the man's eyes light up as he looks at her, the chain still dangling from his hand. I'm absolutely sure that it's affecting his decision. *I need to do something nice for Ruby with part of this.*

He names a figure easily twice what I expected him to give me for it, and I nod immediately. "That's fine," I say quickly, seeing Ruby open her mouth and wanting to agree before she can try to haggle. "Thank you."

When the cash is in my pocket and we're out of the store, Ruby lets out a sound of protest. "I could have gotten more from him! I'm sure I could have—"

"You got *plenty*," I tell her firmly. "And I want to do something nice for you. *No arguing*," I insist as she opens her mouth again. "Let's get a late lunch before we have to go back to get ready for work. My treat."

It's strange to see someone so appreciative of something so small. In my old life, *doing something nice for a friend* meant letting someone borrow a particularly expensive piece of jewelry, loaning out a yacht for the weekend, or an invitation to someone's vacation home. I would never, in my wildest dreams, have thought that dinner at a small restaurant near Ruby's apartment would be something I consider a treat.

It feels like it's been ages since I've been out to eat. The food, too, is nothing that I would have ever considered special before. It's meat drenched in mushroom sauce, with roasted potatoes and beets, but after weeks of peanut butter and noodles, it and the glass of wine I splurge on feels like decadence.

"You really didn't have to do this," Ruby says, plowing through her own food. "I didn't do anything—"

"You absolutely did. He would have given me as little as he thought he could get away with if not for you and your tits." I gesture towards Ruby's neckline, and she laughs, adjusting it playfully.

"They are pretty great." She grins. "And they're going to make me a *ton* of money with this new guy, in the dress you helped me pick out. As long as I can get him out on that date."

"I'm sure you've got it in the bag." I finish my food, putting the money down on the table to pay for it. "We should probably get going, though. We have to be at work in just a few hours."

"Igor's going to be annoyed after sending you home yesterday." Ruby looks at me, a hint of worry in her eyes. "You should have just kept the extra money. You could have stayed home tonight—"

"It wasn't *that* much. He'll get over it as long as I make him money, and I will tonight. I won't let myself get distracted."

"You should think about what I said," Ruby urges gently. "If he comes back. I'll do some asking around like I promised, try to make sure he's safe. But a man like that could be worth a lot—to *you*. I don't know what it is you're working so hard for, but I know it isn't to stay here."

The words stick with me as I pack my bag for work, lingering. *A man like that could be worth a lot to you.*

Not doing more than the club required had been a point of pride for me when I started, a way of clinging to some semblance of my former self. I'd been a dancer before, so I could be a dancer now, just a different kind. I didn't want to be an *escort*.

But is it really so bad? Ruby does those things, and it doesn't make me think any less of her. I think of how it had felt to pocket the extra money from the chain, and I imagine bringing more home, enough to really put me on the path to getting free of this place.

I don't have to decide now. Just think about it.

I throw my bag over my shoulder, heading out of my apartment and down the stairs, telling myself firmly that I won't be taking a cab tonight, no matter what I hear.

I'm half a block down the sidewalk when I hear a man's voice behind me that makes me freeze in my tracks.

"Athena?"

I know the voice, smooth and low and arrogant, and I hate the way it makes my heart stutter in my chest and my blood fizz in my veins. For just a moment, I consider continuing to walk down the street without giving him another moment of my consideration—and then I slowly turn around.

Mikhail is standing there, as I'd known he would be, keys in his hand and a car idling at the curb. He's wearing a dark red button-down tonight, tucked neatly into black trousers, rolled up to show those muscled, tattooed forearms. A different bracelet is around his wrist, silver this time instead of gold—or more likely platinum—and the same watch is on his other wrist, shining in the dim light of the street.

"I didn't expect to see you here," he says smoothly. "But now that I have—can I offer you a ride? I imagine you're on your way to work."

Yes, because some of us have to work for a living. The words bite at my lips, acidic and sharp, but I hold them back as a different suspicion takes deeper root. "What are *you* doing here? This doesn't look like the kind of place where you take a casual night's drive."

He smirks. "What if I said I was on my way to the club, too? Would you get in the car then?"

That would make sense. "Are you?" I can't quite keep the bite out of my words.

"No." He says it casually as if the answer means nothing. "I hadn't planned to come by tonight. In fact, I have other errands to run. But one of them brought me here—which seems lucky, since such a beautiful woman shouldn't be walking alone in the dark."

He steps back, tapping the hood of the car. "It's just a ride, Athena. A *free* one. I'll be a perfect gentleman."

There's no such thing as a free ride. Even in my old life, I knew that. Everything costs something. What this will cost, I have no idea. But Ruby's words are still lingering in my mind, and more than that, I don't want to keep walking the several blocks remaining to the club.

And what if he's the one who's been leaving threatening messages? What if he left the chain? What if you're walking into a trap, stepping right into the car of the man who's threatening you?

Well then, the other half of my mind retorts, *all this will be over, and I can stop fearing what comes next.*

If he does want to hurt me, then he's already found me—it would only be a matter of time before he catches up. And if he is actually only interested in me because he wants *me*, then I have a different decision to make. One that could mean my freedom.

"I'll wait here as long as you need," Mikhail says, an easy smile on his face, and somehow that makes the decision for me.

I step off the curb, walk around to the passenger's side and yank open the door. "Thanks," I say quickly, slipping inside. "I'm almost late as it is."

"Well, we can't have that." He pulls away from the curb and back into the street, the car gliding smoothly forward. I breathe in the smell of new, expensive leather, my fingers tracing the buttery edges of it. In one brief moment, I'm transported back to my old life, my old place in the world, and a cramp of pain grips my chest at the sudden longing for the time when I thought I had so much to worry about, with no idea of how much more there could be.

As much as I wavered about getting into the car at all, the ride feels far too short. Mikhail is, as he promised, a perfect gentleman. His hands stay on the wheel, on his leg, not even twitching in my direction to touch me. His eyes remain on the road. He could be a cab driver, in terms of the respectful distance that he keeps. All too soon, he pulls up at the back door of the club, letting the car idle.

"Your destination, madam." He smiles at me, flashing those perfectly white teeth, and I hesitate.

"You're not stopping by tonight?"

His smile widens. "Why? Do you want me to?"

Something about the self-satisfied smile, the arrogance in his voice, wipes away all the goodwill I feel towards him in an instant. "No," I snap irritably. "I just wanted to know, so I could make sure I was busy elsewhere."

I push the door open, sliding out. My feet instantly hit a puddle in the pitted concrete, which pisses me off that much more. "Thanks for the ride," I throw over my shoulder, letting the car door slam shut.

Fuck.

I let my temper get the better of me with him again, reacting and speaking before I had a chance to think. *Now he's never going to come back.*

Do you even want him to?

I huff out a frustrated breath as I walk up the stairs to the door leading into the dressing room. No man has ever taken up this much space in my head before, and it irritates me to no end that Mikhail is the one who is taking up residence there, rent-free.

At least I won't have to see him tonight.

It should have made me afraid that he showed up there, in my neighborhood, and it does. Even with his excuse of *errands*, something about it doesn't quite feel right. The coincidence is too great.

But at the same time, I'm not convinced that it's him leaving the threatening messages.

There's something else to worry about, too—the *thrill* I felt when I heard his voice. The way just the sound of it had run over my skin, making me feel alive.

No one has ever given me that thrill. *Nothing* has, except—

I have a sudden, stark memory of descending into my father's compound with Levin and Max, a gun gripped in my hand. I remember the trigger squeezed under my finger, the sharp acrid smell of gunpowder, and the smoke filling the air. The thud of bodies as they hit the concrete, the *power* of it. The shock on my father's face when he saw what I'd done. When he knew I was no longer his.

That's the thrill Mikhail gives me. A feeling of power and weakness all at once, the feeling that the same thing that thrills me could also pull me under, overpower me. The sense of danger that cuts with the same edge that allows you to make others bleed. It's a feeling I've never found in a person.

I don't want to find it in him.

I'm not supposed to be at work tonight, so I have to request my time on stage. I pick my old familiar song, the one I can get through without really thinking, trying to give myself the best chance of making it through the night without pissing Igor off again.

When I step out onto the stage, I nearly freeze in place halfway to the pole.

He's there. At the front of the crowd gathered around the stage, looking directly at me. His ice-blue eyes meet mine, and a cold shiver runs over me.

Anticipation and fury wrap themselves around each other, blazing their way through me as I grip the pole. *You said you weren't coming here tonight, you fucker.* Without a shadow of a doubt, I know why he's standing there, a wicked gleam in his eyes as he watches me. Instead of putting him off, he'd taken my parting words as a gauntlet I'd thrown down, a challenge.

He'd changed his plans to come in here and taunt me. It infuriates me–and inexplicably, it turns me on.

Fuck you.

I try to look anywhere else, focus on anyone else, but he feels like a magnet, pulling my attention back to him. I fling myself into the familiar steps of the dance, swinging myself around the pole, but like a compass, I keep ending up facing him.

His eyes never leave me, just like that first night. I can see other hands waving money in my direction, and I sway past them, pausing ever so briefly before moving toward the end of the stage where Mikhail is standing. I feel hands push bills into the taut string of my panties and more cash under the heels of my shoes, but all I can see is him.

You want to play this game? Fine. I'm going to win. I'm going to take you for everything you fucking have.

I swing around the pole again, coming down in a split, swinging my leg forward to crawl on my hands and knees towards him, my back arched. I slide forward, ass high in the air, and something sparks to life in his eyes that I don't entirely understand, as if he's remembering something.

It's almost as if he's remembering someone *else*, someone he went to bed with, maybe, imagining the arch of my back and the sway of my ass belonging to some woman he fucked.

White-hot jealousy that has no business existing flares to life in my veins, and I meet his gaze with my own, letting that heat seep into it. I think I see his eyes widen for a fraction of a second, but his arms stay crossed over his chest as he watches me.

Just like the first night, he doesn't tip. He doesn't fling money onto the stage or try to stuff it anywhere in my lingerie. He does nothing but watch, his eyes burning into me no matter where I turn or look, and I know in the back of my mind that this isn't good.

Right now, he isn't a paying customer. And I'm ignoring the ones that are.

I regain a little of my senses, turning towards the left of the stage, but it's all but too late. The last beats of my song are playing, and I have a sick feeling in my stomach even before I turn towards the steps that will take me off the stage that Igor is watching.

Once he found out I was dancing tonight, he'd want to see if I was 'recovered.' My performance just now might have sealed my fate.

Fuck you, you fucking–

I hiss through my teeth, wanting to push my way through the crowd and find Mikhail. I want to get my hands around his throat, scream at him, but in the end, it's only my fault. He might have taken the bait I hadn't meant to put out, but I allowed myself to be distracted.

Igor points at me from where he's standing at the bar, crooking his finger the same way he had before, and I let out a sigh.

I'm fucked.

I start mentally going down the list of other clubs as I walk toward him, trying to think of which one might not be the worst. *Maybe Ruby can give me some insight as to where I'm the least likely to end up as a human trafficking victim.*

"I thought I told you to take a few days off, recover from whatever–" he waves a meaty hand in my general direction. "Whatever is bothering you."

"I'm fine," I say as convincingly as I can, which isn't as much as I'd like. I'm decidedly *not* fine, but it has nothing to do with being sick and everything to do with the infuriating man who has decided, out of the blue, to fixate on me.

He's hardly the first. He's just the first one you're actually attracted to. This is as much on you as it is him.

"You're not." Igor's normally heavy Russian accent thickens even more, a clear sign that he's pissed. "Two nights in a row, you don't play the crowd. You are in another world as you dance. That might work on another kind of stage, *devochka*, but not here. Here you must make them want you. You must pay attention to the ones who do. You are here to make money, yes? For yourself–and for me."

"Of course." My mouth feels dry. I can tell he's angrier than before, and I can see a red flush creeping up his neck. "I'm sorry. I'll be better–the crowd was so large tonight, it was overwhelming–"

"These are excuses." His lips thin, his eyes narrowing at me. "I think perhaps this is not the right place for you, *devochka*. I need girls who listen. Who perform."

My heart skips a beat, stuttering in my chest. "I'm sorry," I breathe, my eyes widening. I've never begged a man for anything in my life, but I can feel myself on the verge of breaking that now. "Truly, I am. I'll be better. I'll ask Ruby for advice; the other girls—"

"Now, you wish to distract my other dancers?" Igor shakes his head. "I think you should go—"

"I'm sorry to interrupt."

I go very still at the sound of Mikhail's voice just beside me. I don't dare look at him, but I can feel his heat, the smooth fabric of his shirt almost brushing my arm as he stands next to me.

Igor's brows draw together in irritation, but his attention turns fully towards Mikhail. If there's one thing Igor excels at, it's recognizing an opportunity. "Yes, *syn*?"

"I don't mean to interrupt your conversation with the lovely Athena, or to eavesdrop, but I think I might be at fault here."

"How so?" Igor grunts, looking between the two of us. "Athena, you know him?"

"He's been here once before," I say quickly. "He bought time in the champagne room."

"And I'd like to do so again," Mikhail interjects smoothly. "At double the normal price, to make up for distracting your dancer during her set. Of course, I'd hope that would be enough to put to rest any ideas of letting her go."

Igor's eyebrows rise at that. "Of course. Double, you say? For the hour?"

"Double for the hour," Mikhail confirms. "No interruptions."

"Well then. I think this has all been a misunderstanding." Igor looks at me pointedly. "Take him to the back, Athena. Make sure he has no cause to regret it."

"Of course." I nod to Mikhail, gesturing towards the curtain dividing the main floor from the hall leading to the champagne rooms. "This way, *sir*."

Natalia

I see his mouth twitch in a smirk at that, but he follows me as I lead us back. My heart is still pounding in my chest from the near-miss of being let go, as much as Mikhail's sudden appearance. *He paid double,* I think, as I push the curtain aside. *Maybe there's something to consider about what Ruby said earlier.*

I take him to the first available room, which is bigger than the one we'd ended up in the first time. They're all roughly laid out the same: stages with half-moon sectionals wrapping around half of the stage, but each has different lighting, and each is a different size, meant to be able to accommodate different party sizes or numbers of dancers. This room lights up a soft pink when I switch the lights on.

The music I pick has a steady, hypnotic beat, and I half expect him to approach me the way he had the first time. As much as he'd paid, I *definitely* expect him to try to take advantage.

Instead, he walks past me, going to sit on the couch.

Not just sit. He *lounges,* sprawling expectantly on the white leather as he watches me, his gaze as predatory as I remember it. I have that feeling of being watched, of being prey, but it doesn't spark the same fear that I feel when I'm walking home alone.

It should. I *know* that it should. It's as if every self-preservation instinct I have switches off when I'm close to him.

In a situation like yours, that's very, very bad.

I can't let my guard down, but it feels as if it crumbles when he looks at me. The only way I can seem to keep it up, to stay guarded, is to be angry with him. Most of the time, he doesn't make that very difficult.

If I make him angry now, though, and he leaves–I'm out of a job. I'm on my last straw with Igor, and I know it.

Even as I think that, though, the possessive gleam in his eyes rouses the same anger I felt in his car, felt on the stage.

Who the fuck do you think you are?

"Just because you paid more doesn't mean you get more than a dance, you know." The words tumble out as I stride towards the stage, hips swaying. *He likes it when I challenge him. You can push a little. Just don't offend him too much.*

I grab the pole, swinging myself effortlessly up onto the stage. I arch around it, swaying towards him, and I see the heat in his eyes as he watches me, his gaze raking down my body.

"Nothing else was negotiated," I continue, gazing down from my position on the stage. I let my hands slide up, over my head, arching back against the pole. His gaze slides down, settling between my thighs before it returns to my face, and I see him shift where he sits, clearly aroused already.

He grins, cocking his head to one side. "You look gorgeous in that lingerie," he says offhandedly, raking his eyes across me again. "How much for you to take it *all* off as you dance? I want to see you entirely naked, dancing for me. How much will that cost?"

I feel myself flush, heat creeping up my neck and into my cheeks. My first instinct is to tell him no, that I'm here to dance and nothing else. That I work within the rules of the club and nothing else. That he'd be better off finding one of the other girls here.

The words die on my lips as I look at him. *I hate you*, I think, tangled feelings of anger and jealousy and fear twisting in my chest. No one has ever confused me as much as he does. I have no reason to care if he goes to someone else for favors, but I do. I should want him gone, want to never see him and his arrogant, cocky, all-too-handsome face again, but I find myself considering his proposition.

He could be worth a lot to you. Ruby's voice echoes in my head, and I hesitate.

"Tell me how much," he urges, his voice deeper suddenly, silkier.

I suck in a breath and name a figure that seems outrageous to me. *He'll say no.*

Mikhail laughs. "Take it down by a quarter, and I'll agree," he says, but even as he tries to negotiate with me, I see the lust in his eyes.

He wants this. He wants it badly enough to pay.

"That or nothing," I tell him, circling the pole, my body swaying in time to the music. "And every time you ask for something more, the price doubles." As I say it, I hook my fingers in the straps of my panties, pushing them down a little on my sharp hipbones, rotating as I tease him. "How badly do you want it?"

He laughs again, with real feeling this time. "You drive a *hard* bargain," he murmurs, shifting on the couch again, as if my attitude turned him on even more. "Fine. I'll pay exactly what you asked for. But you strip it all off. Slowly. You let me see *everything*."

I nod, feeling my heartbeat speed up in my chest. *This is a transaction*, I tell myself, but it feels like more. The room, large as it is, feels suddenly small and intimate as the music changes to the next track, the beat the tiniest bit slower, still hypnotic and seductive. I swallow hard, my body moving automatically to its rhythm, trained for so long to respond to music as if it were a part of my very blood and bones.

"That's it," Mikhail murmurs, his hands flat on the couch on either side of his thighs. "Dance for *me*, Athena."

His voice is so low I'm almost not certain I heard him correctly, his words lost in the music. I don't start to strip at first, moving through the rhythm of the dance first. I run my hands over the pole, wrapping my leg around it as I spin, watching his face heat and tense with anticipation as he waits for me to give him what he bargained for.

I'm not wearing much to begin with. Slowly, I turn to face away from him, arching toward the pole as I slide my fingers up my spine toward the hooks of my bra. I flick my fingertips over it, tugging, teasing, making him wait until I finally unhook it deftly–better than any man ever has–but I don't drop it yet.

I hold both sides, opening the straps, bringing my elbows in to hold the cups against the sides of my breasts as I move to the music. I let the straps slide down my shoulders, and slowly, very slowly, I turn to face him with the shimmering cups of the bra still held against my chest.

He looks at me with a hunger in his eyes that startles me, making me want to step back. He's very still, watching me, as if he's afraid he might spook me if he moves. I've never felt so hunted, so *aware* of the danger of the man sitting close to me, but every instinct in my body screams at me to run.

I drop my hands, and the bra falls to the stage.

He swallows, hard, his adam's apple bobbing in his throat. I see his fingers flex against the leather as if he wants to touch himself, but he doesn't. I know, as my fingers reach for the edge of my panties, that he must be achingly hard.

I wait for him to ask *how much*. How much to get his cock out and stroke it while I dance for him? How much for his pleasure?

He says nothing. His eyes stay on me as I grind against the pole, my body moving to the beat as I start to push the fragile fabric of my panties down my hips. I pause when the top of it brushes against my pussy, teasing him for just a little longer, and then I let them slide down my thighs, leaving every inch of me bare except for my high heels.

I can tell that he's trying to play it cool. He doesn't want me to see how much this is turning him on—I can see it in the twitch of his fingertips against the leather couch, the tenseness of his jaw, the way the small muscle there leaps as his eyes drag down my naked body and up again. He doesn't even look at the scrap of fabric that is my panties as I step out of them and kick them aside, his eyes hungrily feasting instead on all of the bare flesh on display for him.

The lights shift around us, darker pink and then lighter, playing over my body and his, and I can see how hard he is. His cock is thick and long, straining against the black fabric of his pants, and I know he must be aching, so hard that all he can think about is how much he needs his cock touched, stroked, sucked. How badly he needs to come.

That thrill of power spreads through me as I spin around the pole, the knowledge that I've turned him on so much, and yet he can't do anything about it without permission, without paying more for the privilege. I feel my skin flush, my blood pumping hotly in my veins, a steady throb of arousal growing between my thighs.

I slide down the pole, turning, gripping it as I bend down. I know what he's seeing, the slender curves of my ass on display for him, the soft pink folds of my pussy just peeking out from between my thighs, and I know, if he looks closely enough, he'll see the glistening hint of arousal.

Slowly, I go down into a split, still facing away from him as I bounce on the stage, giving him a view of what it would look like if I rode him in reverse, bouncing on the cock that I know must be throbbing right now. I draw it out, enjoying the knowledge of how I'm torturing him, and then I slowly bring my legs together, turning and sliding off the stage exactly on beat, just as the music changes to the lap dance portion of the hour.

I can see how taut his expression is as I sway towards him, entirely nude. He swallows hard, his hands tensed on either side of him, as I stand inches away and slowly begin to dance, closer to him than before.

"You're too beautiful for this place," Mikhail murmurs, his eyes raking over me greedily. "Perfect breasts, a perfect body, that perfect bare, pink pussy. You're wasted here, Athena. That asshole out there doesn't deserve you."

"I choose where I work," I breathe, still moving to the music. "This is better than the other options."

I lean forward, gripping the back of the couch as I sway over him, my feet on either side of his, my breasts close to his face. "Let's not talk about work," I murmur, arching my back. "Let's talk about something else. Tell me about yourself."

If there's one thing I know about men, it's that they *love* talking about themselves. They love it even more when they think a woman really is interested in what they have to say on the topic. But Mikhail just smiles, tipping his head up to look at my face as I gyrate over him.

"I'm not very interesting," he says smoothly. "Just a man with too much money, who's found a beautiful woman he can't stop thinking about. In fact, I'm much more interested in *you*, Athena."

Something about the way he says it sends a warning flicker through me, something pinging at the back of my mind. "What do you mean?" I breathe, pushing away from the couch and stepping away several inches, turning so he can see the view of my ass as I dance. "I'm just an exotic dancer. Nothing all that interesting there–same old story."

"I don't think that's true at all. You're too beautiful, too fascinating. How does a girl like you end up in a place like this?"

"That's a ridiculous line," I tell him, turning back towards him. "And you paid me to dance, not to tell you my life story."

He smirks. "Well, you said the price was doubled every time I asked for something else."

I raise an eyebrow. "You want to pay me to tell you about myself? Twice as much as you paid me to strip naked?"

For a moment, I think he's going to say yes, and I want to laugh. *That much money and he thinks I'm really going to tell him the truth?* I wouldn't tell him who I really am or what's really happened to me for all the money in his bank accounts, not unless I could ensure his silence forever. Still, I hardly have to tell him anything that isn't entirely fabricated. I can lie for the rest of the hour, and I'll come out of this with the best night I've had since I started.

Then his smirk spreads, his lips curling upwards lasciviously as his eyes heat, and he laughs softly. "No, Athena. I want to pay you that much to touch yourself while you dance for me. I want you to finger that pretty pink pussy, and come for me before the hour is over. For that, yes. I will pay you double what I already agreed to, for you to take your clothes off."

An inexplicable throb of heat pulses through me at the idea. I should be horrified, but instead, I feel the arousal gathering between my thighs, wet and slick. "You won't be allowed to touch me."

He smiles. "That's fine. I like watching."

I go still for a split second, remembering last night, the strange and unsettling feeling I had that someone was outside my window. The dream that I woke from, of ice-blue eyes hovering above my head.

It's just a figure of speech, Natalia. He can't actually have been outside your window.

I should tell him no. I *know* I should. This has already gone too far, crossed lines that I said I wouldn't, and with every boundary that I let him break, I know he's going to keep pushing. I'm coming to realize that part of the game for him is seeing how far he can make me go, how he can break through my defenses and boundaries, and what my price is for that.

Double what he paid for you to strip. For you to do the same thing you're going to do alone tonight in your bed—thinking of him, no less—you just have to do it with him watching. Is that really so bad?

That flush of heat spreads through me again, an ache growing between my thighs that makes me *want* to do it, just so I can relieve the need that's rapidly building. My clit feels swollen, pulsing with the need to be touched, and I nod, my voice coming out more breathless than I mean for it to as I agree.

"Double," I manage, my hands slowly sliding up my thighs to tease him further. "And I'll masturbate for you."

His eyes gleam. "As long as you orgasm, Athena. I want to see you come—and I'll know if you fake it."

Something about his words sends a frisson of lust over my skin, prickling it from my head to my toes. I can feel how wet I am, drenched with arousal from the sound of him demanding my orgasm.

I think of the way his voice made me feel earlier tonight, out on the street. Of how he was inexplicably in my neighborhood, right behind me, how he just *happened* to be there.

I think of that feeling of being watched again, of eyes on me.

What if this is all him?

Or what if you're just being paranoid, and you lose out on a chance to strike gold?

I've heard all the girls talk about these types of men, the ones they call "whales," with the kind of reverence normally reserved for a religious experience. Men who throw unbelievable amounts of money at them, men who pay for their rent and clothes and anything else they want, for the period of time that they stay obsessed. They never last forever, but while they do, they can change a girl's life.

If that's all Mikhail is, if I'm just being paranoid, then he could change *my* life.

I've never felt more confused.

What's even more confusing is how the fear feels to me. I'm afraid he might be the one stalking me, that I might be walking into a trap, and yet it doesn't make me *less* aroused. The danger just seems to heighten everything, making my heart race and my palms tingle, making me want to dance that line of seeing how far I can take this. What will happen next?

I feel alive, on a razor's edge of desire and danger, and I know if I fall off, it could be deadly.

"Well?" His eyebrow raises, and I know I'm not going to tell him no.

"Agreed," I whisper. The music is still playing, slow now and hypnotic, and I feel it pulse through me as I slide my hand up my inner thigh, teasing. My other hand goes to my breast, playing with my stiffening nipple as my fingers move upwards towards my pussy, feeling the stickiness of my arousal on my skin.

"That's it," Mikhail breathes, as I spread open my smooth pussy lips with two fingers, revealing my swollen clit. "God, you look fucking delicious. So fucking beautiful—"

He trails off with a groan as I flick my finger over my clit, and I suck in a breath between my teeth as the pleasure jolts through me.

I've masturbated countless times. I know how to make myself feel good, what touches and pressures feel the best, and exactly how to find the right rhythm. But the moment I rub my fingertip over my clit with Mikhail's eyes on me, I know I should never have agreed to this.

Touching myself like this, with him watching me, is better than anything I've ever felt alone.

This was a mistake.

I'm never going to be able to forget how this feels. I can't pretend like this never happened.

Mikhail

I'm harder than I've ever been in my entire fucking life, even harder than I was watching her through the bedroom window.

It's all I can do to keep my hand off of my cock. I watch, entranced, as she spreads open her pussy for me to see, teasing her nipple with her other hand. She's soaking wet, her clit hard and swollen, and I want to reach out and grab her by the thighs, pull her astride my face, so I can devour her.

I hear her sharp indrawn breath as she starts to rub, her body still swaying gently to the music. I have half a mind to ask her to turn it off–I want to hear the wet sounds of her fingers on her pussy–but I don't want to ruin the moment. She's devastatingly beautiful like this, her pale skin flushed with heat, her two fingers rubbing over her clit, her thighs trembling gently as the pleasure sweeps through her.

She moans, soft and breathless, and my cock throbs. *Fuck.* My balls are drawn up tight against my body, swollen and painful, and I need to come. I can feel the deep, threatening tingle at the base of my cock that warns me how close I am, that I might lose control and come just at the sight of the goddess in front of me pleasuring herself.

She'd chosen her stage name wisely, because she *is* a goddess. I've never seen any woman more beautiful. Her hair falls down her back in a waterfall of black as her head tips backward, her back arching as she rotates her hips, grinding onto her hand. "Ohh–"

Her moan nearly pushes me over the edge, without having so much as brushed a finger against myself. My pants feel too tight, the friction of the fabric as my cock twitches and lurches almost enough to make me come. I know I'm torturing myself, but it's the sweetest fucking torture I've ever experienced.

Every inch of her is perfection. Her body was made to be touched, pleasured, *owned*. *I want her to be mine*, I think with a ferocity that I've never felt, as she sways towards me, her fingers still moving against her clit. *I want to make her scream with pleasure before I make her cry in pain. I want to torment her in every way possible. I want her body to belong to me and only me, for my pleasure and my vengeance.*

If it's her—it has to be her. I need *it to be her.*

If this woman isn't Natalia, I have no reason to continue doing this. No reason to keep following her, watching her, paying for her company. No excuse to find a way to capture her and use her.

"Do you want me to come on the stage?" she asks, hovering in front of me as her fingers make slow, torturous circles around her clit, her voice thick with pleasure. "I can sit there, spread open for you, so you can see *everything* as I come. Every clench and spasm–"

Fuck. Oh god, fuck– My cock jerks, and for a moment, I think I'm going to lose control, just at the thought of watching her perfect pussy clenching around her fingers as she comes.

"Or–" she breathes, so close that I could touch her if I wanted to, if I were *allowed* to. The thought makes me feel almost feral, grating at me that I can't have what I want, take it, that I have to keep playing this game with her. *If we were really alone right now, you wouldn't be teasing me like this.*

"I can do this—" She moves closer, one heeled foot suddenly on the couch next to my hand, her pussy inches from my face. Her folds spread open like a flower as she opens her thighs, her fingers scissoring around her clit for a moment, so I can see it, slick and hard. "You can watch while I do this—"

Two fingers of her other hand circle her entrance, and this close, I can hear the sound of how wet she is. My throat tightens, my cock close to bursting, and my mind feels thick with fog, with *need*. I can smell the sweet scent of her, and I can't think past how aroused I am.

"If you pay," she breathes, and I nod before I can even really make a decision. I need to *see* her come, to hear it, to breathe in her scent as she orgasms, and I would pay any amount of money.

"Yes," I groan. "Double again. Slide your fingers inside yourself, Athena, and let me watch you come for me."

She gives me a sultry smile, but I can see something victorious in it. It should piss me off, knowing I've been toyed with, played, but it only turns me on more. She's only giving as good as she's getting, and the fact that she's a match for me, that she isn't letting me manipulate her so easily, is driving me insane with want.

Her fingers slip into her wet pussy, and I'm flooded with the memory of watching her, of her ass in the air as she slammed her fingers into herself from behind, grinding against her hand. Her foot braces against the couch, her hips swaying as she thrusts her fingers upwards, her other two still circling her clit, and I hear her breathy moan.

"I'm so close—yes—" She lets out another gasp, and then she drops down, her knee next to my arm as she straddles my lap. My hands are suddenly trapped at my sides by her legs, held prisoner as she hovers over me, her hand that's fingering herself just above my cock. She bounces on her own fingers, her expression taut with pleasure as her wide blue eyes stare down into mine, her perfect, full lips parted.

"I'm going to come," she moans. "I'm going to come on your fucking cock, yes—oh!"

It's so fucking easy to imagine. The way she's hovering over me, the way I can feel the impact of her fingers inside her tight, hot pussy, the rhythm of her stroking her clit. It's almost as if I'm fucking her, and as she arches her back, her thighs squeezing against my arms as she throws her head back, I know I'm going to lose it.

"I'm coming! Oh god, I'm coming—" She cries out, her entire body shuddering above me, nothing touching me except her legs against my arms, but in my mind, I can *feel* it, her tight inner depths clenching around my straining cock, rippling, *squeezing*.

My cock spasms, losing control as I groan, spurting hot cum without ever having been touched. I hear her moaning as my cock jerks and shudders, my orgasm coming with hers. I feel the heat of her release soaking into the fabric of my pants, too, intensifying my pleasure. She grinds above me, thrusting against her hands, and my cock keeps spurting cum, my fingers clenched against the couch. I can't breathe, can't think. All I can see is the gorgeous woman undulating above me, lost in the pleasure of an orgasm that I know beyond a shadow of a doubt is real. All I can feel is the loss of control as I come without having been touched for the first time since I was a fucking teenager.

I'm still fucking hard, I realize in disbelief as she goes still, her body giving one last shudder before she gracefully slips off of my lap, her hands sliding out from between her thighs. No other part of her body touches me, and she steps backward, her eyes flicking to my lap.

"You can leave the money there," she says, nodding towards the table to the right of the stage. "The time is up."

There's a wicked, victorious gleam in her eyes. For a moment, I want to lurch across the room and throttle her, wrapping my hands around her slender neck and squeezing until she learns what it means to wonder if she'll ever breathe again.

Instead, I stand up, feeling the wet fabric of my pants clinging to my groin and thighs as I fish my wallet out. I pull the money out, throwing it down on the table.

"I'll see you again," I murmur, my voice low. I think I see her flinch as I stride out.

Good.

I slam the door behind me as I stride into the bathroom, furious with myself.

You had a chance, and you threw it away, you fucking idiot! I glare at my reflection in the mirror, teeth gritted, gripping the edge of the black lacquer countertop. *You could have paid her to talk, and instead, you paid to watch her come.*

She would have only given me bullshit, anyway. It wasn't worth it.

You could have read between the lines! Tried to catch her slipping up! Instead, all you could do was think with your fucking cock. A wasted opportunity.

I clench my teeth so hard I feel my jaw pop, holding back a scream. I'm still fucking rock-hard, and it takes everything in me not to slam my fist into the mirror.

She'd played me exactly as she was meant to, and I'd fallen for it. Even now, I want to go back into that fucking room and repeat the experience. I've never seen any woman so beautiful, never met any woman who made me so fucking hard, who made me feel like I was fucking drowning in the scent of her, desperate to see her come for me.

If she's Natalia, she's going to fucking regret this.

I pivot on my heel, throwing open the door to one of the stalls and stepping inside, slamming it behind me. I jerk open the damp fly of my jeans, the scent of her cum and mine mingled together, filling the small space as I yank out my hard cock, my fist closing around it. It's slick with cum, and I stroke furiously, my teeth gritted to the point of pain as I scream at myself internally, squeezing my cock in a punishing grip.

You should have been focused on getting information out of her, not on how caught up you were in seeing her fucking pussy. You should have used that time wisely. It's going to fucking cost you to see her again.

I bite back a groan at the thought of seeing her again, watching her dance. My hand slides up and down my aching shaft, my hips shuddering forward as I remember the slick pink flesh, how sweet she smelled, the sounds of her moans–

A waste of money, a waste of time, if this isn't going anywhere–

"Fuck–" I curse under my breath, my other hand gripping the back of the toilet as I jerk my cock harder. *I'm creating a relationship with her. Getting her to trust me. To believe that there's nothing suspicious about me, that I'm infatuated with her, that that's the only reason I keep coming back.*

Not hard to believe at this point.

I have to build trust. I have to make her trust me. Then she'll be in the palm of my hand, and I can do anything I fucking want to her.

My cock throbs in my fist at the thought, at the idea of Natalia at my mercy. Except–

What if she's not Natalia?

The disappointment and the resistance that I feel at that thought tells me all I need to know about how close this is coming to an obsession that's going off the rails. My hand clenches around my cock, feeling it swell with another oncoming climax.

What if she is? What if she's right here, at the tips of your fingers? Right here for you to convince her that you're harmless…until it's too late for her?

I bite back a snarl of pleasure as my cock erupts, the sensation spreading through me in a hot wave as my toes curl and my hands clench, my cock spurting at the thought of her for the second time in mere minutes. I come hard, as if I haven't come in weeks, the thought of her bound and at my mercy driving me wild with need.

I'm losing control. I tuck my finally-deflating cock back into my pants, unclenching my jaw. *I'm letting her consume me, not thinking about this rationally.*

The idea that the woman who just danced for me so sensually, who straddled my lap and came atop me, inches from me, who so lewdly moaned and writhed and soaked me in her release—the idea that *she* is Natalia Obelensky, a Bratva princess and former prima ballerina, is ludicrous on the surface. It's ridiculous.

She wouldn't be in a place like this, negotiating her body for a price that she would have scoffed at before. I was right in my first instinct when Yuri showed me the picture. Surely. It's not her.

I'm not sure I've ever felt so frustrated in my entire fucking life. Common sense says it's not her, that she'd never stoop so low, that she likely didn't even come back to Moscow. But even as I think it, I waver.

If she *had* come back, it's true that she would be in hiding. *She has no access to her money or connections, so she would need a way to earn a living that would stay under the radar. She'd believe that no one would look for her here, for exactly the reasons that you're unsure that it is her.*

She doesn't belong here. You know that's true.

I've been in seedy strip clubs before, plenty of them. I've never seen anyone with the grace and poise that this woman who's styled herself *Athena* has. She sticks out, even as she's so clearly trying to blend in—as she's trying to *hide*.

It could be her. But you have to be sure. You have to get closer—but you also have to keep control.

I wash my hands, rub them over my face, and look at my reflection in the mirror. I'm not so blind as to lie to myself about why I'm still here. Natalia or not, this woman has captivated me in a way that I know is dangerous. I know, too, that I'm enjoying the game of finding out. I haven't had something like this to capture my interest in far too long. And if it *is* her—

If she is Natalia, then the game will only make it better in the end. If she is the woman I seek, and I can gain her trust, make *her* want me—

My revenge will be all the sweeter in the end.

Natalia

"You're coming tonight, right?"

I glance over at Ruby as I hook my bra, letting out a sigh. "You're not going to let me off the hook, are you? Even though we don't get out of here until *two in the morning?*"

"Not a chance," Ruby says with a smirk. "Besides, neither of us is scheduled to work tomorrow. You can sleep all day and night if you want. You *promised* you'd come to the party. You've never even seen my place."

"I was going to pick up a shift tomorrow. Crystal is sick—"

"That's on you," Ruby says primly. "If you want to dance tomorrow, dance. But you *can't* miss the party. It's going to be a rager."

That's what I'm afraid of. The last thing I feel like doing tonight is going to a house party full of all the other girls from the club. I don't have the energy to mingle or remember my lies about who I am and why I ended up here or listen to others talk. I *can't* get drunk, lest I slip up and say something that would give away one of the many, many secrets that I have now. Partying after a Saturday night shift is the last thing I want to do.

Especially when it's been two days since Mikhail bought that time with me in the champagne room, and I'm once again itchy and on edge, wondering what's going on and pissed off at myself for caring. *It's just because he spent so much money,* I tell myself. *It sucks if that was a one-off thing. If he got what he wanted and now he won't come back.*

I should have teased him more, done it on the stage instead of up close. I should have saved that. I'd gotten carried away, too into the pleasure and thrill of it. I could have lured him back with the promise of more.

Too late now.

Thankfully, despite my mood, I've managed to keep my attention on the other customers. I know I won't get another chance with Igor, and I can't count on Mikhail swooping in and saving me. The last couple of nights haven't been windfalls, but they've been decent enough to please Igor and make my nights profitable, and I hope tonight will be better.

By the time two a.m. rolls around and the bartender shouts last call, I'm pleased with how it's gone. I'm tired, my body sore, but I'd taken two customers back to the champagne room and had a second solo on stage requested, along with endless floor dances. When I count out my tips for the night, it's more than I made all week, excluding Mikhail's contributions, and I'm not upset with it.

"I'm not letting you out of my sight," Ruby says, popping up near my elbow and making me jump a little. "I know if I do, you'll slide right out of here, and I won't know where to find you, since I don't even get to know where you live."

She loops her elbow through mine as I fold up my tips, leading me back to the dressing room. "Come on. I'm going to give you something to borrow for the party. You can't wear those baggy street-rat clothes you wear all the time to this. Who knows? Maybe you'll meet the love of your life there, and he'll sweep you away from all this." She rolls her eyes dramatically, and I groan.

"There's going to be guys there? Ruby–"

"What? You thought it was just girls' night? This is a *party*. I know you've been to a party before."

Not like this. The parties I've been accustomed to have been elegant, expensive affairs, full of designer gowns and gossip, string quartets, and expensive catering. This isn't the sort of party I've *ever* been to, and I feel a shiver of nerves that I hadn't expected.

I'd very much like to go home and go to bed.

I don't want to disappoint Ruby, though. I remember standing in the charity shop with her, looking at clothes, wondering how I could be the sort of friend to her that she's been to me. I know that this is the answer. I can swallow my nerves and my desire to hide away in my apartment and go to her party. No one will be there who can hurt me, who will know me, who can blow my cover. There's no real reason not to go.

I plaster a smile on my face. "Of course, I've been to a party before. What am I borrowing for this one?"

Ruby grins, reaching into her bag to fish out a black sequined dress that sparkles in the dressing room light. She holds it out, the fabric rustling. "Here. This should fit you, and it will look *fantastic*."

I reach for it a tad reluctantly, pulling it over my head and shimmying into the tight fabric. It clings to me, holding on by thin straps at my shoulders, and when I turn and look in the mirror, I have to admit it does look good, even though I'm not sure it suits *me*. It's flashier than anything I would have worn in my former life and makes me stand out more than I'm comfortable with now. Paired with my black hair, pale skin, and red lips, I look like a femme fatale, albeit one who sparkles a little bit more than strictly necessary.

"Here." Ruby holds out a pair of silver hoops in my direction. "You need jewelry."

She changes into a gold dress made out of some kind of shiny, stretchy material that folds and drapes over her curves and clings to her thighs even higher than the dress I'm wearing does on mine and slips dangling earrings into her ears before packing up her bag and turning to me with a bright smile.

"Let's go. We're stopping at the liquor store first."

"We shouldn't be walking out on the street like this, especially not so late." I feel a sudden cramp of fear in my stomach, longing for my loose clothing. I remember the panic of those footsteps behind me earlier this week all too well, and I haven't forgotten Mikhail's appearance either. I can't reconcile him showing up so close to where I live, no matter how I try or how hard I try to pretend like it's not strange. All complicated thoughts of the way it made me feel aside, there was no reason for a man like him to be in a place like that, that I can think of.

Unless—

He might not be stalking you. It might have had nothing to do with you. It could really have been a coincidence—if he's the kind of man who does work for men like your father used to be. If his "errand" in that part of town was someone, not something. Someone who needed dealing with.

If that's true, then it's not any better. If he works for the Bratva, *any* Bratva, and mentions me…

Cold fear licks down my spine, and it takes a moment before I realize that Ruby's talking and I haven't heard a word that she said.

"I'm sorry," I say quickly, seeing a flicker of annoyance on her face when she realizes I zoned out. "I'm really tired. But I'll rally, I promise. What did you say?"

"I said we'll take a cab. My treat. There's no way we'll be walking out this late." She tugs on my elbow. "Come on. People will be showing up soon, and I need to have everything set up."

She hails a cab when we're outside, giving the driver directions to a nearby liquor store. It's starting to lightly rain again as he pulls up in front of it, and we make a dash for the door, not wanting to get soaked. We're both laughing as we step inside, and it takes me a full second to realize that the voice I hear as we walk in is one I know.

What the fuck?

The man standing at the counter, his palms on the glass as he leans forward, urgently talking to the man behind it, is Mikhail. I know it's him, even with his back turned. I know the sound of his voice.

What is he doing here?

I dart behind a shelf of bottles, but not fast enough. I see Mikhail turn at the sound of our footsteps and laughter, the bell jingling at the top of the door, and his eyes light on me a second before I disappear.

Fuck.

Ruby is already aisles down, completely oblivious. I feel my hands shaking slightly as his footsteps come closer, and I know he's going to come and talk to me. I don't know what to say.

You don't belong in this part of town. Explain why the fuck you keep popping up where you shouldn't be...where I am.

Except there's no way he could have known I was coming here. *I didn't even know I was coming here until fifteen minutes ago.*

"What a lovely surprise." Mikhail's deep voice, low and intimate, ripples over my skin. It's as if he's speaking just for me, a conversation meant for our ears only. "I didn't think I'd have the pleasure of seeing you tonight, *Athena.*"

There it is again. The way he says my name, sticky sweet and lingering, with that emphasis that says he knows, of course, that it's not my real name and that he would very much like to know what it *is*.

I swallow hard, trying not to look as unsettled as I feel. "You can see me any night you want," I say coolly, tilting my chin up to meet his gaze. "All you have to do is come by the club, and I'm almost always there."

"There's a certain spontaneous pleasure about running into you so unexpectedly, though." Mikhail takes a step closer, and I can feel the heat of his large, muscled body. I can smell his cologne, rich and spicy, and desire ripples through me in a way that makes me feel flushed and angry all at once.

"I have places to be, so I'm afraid the pleasure will have to be brief." I step back, away from his overwhelming presence. "But I'm glad you enjoy my company. You really should come by the club again, so you can enjoy more of it."

I pivot on my heel, turning away from him, and a small part of me wants nothing more than to feel his hand close around my wrist, pulling me back. I can imagine it, the strong grip, the rush of fear and adrenaline, the heat of his hard body pressed against mine as he holds me against him, unable to pull away–

What the actual fuck is wrong with you, Natalia?

It's a good question, especially considering the disappointment I feel when no hand touches me and nothing stops me. I hear silence behind me for a moment, as if he's watching me go, and then the sound of his footsteps retreating in the opposite direction.

You're losing your mind.

I find Ruby perusing a wall of tequila bottles. At first I think she missed the entire encounter, but then she turns to me with wide eyes, and I know immediately that she didn't.

"Was that–"

I nod. "It was." I bite my lip, about to insist that we don't talk about it, but something nags at me. *If anyone would have an opinion about this that you could listen to, it would be Ruby.* "It's weird that he was here, right? A man like that, with that much money–he doesn't need to buy his own liquor. He definitely doesn't need to be here, arguing with someone behind the counter about god-knows-what. Isn't it strange?"

Ruby pauses for a moment, as if she's thinking, and then shrugs as she plucks two bottles off of a shelf in front of her. "Maybe not," she says contemplatively. "Maybe he owns this place? He might have been upset about something with the business. It's entirely possible."

"He showed up out of the blue as I was walking to work, a few nights ago," I blurt out, feeling that creeping sensation of fear and paranoia all over again. "You don't think it's a weird coincidence? You think there's a normal explanation for it?"

Ruby shrugs again. "He might own any number of places in this area." She purses her lips, thinking. "I did ask around with some of the other girls I know, like I said I would. None of them knew anything about him or had seen him—but he could be a silent partner. Or maybe he's in the liquor business, and that's why he's been around here multiple times. Maybe he supplies to the clubs, and that's how he happened to be there to see you that first night. There could be all kinds of reasons, Athena. I don't think it's anything to worry about."

She slides one of the bottles under her arm so she can pat mine, giving me a reassuring smile. "Men like Igor—there's always someone over them, someone with bigger purse strings. This guy is probably one of those. You haven't been doing this all that long, but you'll see. I don't think this is anything out of the ordinary."

I nod, trying to feel confident that she's right. "If you think so—"

"You just have a whale on a line, that's all," Ruby says confidently. "Now you just have to reel him in."

"Of course." I try to sound as sure as I know she wants me to feel. "It's good that he ran into me, then. He'll wonder where I'm going dressed like this, what I'm doing. It'll add a little mystery."

"There you go!" Ruby grins at me. "Now you're catching on." She hands me the tequila bottles, gesturing towards another shelf. "Come help me pick out some vodka."

I tell myself, over and over as we pick out the liquor for the party, that she knows what she's talking about. That I'm overreacting, and there's nothing to fear.

But I can't help wondering that if Ruby knew who I really was, if she knew my past, if she'd have the same answer. If she'd be so quick to dismiss it.

And that, I can't reconcile.

Mikhail

I can't get the sight of her in that little black dress out of my head.

It sticks with me all day, all the way into the evening's twilight, as I get ready for the job I have to do. It's strange, that I'd be so aroused by her clothes, but somehow the sight of that gaudy fabric clinging to her body was more erotic than the lingerie I see her in at the club. *I know what's beneath that,* I couldn't help but think as I looked at her, hot lust throbbing through my veins. *I know how your most intimate flesh looks, the sounds you make as you come, the very scent of you.*

If tonight pays off, I very well might know for sure if she's who I'm looking for. The anticipation is almost unbearable.

I'd come again last night thinking about her in that dress. I'd barely been able to wait until I was home, feverishly stripping off my clothes and only making it as far as the couch before I had my cock in my hand, stroking myself hard and fast to the thought of tying her to my bed and cutting that tight dress off of her, leaving her bare to my every desire. *I'd have the power, then. No making me pay for the pleasure of your attention, for you to grace me with the favor of letting me have what I want. No more rules except the ones I make. Nothing between you and me—and my revenge.*

I can feel my obsession, my *need* reaching a breaking point. I avoided the club for the past few days for exactly that reason. Soon, I'll know the truth, and I can decide what to do next. Until then, I knew I needed space. I thought it would help to cool my head.

Instead, it had only intensified my lust, and seeing her unexpectedly outside of the club had made it worse still.

I look down at the address on the slip of paper in my hand, another bit of information from Yuri. *This better be good, you bastard, or I'm going to take it out of your hide slowly.* I don't care for the man, but he's been a primary informant for me. The fact that he's going to die soon because he angered Valeria is an inconvenience that I'm going to have to find a way around. I have other sources I'll have to lean on more often.

Or maybe not. If this information is good, and it leads me to an answer about Natalia, my time here might almost be over.

I slip out of my apartment, keys in hand. I still have the rented car that I'd been driving the night I gave her a ride, rented under a fake name, nice enough to not draw suspicion but not such a luxury model as to make me stand out. Years of this kind of work for Viktor has paid off for my own purposes, and all of this feels as easy and natural as breathing.

This is who I am—a shadow in the dark, a knife in the night, the devil that you don't want to anger. Natalia will find out that truth very soon, if I'm correct, and she is the woman working at the *Cat's Meow*.

The address that I was given belongs to a club in a slightly better part of town than where "Athena" works, a two-story building that I recognize. It has a bar and nightclub in the basement, dancers on the first level, and rooms on the second for customers to take their choice of women for the evening. I park my car half a block away in the shadows, away from any streetlights, and slink along the walls toward where I should find my mark.

Yuri's information was good. The man is exactly where I was told he'd be at this time, around the back of the club, smoking a cigarette on his break. He's leaning against the wall, blowing smoke out into the darkness as if he has nothing to fear, relaxed and at ease.

He never sees me coming.

I'm at his side before he can react, a needle sunk into the fleshy muscle of his arm. He grunts in surprise, turning sharply towards me, but before he can hit me, the drug is already taking effect. I dodge back, out of his reach, and then forward again to catch him as he falls.

It's a matter of moments to move him to the other side of the dumpster on the other side of the building, out of sight. I jog back to the car, pulling it around, and then bind his wrists and ankles with plastic zip-tie cuffs, hoisting him into the trunk of my car.

Easy and quick. *I've still got it.*

From there, it's just a matter of driving to the warehouse that I rented under a different fake name for exactly this purpose. I've only had a few jobs over the past year that required it, but I'm absolutely certain that I won't be found here for as long as I need to stay. No one will hear the screams, and no one will come to investigate.

The hardest part is getting the bulk of the man out of the trunk and to the warehouse. He's tall and heavily muscled, but fortunately, I'm not all that worried about what kind of shape he's in when he wakes up. As long as he talks, that's all I give a shit about.

I've already prepared the room in the warehouse with plastic sheeting, a chair in the center of it with cuffs dangling above from the ceiling. I cuff him to the chair for now, wrists and ankles, and leave him there while I move the car far enough away for it not to be seen at the warehouse. By the time I get back, he's starting to come to–right on schedule.

"What the—" the man's voice is thick and slurring as he wakes up, his eyes foggy as he looks around, but I can see the dawning awareness there, the first hint of fear.

Good.

What made me effective in Viktor's employ, was that none of this bothered me. Blood, gore, screams, pleas for mercy, none of it affected me in the slightest. Once someone was handed over to me to extract information, to punish, to execute, they became a job, not a person.

And I've always been very, very good at my job.

"I—fuck—I don't know—what do you—" The man is spluttering already, his voice fearful, and it calms me. *Good. He's already afraid. That should make this easier.*

"What's your name?" I don't personally care to know. I'd rather remain detached. In the beginning, when I started this kind of work, I never asked for names. I wanted them to remain as much an object as possible, divorced from any kind of humanity. But in time, I learned that asking their name softened them. It gave them hope, made them think I *wanted* to give them their freedom. That I care about their pain, their future after this. That I want to see them as a person, and if they'll only cooperate, this can all be over.

So I started asking for names.

The man swallows hard. "J-Jakov. Please, I—whatever you want, it has nothing to do with me. I'm security, that's all. Whatever is going on in that place, I know nothing. They tell me nothing. Please—"

"This has nothing to do with your current job." I get up, pushing myself to my feet, as I start to circle him. "You were in the employ of Adrian Drakos before this, were you not?"

The man goes very still. "I—I don't see what that has to do with anything."

My fist connects with his jaw, hard. His head swings sideways, and he coughs, spitting up blood.

"That's not how this works, *syn*," I snap, circling to face him. "I ask questions, and you answer. If you do that, then you will feel less pain. Trust me, that was only a very small taste of how much I can make this hurt if you refuse to answer my questions–and I have *many* more questions."

Jakov looks at me, his eyes widening. Blood is slowly trickling from his lip, and he swallows convulsively again. "Please–can I have some water. My mouth–"

I hit him again, this time on the other side of the jaw. "*I* ask the questions. Did Drakos fire you because you were too fucking stupid? It's starting to seem that way."

"N-no." Jakov shakes his head. "He actually–I came quite highly recommended to him."

"Good for you." I take a step forward, and Jakov flinches. *Good. He believes you're serious.* "What did you do for him, when you worked there?"

I can see the gears turning in Jakov's thick skull, trying to decide whether this is a safe question to answer, if giving me something will soften me towards him. He still believes he's getting out of here alive. A man with hope to live who once worked for a dangerous man will try to keep that man's secrets, lest something else terrifying chase him down in the dark.

In time, tonight, he'll realize that I am what he needs to fear most. And when the moment is right, I'll let him know that he won't be leaving this place.

I can see the decision click into place. "Security," Jakov says thickly. "I was part of his security team."

"A career man. Good. It must have been a lucrative position."

"Is that a question?"

My fist slams forward, directly into his mouth and nose. His head snaps backward, and he lets out a cry of pain.

"My nose!" Blood is streaming down his face. "Fuck, why–"

"You don't talk back to me, *suka*." I punch him again, hard, and then again before he can recover, leaving him reeling and breathless from the pain. Once upon a time, I left jobs like this with sore hands and bruised knuckles, but now I hardly feel it. My hands, like the rest of me, have hardened over time.

"Are you ready to be polite?" I loom over him. "You are a guest here. Is that how you behave in someone else's home?"

He sneers at me, and it's all I can do not to laugh. *This one is so predictable.* I can see him going through the stages that so many of them do, in this position. He began with fear, and now he's shifted into anger. *We'll see how long his resistance lasts.*

"This isn't your home. Or if it is, no wonder you're such an asshole. It's a fucking dump."

Another blow, and another. His lips begin to swell, and I refocus my attention elsewhere. He has to be able to speak–although all that really means is leaving his tongue intact.

"You should use that tongue to answer my questions, instead of insulting me." I reach for his bound hands, undoing them from the chair. He starts to struggle, twisting, but he's at a disadvantage and in pain. I deliver one hard blow to his gut, and while he's wheezing, I drag his hands above his head and chain them. His feet are still touching the ground, unbound from the now-discarded chair, but if need be, I can drag the chain higher.

"Answer my question," I repeat, as I see the reality of what's happening begin to settle over his face. "Did Drakos pay you well?"

I can see him once again weighing the risks of answering. "Well enough," he says finally. "Not enough to make any of us rich, but room and board came with the job, so I guess all added together, it was pretty comfortable."

I nod. "So why did you leave the position? Was it too dangerous?"

That strikes a nerve. "Fuck you!" he snaps, twisting in the chains. "I'm no fucking coward. I would have stayed there as long as I could have. Working in a place like Santorini—"

"Ah, so you worked for him *recently*." I smile at him. "I knew that already, of course, but it's good to hear you are beginning to be more forthcoming. So you didn't leave. You were fired."

Jakov's expression turns sullen. "I don't see what that has to do with anything."

"That's not for you to understand. All you need to do is answer questions."

I can see the moment that his courage rallies a little, his anger warring with his fear. "Fuck you, man," he spits out. "I was having a perfectly decent night at work. Even had one of the girls show a little interest for free, if you know what I mean. I don't know what fucking information you think I have, but I don't know anything—"

He splutters as I grab his chin, reaching for one of the implements on the nearby table. I see the sheer terror on his face as I reach upwards with a pair of pliers and feel the shudder that goes through him at the scrape of metal against a tooth.

"Think harder," I advise, and yank.

Blood runs down his face as he screams. "Fuck! What the fuck!"

"Were you fired?"

"Fuck you!"

I shrug and pull out another tooth.

Three later, Jakov is sobbing. "Fine," he splutters through blood and saliva, the smell of piss beginning to fill the air.

My least favorite part of the job.

"Fine," he sobs again. "I was fired. Drakos fired me."

I hold up the bloody pliers, and he makes a choked sound, shrinking backward as much as he's able in the chains, tears streaming down his face. "Why?" I ask flatly, and I see something give in Jakov.

"I had gambling debts. I'd lost all my money and then some." The words come out wetly, half-slurred, and thick with pain. "I was fucking broke."

"I can see why. You have a shit poker face."

There's a brief moment where I can see him trying to rally, to gather his courage to find a retort, and then he slumps again, looking at me through swollen eyes. "Whatever."

I click the pliers, and he lets out another sob. "What did your gambling debts have to do with it? Drakos have something against gambling?"

Jakov sags forward in the chains, trying to speak between gasps of pain and tears. "I stole something from him. A piece of jewelry–this pearl ring. It was worth a lot; I heard him talking about it. I figured I could sell it, cover the worst of the debts until the next payday. I'd blame it on someone else. I thought for sure I could pull it off. I knew all the alarms, the security shifts, and his routines. Everything. But I guess someone was suspicious. Maybe they knew about the debts, or he did. Maybe someone was fucking watching me. I don't fucking know. But I got caught.'"

It takes a long time for him to get all of that out, the words coming in fits and starts. When he finally goes silent again, I look at him, clicking the pliers together. "So you lied to me."

His eyes go wide. "What? What–no! I haven't…please, no–"

"You said you were fired." *Click.* "But a man like Drakos, if you steal from him, he doesn't just fire you. I know that. So that was a lie."

"No!" Jakov screams as I grab one of his feet, still bound together at the ankles, dragging off his shoe. "No, no, no—"

It's a good thing, I reflect, as I tear off the nail on the big toe, *that no one will pass by out here to hear the screams.*

"Understand," I tell a weeping Jakov as I hold up the bloody nail, "that a lie will make this all so much worse. Refuse to answer, and it will hurt. But it will be so much worse if you answer, and I discover it's a lie."

"I didn't, I didn't mean to—"

"It doesn't matter," I tell him gently as I reach for his foot again.

When he's stopped screaming, and I think he can speak again, I set the pliers down, crossing my arms over my chest. "I'll give you a chance to redeem yourself," I say flatly. "Tell me what happened after Drakos caught you stealing."

"I—oh, fuck." Jakov squeezes his eyes shut. "I wasn't caught exactly. I wasn't lying!" he adds, screeching as I reach for the pliers again. "God, just fucking *listen!*"

I press my lips together tightly, trying hard not to laugh. "Fine. Convince me as to why that wasn't a lie."

"It was a–a simplification." *Big word for Jakov.* "I did get caught trying to get the ring, but they didn't catch me when I made a break for it. I had my papers on me, just in case something went wrong. My passport, all of that. I ran and managed to get out the window. Not with the ring. But I had a little money on me. I made it to the airport and got on the first flight out. I'm not from Moscow—he didn't think to look for me here."

"But there's a price on your head, surely?"

"I don't know," he says, letting out a shriek as my fingers touch the pliers. "I don't! I haven't heard anything. I've been hiding out here, working at the club. Hoping he has bigger things to deal with. He—well, the night before—"

Abruptly, he stops talking, and I know I've bumped up against something important.

"Keep speaking, *syn*, if you know what's good for you."

Jakov swallows hard, terror written over every part of his face, and I can hear the sound of him starting to piss himself again. "I can't," he mumbles thickly. "If I say–I won't–I can't–"

"You can, and you will." I reach for the pliers again, ignoring his pleas.

"No, no–" He shakes his head, when there's only one nail left on the right foot, and I raise an eyebrow. *It must be good for him to hold out this long.*

It's time to let him in on the secret of how tonight will go.

I set down the pliers, giving him a sympathetic smile. "Listen," I tell him slowly. "I know you fear what Drakos will do to you if you tell me the truth. But there is no reason to fear."

He looks at me, uncomprehending, and I step closer.

"You will not live past this night." I reach out, tipping Jakov's bloody, swollen face up into the light. "Your life is over, *negodyay*. You only have the means of how it ends left to negotiate. There is no reason for you to fear Adrian Drakos any longer." I squeeze his jaw, pressing in on the places where his teeth once were, and he lets out a moan of pain.

"You only need to fear me, now. I will end this, if you tell me what I need to know. Quick and clean. If you continue to drag this out, I can take you apart in so many pieces that you will look at them scattered about as you die. Make your choice, *syn*, or I will make it for you."

I can see the moment it clicks, the sheer terror, the hopelessness, and then the resignation that settles over his face, each emotion clear and vivid. I can see the precise second when he realizes that he *will* die, that the cigarette he smoked outside that club is the last one he'll ever taste, that he will never eat another meal, have another drink, or come inside a woman again. His life, now, is over. He has hours, minutes, seconds, and his last choice will be how many are left and how painful they are.

Tears spill down his face, dripping in a hopeless trail down swollen and bloodied cheeks, and he nods almost imperceptibly. The words come out slowly, halting and pained, but they come without resistance now.

"There was a woman there. Adrian had many beautiful women visiting his villa, but this one was extraordinary. A blonde goddess. She was there with three others."

I feel my pulse spike, a jolt of adrenaline flooding me at the first taste of the information that I'm seeking.

"Others?" I frown at him. "Who? What was her name?"

He shudders, and my hand twitches threateningly toward the table of implements.

"I'm trying–to remember–" He coughs thickly, still weeping, and manages to force out the name. "He called her Natasha…no, that's not right. Natalie–Natalia! It was Natalia. Ob–obe–"

Holy fuck. Yuri's information had been good. I'd been careful not to mention Natalia's name, not to lead Jakov in the direction of his salvation, instead letting him find his way there himself, if he really knew the name.

"And the others?" I press.

"Another big Russian man. I can't remember his name–I can't! Really!" He squeals it out, and I laugh, chuckling as I look at him.

"I believe you. Who else?"

I see Jakov slump slightly with relief at the idea that I believe him. "A priest. And another blonde woman, pretty, but not as gorgeous as the woman Drakos was with."

Fuck. I bite back a groan of satisfaction. With every word Jakov speaks, the more I'm certain that he's not mistaken. "So that's what's occupying him?" I press, leaning in and seeing Jakov shrink back. "He's so busy with this woman that he won't pursue you?"

Jakov shakes his head. "No. She's not there any longer. The night before I tried to steal the ring, she and Drakos had a huge fight. They'd been together for a handful of weeks, but they both had strong personalities. They fought and made up a lot. We all heard it–the fighting and the fucking, but this one was louder than usual. After the fight, she left. That never happened before. Usually, their fighting would end in rough sex all over the villa. We'd all have to stay out of the way to avoid running into them. Drakos would lose his fucking mind if anyone saw her in so much as a nightgown. He was insanely jealous."

It takes a long time for him to get all of that out, but I can be a patient man. When the last words are stuttered out of his swollen lips, I cross my arms over my chest.

"So that's it? She just left? Went to a hotel on Santorini?"

I can see the flicker of resentment across Jakov's face, the moment when he considers retorting back–*how the fuck would I know that*, perhaps. But instead, he just sags in his shackles, his throat convulsing. "I don't know where she went," he groans. "But!" he almost shouts the word as I reach towards the table, babbling a fearful stream of information. "I heard what she said during their fight."

"And what was that?"

"She said something about–" His throat convulses again as if he's trying hard to swallow and can't. "She mentioned Moscow. That she could survive there on her own if she needed to, without his help. She talked about not wanting to spend the rest of her life on the run, going from country to country. How she had no way to start over without help, no money, and no fake passport, and how angry that made her. How she didn't want to be dependent on a man. That especially pissed Drakos off. He said that she should have thought about that before—"

"Before?" I press, narrowing my eyes, and Jakov coughs again. There's a moment of resistance on his face, a last struggle to finish his statement.

"Before she killed her father."

The words come out flat and hopeless, as if he knows they're the last he can give me and, therefore, the end of his life. His eyes shut, tears streaming out faster now, and I reach for the gun on the table, silencer already affixed. I feel the warm sense of satisfaction filling me, the knowledge of a job well done, that I have the information I need.

"Good man," I say soothingly, stepping towards him, and I see his shoulders shake with sobs as I press the muzzle of the gun to his temple. "Shh, it's over now. You've earned this."

He stiffens before the trigger is even pulled, his body reacting with horror to the death he knows is coming, but when it comes, it's quick. A muffled shot, a burst, and then his body sags in the chains.

Jakov is no more.

It's her. I've never felt more certain of it. I could go and take her now, abduct her from the club and bring her here, torment her to her breaking point, and then arrange to take her to Viktor. But even as I think about it, a better idea comes to mind.

She's so close, so *very* close to trusting me. *The revenge will be so much sweeter if she trusts me,* I think to myself as I start to clean up the remnants of the job. I have resources at my disposal, resources that I've tucked away for some time now–but I can use them. I can be the sort of man I used to be, the kind of man that she would see as her ticket out of this place. When she trusts me, when she believes that I'm only there because I want her so desperately, I'll bring the entire house of cards crashing down around her.

Is that entirely a lie? Why are you drawing this out, if not because you want her, because it's clouding your judgment, making you want to delay the moment when she's no longer available to you?

I ignore the needling voice in my head, the plan forming in my mind instead. A plan to make Natalia Obelensky feel safe, wanted, and *desired*, a plan to give her a window into her freedom–

And then snatch it from her, and watch her shatter.

Natalia

My mind is still on Ruby's party as I dance for the gentleman sitting in front of me on the champagne room couch, his hand on his thigh as he watches me twist around the pole. He's sixty years old if he's a day, and I see his fingers twitch again and again towards his groin, as if the not-so-subtle hint will encourage me to tell him, *by all means, go ahead and jerk off while I dance. I'd love that.*

Fucking disgusting.

Ruby had tried to push me toward some of the guys who were at the party, urging me to flirt, have fun, make out with someone. I hadn't entirely been sure why I wasn't able to. It wasn't that none of them were handsome—in fact, a few of them had been exactly the bad-boy type I've often been attracted to, but with a rougher edge that I would never have found in my old life. It wasn't even that I was worried about my cover being blown—none of them would have had a reason to suspect me.

In fact, a good meaningless fuck might have been exactly what I needed. A perfect excuse not to go home alone again, imagining blue eyes and demanding hands that I should be afraid of, not fantasizing about.

The one man I nearly approached, though, had been all wrong. Light blond hair, long on the top and shaved on the sides, and those pale blue eyes that sent a shock to my soul when he'd turned to look at me. I felt a chill go down my spine. Even though his eyes had raked down my body with the kind of blatant interest that told me I could have ended up in bed with him, all I'd been able to think about was a different pair of icy eyes, a different man looking at me with that same blatant lust.

I turned away instead, going to find Ruby, my body throbbing with a need that frustrated and pissed me off. Now I'm here at work again, wound tighter than a guitar string, thrumming with the need for something other than my own fingers to get me off. I need to get laid, but I feel as if Mikhail has cast some strange spell over me, invading my thoughts until it's only him that comes to mind.

Which makes me angrier still. I shouldn't want him like that. I shouldn't even entertain the thought. I should have the same distaste for him that I have for the man staring at me right now, and in so many moments, I *do*. But it's all tangled up with a fretful lust that makes me feel cold and hot by turns, feverish and frustrated.

Fucking hell, I need to just get laid anyway. Maybe then I can stop thinking about it.

I'm sliding down the pole, twisting with my back arched and my hands above my head, facing away from the man on the couch, when the door to the champagne room suddenly flies open.

I flinch in shock, managing not to fall only by virtue of excellent reflexes and long practice. I land on my feet like a sinuous cat, hearing the surprised grunt of the man behind me on the couch, as the last man I expected to see right now steps through the door as if I summoned him with my thoughts.

Mikhail strides in, cool and casual as if he belongs here, coming up short when he sees the man on the couch and me mid-dance.

"What the fuck?" I hear the man behind me growl angrily, his voice raspy with age, and I let go of the pole, glaring at Mikhail.

I swear to fucking god, if you get me in trouble with Igor again—

"That's a good question," I snap, narrowing my eyes at him. "What the fuck? I'm with a customer—"

"I was told to go ahead and go in," Mikhail says smoothly, taking another step forward. "I assumed you were done, but seeing this—" he shrugs. "I can only assume that since I paid extra for your time again, I take precedence over—whoever this is."

His eyes slide down my body slowly, possessively, sending a shudder through me. Fear and desire twist together in my belly, that feverish chill sliding over my skin, disturbing me. The way he looks at me, as if he can buy me, as if he *owns* me, makes me want to grab him by the throat and strangle him. *No one owns me*, I think furiously as I stare him down. Yet, that blatant possessiveness sends a flush of heat through me that pools between my thighs, making me feel faintly dizzy with the desire to find out what he might do to me if I let him.

"Get out," Mikhail snarls, craning around me to look at the man on the couch. "I've bought her time. It's mine now. Get the fuck out."

"My hour isn't up—"

"It is now." Mikhail stalks forward, his eyes narrowed dangerously. "I was told she was ready for me. Which means it's time for you to leave—unless you want me to help you out of the room, old man."

The tension crackles in the air for a moment. A part of me wants the old man on the couch, disgusted as I am by him, to tell Mikhail to go fuck himself. *It would serve him right.* But instead, I hear the soft leather rustle and squeak as the man gets up slowly, walking past Mikhail.

"I'll be sure to mention this to Igor," he rasps, looking between Mikhail and me, and I feel a cold knot in my belly. But Mikhail just shrugs.

"Do that. I guarantee he won't give a fuck, after what I just paid him."

"What the fuck was that?" I gasp, wheeling on him the moment the door shuts behind the other man. "You can't do that! You can't just—just come in here, not wait your turn, and be rude to other customers! This is my fucking job!"

"And I'm paying." Mikhail steps towards the stage, his gait cool and careless, his full mouth smirking slightly as he gives me another of those possessive looks. "I don't like seeing you with other men, Athena." He steps closer still, up to the very edge, inches from me. Every part of me wants to step back, away from him, but I'm frozen in place.

"I didn't like seeing you dance for him," he continues, his voice sharp, almost angry. "I didn't like the idea of you so close to him—like you were with me the other night. Would you have danced for him like that, Athena? Would you have gotten *so* close to him, so close that he could smell you, almost *taste* you?"

A shudder goes through me, but I feel a pulse between my thighs at the memory of that dance, the orgasm that had torn through me as I gyrated above him, how fucking *good* it had felt.

I swallow convulsively, still feeling as if I can't move. "It's my job," I manage finally, looking down into those pale, jealous blue eyes. "You're a customer like any other, *Mikhail*," I say his name with the exact opposite intonation of how he says mine, sharp and cold, without any of the sticky, clinging sweetness that he always coats *Athena* in.

Mikhail raises an eyebrow slowly, that possessive sheen still in his gaze. "Aren't you supposed to make your customers feel special?"

Slowly, he reaches out, his fingers coming very close to my calf. His hand hovers there, so close to my skin that I can almost feel his touch without any actual contact, and another shudder runs through me. I feel as if I'm vibrating on the inside with nerves, the tension between us stretched so tight that I feel as if any moment it will snap. I know instinctively that it will be me that it hurts when it does.

His fingers graze my bare skin, ever so slightly, and it feels like an electric shock. It tingles up my leg, making me step back, nearly tripping in my haste to get away from him.

"You're not supposed to do that," I gasp, stepping out of reach. "I could have you thrown out of here for that, with no refund. Is that what you want?"

His smirk grows, and he folds his arms over his chest, still standing at the very edge of the stage. "Would you rather be touching yourself?"

I *feel* myself flush bright red, the color beginning at my neck and rising up into my cheeks, and I hate both myself and him for it. "Fuck you," I hiss. "You paid me to do that, and you know it. All that means is that you can't get a girl to masturbate for you in real life, so you have to pay me to fulfill your sick fantasies."

It's as if my words go right through him. He just grins, laughing softly, his eyes sliding over me and back up to my face. I can see the growing hunger in them, the way it rises as what must surely be a game to him continues–but it doesn't feel like a game to me. Not any longer–if it ever was. This feels dangerous, and yet, it's that very reason that I don't shout for Davik the way I would if it were anyone else.

"I know you enjoyed it," he says silkily, his words rippling over my skin. "I know it wasn't just all an act. No woman comes like that just because she's getting paid."

He breathes in deeply, his eyes heating. "I still remember how you smelled. So aroused, so *needy*. You can't fake that, *kotenok*."

I can feel the burning flush of anger flood through me, because he's right, and it fucking pisses me off. I curl my lip, glaring at him; some of my desire cooled with the fresh fury that he always seems to incite, eventually.

"What do you want?" I snap irritably. "It can't be just to stand here and piss me off, unless that's a kink you haven't told me about yet. So what did you pay extra for tonight?"

He grins, shrugging as he walks to the couch. "A dance, *dorogaya*, that's all. You can even leave the lingerie on. You look beautiful in red, by the way. Did you borrow that from your friend? The one with the bright hair?"

I flinch, seething at how quickly he picked up on it. I *did*, in fact, forget my lingerie tonight–or rather, I'd forgotten my bag. I left it here when Ruby had dragged me off to her party, flustered and distracted, and when I'd come back tonight, the set that had been left inside was missing. It had started off my night on the wrong foot–especially since the only reason it could be gone is that one of the other girls stole it–and it's only gone downhill from there. I had to borrow something from Ruby, which doesn't fit as well as it should, considering the difference in our builds. I already feel off, less confident than usual, and having him point it out only throws me off my game even more.

Just forget about it, I tell myself. *Dance, and hope he doesn't want more.*

But I've never known a man to not keep pushing once he's found the edge of a boundary. And Mikhail, especially, feels like the kind of man who won't stop.

The problem is, I'm no longer sure if I want him to.

Mikhail

She's a vision in red.

I grin to myself as I slouch back onto the couch, watching her step off of the stage to change the music to the sultry, smoky beat that she prefers when she dances for me. *See, pretty one, little* kotenok? *Already, I've learned things about you. Already, I'm beginning to know you.*

She would have blamed one of the other dancers, by now, for the loss of her usual lingerie. My reasoning for sneaking into her dressing room and stealing it in the wee hours of the morning after I finished cleaning up the mess that had once been Jakov was three-fold.

I wanted to unsettle her. I wanted her to wonder who would have touched her things, stolen them. I wanted her to feel slightly adrift, in need of someone else to trust.

I wanted her lingerie for myself, to keep along with the panties that I'd stolen from her apartment. A trophy of sorts to mark the next step in my plan. I gathered up the lace and thin fabric in my hands, feeling my cock throb as I imagined that it still felt warm from her skin, her scent emanating from it—sweat and flesh and sweet perfume. But that hadn't been all.

It had been obvious that she would have borrowed something from the bright-haired dancer, the one who calls herself Ruby. She's the only one, from what I've seen, that Natalia actually trusts. I wanted to see her in something else, to feel a measure of control over her. *You're wearing borrowed clothes because of me*, malen'kiy.

It's hard to restrain my need as I watch her ascend the stage again, her body already moving sinuously to the beat. The lingerie is ill-fitting, but it doesn't matter. She might as well be naked for me, with how strongly I can feel myself react to her. The memories of what I'd done when I returned to my apartment with her things surface, fueling my arousal as I remember the scratch of lace over my sensitive, aroused flesh, the flood of release as I'd come, the lingerie wrapped around my straining cock, my hands still bloodied from Jakov.

A night spent extracting information always makes me needy for the pleasures of the flesh, and that was no different. It had been all I could do not to go back to her apartment and take her then and there, sweeping her away to the secluded place where I could do all I wanted to her and more.

I had to force myself to be patient, to remember how much more gratifying it will be this way. If I'd gone for her that night, she would have been terrified, but she would have thought, *of course, yes, I was right all along to mistrust him. He was always a danger.*

If I can make her trust me, *give* herself to me without force, it will be so much sweeter to see her break, to see her realize that she made a mistake. It will be so much better when she realizes she wanted the same man that will destroy her.

I shift on the couch as I watch her dance, desire thrumming through me like the heavy beat of the music, heavy and hard to restrain. It grows worse with each passing day, the need more and more unbearable, but I remind myself that the plan is set in motion tonight.

Soon. Soon, I'll have what I want. What I need.

She throws herself into the dance, but as always, I can't be sure what is real, and what's by virtue of her having been paid. I want to *know*, before I break her. I want to know beyond a shadow of a doubt that she's given in to what I know she wants, that she's fallen thoroughly into my trap.

I hear the shift in the music as she comes down off of the stage, her skin faintly glistening with sweat, her lovely blue eyes fixed on mine, sultry and warm. I can feel the throb of lust in my veins as she comes closer, gyrating over me, and the temptation to negotiate for more is almost too much. I could have her moaning above me again, hear the wet sounds of her fingers against her flesh, could feel her heated release soaking through the fabric of my pants onto my cock. I feel myself throb and harden even more at that memory, at the memory of stroking myself in the bathroom with my flesh wet from her orgasm.

Wait. It will be sweeter if you wait. If you ask for more now, she will only ever see you as a customer. You want her to desire you as more than that.

I can tell she's angling for it, whether out of her own personal desire or a desire for more money tonight; I'm not quite sure. And I want to be sure. She sways over me, arching her back, her small breasts pushed forward, so they're very close to my face. When she turns, gyrating above me, her ass is so very close to rubbing against my aching cock that it hurts.

By the end of the dance, she's straddling me without actually touching me, her hands gripping the back of the sofa as she rolls her hips above mine, her legs spread so that no part of her brushes against me. It's sweet torture, the warm scent of her sweat and perfume filling the air, and I resolve to make it home before I come tonight, to use her lingerie again so I can keep that scent in my nostrils as I find my release.

As the music slows, she slides away from me, gracefully slipping out of reach. "What else do you want tonight?" she asks, her voice still smooth and sultry, but I can hear the hint of irritation in her voice.

This is exactly why I can't ask for more tonight. She sees me as something to be finished with as quickly as possible. A way to make money and then get rid of me, because she can't reconcile how I make her feel.

I want her to feel the same desire I do, the same painful, consuming ache—and then I want her world to come crashing down around her as she realizes the mistake she made.

"Nothing," I tell her simply, and I see the startled look in her eyes in the instant before she smooths it over. "The dance was enough. Nothing more...for now."

"That can't be true," she says with a laugh, tossing her hair over one shoulder. "Men like you always want more. They're never satisfied with going backward, once they've crossed a line. They always keep pushing."

She steps back, leaning against the stage, still perfectly posed. "So what is it you want, Mikhail? I know you didn't pay extra only for me to do the exact same thing you could have seen on the stage outside, but in private. We're past that now."

"Alright, then. If it's honesty you want from me, then I suppose I can give it to you." I give her a half-smile. "It's a bit embarrassing, honestly."

She rolls her eyes. "I've heard it all in here. But there are no promises. You might have all the money in the world, but in here—" Her tongue flicks out, dragging over the swell and curve of her lower lip, and I know it's on purpose. "I decide what I do and don't do."

"Oh, it wouldn't be in here." I grin at the flicker of uncertainty that crosses her face. "I want a date with you, *Athena*."

I see it again, that hint of nervousness at the way I say her name, the emphasis I put on it, letting her know that I want to know who she really is. That I don't buy the fake stage name, that I don't even *pretend* to, the way some men do.

It pleases me how much it catches her off guard. She takes a full second to respond, as if that were the last thing she ever expected to hear coming out of my mouth.

"That's out of the question." She bites off each word, flatly, as if to close the topic before it can even really be explored. But I'm not so easily dissuaded.

"I'll pay for it, of course, if that's what you want." I lean back against the couch, watching her carefully. I don't want to miss a single reaction, a single expression on her lovely face. "For your time," I add quickly, as if it's an afterthought. "Nothing more, if you don't want it."

She shakes her head. "That's ridiculous," she says flatly. "Why would you do that? To spend an evening with me? I'm not that easily fooled, and frankly, I'm offended that you would think I would be."

I shrug casually. "You can believe me or not, of course. But it's the truth, *Athena*. You don't belong here, in this seedy place. I want to take you out somewhere nicer than this. Somewhere that I can enjoy your company without being reminded of how very–*transactional* this all is." I wave a hand around the room, as if all of this feels distasteful to me.

She narrows her eyes, but I can feel her wavering. It was a calculated ask, because I know if she is Natalia, as I believe her to be, she must miss the trappings of the life she had before terribly. I remembered the way she'd breathed in when she got into my rented car, her fingers sliding over the soft leather as if she *needed* the caress of it, and now it all makes sense. She's a diamond lost in a coal mine, and she needs a night to sparkle, to remember what she used to be.

"Just one night," I coax gently. "A five-star dinner, paid for in full, and then more on top of that for your time. An *experience*. You won't get that from any of the other customers here, and you know it."

She sucks her lower lip into her mouth, chewing on it, and I push forward that last bit, naming a figure that I know is ridiculous. "For your time," I tell her, emphasizing the last word. "Only that, if you want it to be that way. If there happens to be more, we can discuss it then."

Her eyes widen at the amount, and I see her hesitate for one final second before she nods.

"Alright," she says finally. "But you pay at the beginning of the date. And it will be only that. Dinner. The rules remain the same as they are in here—you may not touch me."

Oh, sweet kotenok, *you're going to* beg *me for more before the night is over.*

"Of course." I smile at her. "I hope I've proven myself to be a gentleman so far. I haven't taken more than you've permitted. This will be the same."

She glances up at the clock. "Your time is up," she says. "I'm off Thursday night. You can make arrangements then. I'll meet you on the same block where you picked me up the other night."

Slowly, I rise from the couch. I don't hold out my hand to shake on the deal, remembering how she reacted to being touched earlier. Instead, I just hold her gaze, letting the smile teasing the corner of my lips spread over my face.

"I look forward to it."

Natalia

I think I might have made a terrible mistake.

As I walk up the stairs to my apartment, hours before I'm supposed to meet Mikhail for our date, my heart is racing until I feel dizzy. *What was I thinking?*

That feeling is only compounded when I see a long box, white matte with a silvery bow wrapped around it, sitting on my doorstep.

I can't believe it wasn't fucking stolen. This is hardly the kind of place to leave an expensive-looking delivery, which means it can't have been here for more than a few minutes. I glance around nervously as I pick it up, half expecting someone to jump out of the shadows and grab me while I'm distracted. It's hard enough to unlock the multiple locks on my door while holding it, but I don't dare unlock my door first and leave it that way while I pick up the package. I can easily envision someone coming up behind me and following me into the unlocked apartment before I can stop them.

You're paranoid, Natalia.

I have every reason to be.

I quickly step into the apartment, setting the box down and relatching every single one of the locks with a pounding heart. This is very different from the other "gifts" that have been left for me, and my imagination is running wild with the worst things it could be.

I set the box on my kitchen table, ignoring the way it shifts on the shorter fourth leg as I reach for the bow with shaky hands. I expect it to be something terrible—a dead animal, maybe, or something more threatening. When I finally work up the courage to lift the lid, all I see is smooth tissue paper, the same silvery sheen as the bow that was wrapped around it.

What the hell? My hands tremble above it, anxiety flooding me. I'm afraid of pulling the tissue paper back, the irrational fear that something will jump out at me, making me feel shaky and unsteady. I take a deep breath, sucking in air, trying to steady myself. *You can't be afraid of a box and some paper, Natalia. You're tougher than that.*

I reach out quickly, yanking the paper back—and stare down at what's nestled there in the box.

It's a dress. Laid out on silvery paper, made of sleek, soft sapphire silk. I reach for it, my fingers brushing down the length of the fabric. It reminds me of something I would have worn before all of this, something I would have chosen for myself for some after-party or charity gala. My heart skips in my chest, wondering who would have sent this to me. *Who could have chosen something like this?*

I pick it up, lifting it out of the box and letting the fabric ripple down. It's a longer dress than I would have expected, falling to ankle length. It splits up both sides, the deep-cut bodice held up by thin straps, and I know just by looking at it that it will fit me—probably perfectly.

Glancing down, I see that's not all that was in the box. There's a smaller, black matte box and a longer one at the end, all of them nestled inside like a Russian nesting doll. The irony doesn't escape me as I scoop the other two boxes out, carrying them and the dress to my bedroom.

I lay the blue dress on my bed, setting the other boxes down. I reach for the long, thin one first, lifting the lid more quickly this time, not expecting some gruesome thing to frighten me. *The dress could have just been to get your defenses down,* I caution myself, but I'm too curious now to be as cautious as I was before.

It's a pair of shoes. Fine, expensive, and delicate, nude leather and thin spiked heels with straps so slight that the shoes will barely cling to my feet. I feel a moment's hesitation about wearing them–open-toed shoes are the bane of a former ballerina–but they're so beautiful that it's impossible not to want to put them on. I glance at the size–it's exactly mine.

A shudder ripples down my spine, and I drop them into the box, feeling a cold knot tighten in my belly. *How does whoever sent this know? How does he know my shoe size? What* is *this?*

I have a suspicion as to what the last box will be before I even open it, and I'm right. Inside are a pair of drop earrings, a series of sapphires the same color as the dress falling down in a strip of sparkling gemstones, set in what looks to be white gold.

Who could have sent all of this? Any of the items alone are expensive, I can tell that much, but all together, they must have cost a fortune. I set the earrings aside, pawing through the tissue paper in the large box, looking for a note or a card that might tell me.

I find it at the very bottom, tucked away in a spot where I might have missed it if I hadn't been looking. It's printed on thick card stock, and the black script gives me my answer the moment I look at it.

I know these will be beautiful on you.

Looking forward to our date.

Mikhail

Fuck. I sit down heavily on the edge of the bed, my heart beating faster now. I'm on the verge of canceling the date altogether, the gifts striking a chord of terror in me instead of the elation that I'm sure he expected. *My dress size. My shoe size. What explanation is there for this?*

I try to breathe, recalling the conversation I had with Ruby in my dressing room after I left the champagne room with Mikhail's offer of a paid date. I'd been panicking, angry with myself for agreeing, trying to think of a way out without losing him as a customer altogether. I explained what had happened to Ruby, breathless with fear and regret, and she laughed.

"I'm sorry, I'm not laughing at you," she said. *"It's just—this is a good thing! You've got a whale on the hook, just like me. My date went fucking fantastic. He wants to see me again. He's paying me the kind of money we'd never see in this place, not usually. If this man has that kind of money—and it keeps looking as if he does—fucking take advantage of this, girl! Don't let him get bored or offend him, and let some other girl get her claws in him."*

"So this is normal?" I had to lock my fingers together in front of me to stop myself from chewing on my nails, an old bad habit that I thought I'd broken years ago. *"You don't think this is weird? Suspicious? That agreeing might be dangerous?"*

Ruby shrugged. "I mean—there's always a chance that men like this might be dangerous. But you've been in his car once before, alone. If he wanted to hurt you, that would have been an easy opportunity." She let out a long breath, giving me a comforting smile. *"There's always an element of risk. I don't want to tell you otherwise. But this is a good opportunity. And yes, it's normal. Men like that—men with money, they have egos, too. It makes them feel good to get you out of this club, this environment, into their own world where they feel like they have more power. They can buy your time and forget for a little while that they purchased it. The fact that he negotiated for just your time right off the bat—that's a good sign."*

I swallow nervously, nodding. *"I just—this is strange for me. I've never done this before. I didn't think I would—"*

"Growth." Ruby nodded sagely, still grinning at me. "This is good! And you don't have to accept a second date if this one goes badly, or if you feel like you're getting a bad feeling. Get the money for this one, and then see how it goes! Take it one date at a time." She laughed at her own bad pun. "And if you need anything, just ask me. I'm here for you. We've got each other's backs."

Now, staring down at the gifts from Mikhail, I wish I could call her and ask her to come over. I felt this sense of foreboding dread from the very start, a suspicion that this isn't quite right, but Ruby had soothed that. She told me he was just a sugar daddy, just a rich man looking to pay for time with a woman who had caught his attention, who wanted the power of knowing he can buy her time and take her out of the environment he found her in. She'd given me examples of men she'd gone out with, ones the other girls had similar arrangements with, and it had started to soothe those fears. *You're just afraid because this is strange,* I told myself. *Not because there's anything really wrong. And she's right; he had the chance to take advantage when you got into his car. He's been a gentleman so far, in terms of not taking what wasn't allowed.*

What I couldn't admit to Ruby is where the rest of my misgivings are coming from—the fact that deep down, I *want* to go on the date. I want to go out to a fine restaurant again, to eat expensive food, to spend time with a man who seems to be from the world I once inhabited, or at least adjacent to it. I want to see what boundaries he might offer to pay me to cross—and I might want to agree.

I know I shouldn't want that. And now, as all the fears come rushing back, I try to think of what Ruby might say to me if she were here right now, if I weren't afraid to let her come over for fear that she might be seen and targeted by someone, too.

She'd tell me that he's had other girls like this, girls that he kept and spoiled, and that he probably has a type, so that's why he knows my dress size. Maybe he even has an assistant he showed a picture to, a woman who would be more likely to be able to guess correctly. And as for the shoes—

How can that be explained away? I feel my toes curl instinctively, that dread creeping through me. *Maybe he has a foot fetish. Maybe he's just very good at noticing those kinds of things. Maybe that's his quirk, being able to guess shoe sizes. Are you really complaining about a free pair of thousand-dollar shoes?*

If the date goes bad, and I don't see him again, I can sell them. The dress and earrings, too. That, on top of what I make for the date tonight and what I've already tucked away from my nights in the champagne room with him, will make a nice little dent in what I need to escape.

Just one night, Natalia. Get through this, and you'll be well on your way to never having to worry about anything like this again.

I force myself up, quickly stripping out of my loose jeans and t-shirt, and going to the top drawer of my dresser. The dress is too sparse on the top to wear a bra—not that I really need one anyway—and with the way the fabric will cling, I need something that won't show lines beneath it. I find a thin, silky thong in my drawer. I have a sudden thought of Mikhail's hand between my thighs, his fingers finding the slight bit of fabric, and the way his eyes might heat at the realization.

A quick jolt of heat bursts through me at the thought of his fingers hooking around the thin string, pulling it aside, brushing against—

You're not going to make it through tonight if you can't stop thinking like that. Get a grip, I tell myself firmly, slipping the panties on quickly over my hips and reaching for the dress. *Tonight is about getting what you need to escape this place, nothing else.*

The dress fits perfectly, exactly as I thought it would. It slides over me and clings in all the right places, the slits stopping at the tops of my thighs, the fabric swishing between my legs in a way that reminds me of every beautiful dress I chose for myself in my past life. Something in my chest aches, looking at myself in the mirror. If I ignore the black hair, and the sparse, ugly apartment in the background, I can almost imagine that I'm back in my old room, dressing for a night out. Once I slip the shoes on, it's even easier to picture.

I almost feel like myself again.

I skip the heavier makeup that I do for the club. I curl my hair into soft pinup-style waves, pinning it back at the front, and settle for a simple wash of champagne eyeshadow and mascara, with the thinnest strip of eyeliner and no fake lashes. Instead of my usual bold red lip, I dig out an old tube of rose-colored lipstick, just enough to give my mouth a slight flush. When I'm finished, I look so much more like the person I remember being before that I have to blink back tears.

Get ahold of yourself, I warn myself again, swallowing hard as I force the emotions down. *You need to be on your game tonight, or he'll take advantage. He's not doing this for you. He doesn't even know who you are, thank god, and he has no idea what it means to you to be dressed like this, going to a place like this again. Don't let it go to your head.*

Walking down my street to where I'm supposed to meet Mikhail is more than a little nerve-wracking. It's early evening, so there are a few people out and about, and dressed like this, I stick out. I keep my eyes ahead, ignoring anyone who looks at me, and I try not to think about what it looks like as I stand at the corner waiting for him.

In a matter of moments, I see a sleek car pulling up, different from the one he'd been driving the first night I'd ridden with him. This one is a black Aston Martin, and as it idles there, I peer inside, wanting to make sure that it's Mikhail.

I don't have to look for long. His door swings open as he steps out, dressed immaculately in tailored black pants and a charcoal button-down, complete with a silvery grey tie. He circles around to where I'm standing, opening the passenger door as he smiles at me. "I was afraid you might not be here. I've never been so happy to be wrong."

"We made a deal." I give him a small smile as he gets back into the car. "I had to hold up my end of it."

"I'm grateful you did." He nods at the center console. "In there is the money. Feel free to take it, count it, whatever you like."

I glance at him, opening the console to find an envelope clearly filled with cash. "Usually, this is given at the end of a date, from what I hear," I tell him lightly, forcing a teasing note into my tone.

"We agreed on the beginning." He smiles. "I hold up my end of the deal as well. And anyway, I would have wanted to get that out of the way no matter what, so I can pretend I'm getting a *real* date with you. You can't blame a man for wanting to fantasize a little, can you?"

"I'm glad you're a man of your word." I tuck the envelope into my clutch, feeling a little better with that out of the way. Not because I want to pretend it's a real date–*I don't*, I remind myself forcefully–but because now I don't have to worry all night that he'll try to weasel his way out of it at the very end. Ruby had told me not to be concerned with that, but I couldn't help it.

"You know," he says conversationally as he drives out of my neighborhood, "I should know your name, if we're going out on a date. You know mine, after all. It's only fair, I think. If there's a price–"

"Ekaterina." I smile at him, giving the first name that comes to mind and hoping that he accepts it without pressing further. "Does that make you happy? Knowing my name?"

"Very." He flashes me a full grin, and I feel something loosen in my chest, the fear that he wouldn't believe me slipping away. "It's a beautiful name. I knew someone who went by it, once."

"Oh?" I affect a little playful jealousy, glancing over at him. "Was she very important to you? Very beautiful? Should I be jealous?"

He laughs. "I only knew her for a few nights, so no. No need for you to be jealous. No one could be as beautiful as you, and we've already spent more nights in each other's company than I ever did with her. In fact, looking at you, I'm forgetting her already."

I know this is a game. It's a game I've played before, but I can feel myself relaxing and settling into it. It feels good to banter, to be teased and flattered, and I can feel myself forgetting how angry he makes me at times. This feels *good*, normal, to be in a luxury car on my way to a luxury dinner, dressed in designer silk and jewels, sitting next to a handsome, wealthy man. I keep my hands folded in my lap, giving him no reason to touch me, but I find myself wishing he would try as we drive, that he might reach out and run his hand up the smooth bare skin of my thigh.

He pulls up to the valet as we reach the restaurant, coming around to open my door again before the valet can. He hands the young-looking man the keys and pauses, looking at me. "I know we said no touching," Mikhail says smoothly. "But I'd like to be able to touch you, just a little." His hand hovers over the small of my back. "Here, perhaps, if you'd let me. Will you?"

Leaning a little closer, I feel his warm breath against my ear, brushing over the shell of it–but his lips still don't touch my skin. "We can negotiate for it here, if you like–or later."

I feel heat ripple over me, my breath catching in my throat at the nearness of his hand. "You may," I manage, the words coming out with a little difficulty. "We can–talk about it later."

I'm hardly about to stand here on the steps of a five-star restaurant negotiating the cost of his hand on my back, but when he touches me, I almost wish I had. This is all new to me, a dance that I'm not accustomed to, and I hadn't expected the way it would feel.

It's a light touch, just on the small of my back, nothing even remotely erogenous. His hand barely rests against my skin, but it feels as if his touch burns through the silk, making my heart skip a beat in my chest. I almost falter on the steps, and at the slight hitch in my gait, I feel his hand press more firmly against my back, urging me forward.

"Good thing you let me," he whispers against my ear.

Natalia

The warmth of his breath against my ear sends a shiver through me again, and I feel a little dizzy at the sudden desire that floods through me.

I swallow hard, picking up my pace a little, suddenly wanting his hand away from my skin. I hadn't expected such a simple touch to affect me like that, or I would never have allowed it.

"Table for two," Mikhail says as we step up to the hostess stand. "Under Kasilov."

We're led into the gorgeous restaurant, all white marble and black iron with chandeliers hanging throughout, dimly lighting the space. Mikhail's hand never leaves my back, all the way until we reach the table in a secluded corner, where a bottle of champagne is already on ice. Only then does he step away, pulling out my chair so I can sink into it, like the perfect gentleman.

He must see the expression on my face, because he smirks at me, reaching for the champagne. "I told you that you had nothing to fear from me," he says with a laugh. "That I would behave tonight, and I only wanted to spoil you."

He reaches for the flutes, pouring out the champagne. I can feel my mouth water a little at the sight of it—I can already imagine the dry, sharp taste, the fizz of the bubbles on my tongue. It feels like such a long time since I've had good champagne.

Mikhail hands one to me, tapping his glass against mine. "To finally getting you alone," he says with a grin, and I raise an eyebrow, laughing.

"We've been alone before," I remind him. "In fact, we were more alone in the champagne room than we are here, in a restaurant."

He smirks. "Well, I suppose you're right. Then—" he taps his glass against mine again. "To a date with the most beautiful woman I've ever seen—and actual champagne."

"I can definitely toast to that last part," I say with a soft laugh. "I can't remember the last time I had actual champagne."

His eyes narrow just a fraction, and I feel my heart stutter in my chest as I realize my mistake—that the role I'm playing means I shouldn't have *ever* tasted something this good before. *Maybe he won't call me on it,* I think, a ball of ice forming in the pit of my stomach, but I'm not so lucky.

"So you've had champagne like this before?" He swirls it lightly in his flute, a smile still twitching at the corners of his mouth. "What other man has been taking you out for fine dinners?"

I lift my own flute to my lips, buying myself time. I played myself off as being new to this kind of transaction—which I *am*—and now I can see the corner I've backed myself into. "A birthday party, a long time ago," I manage, setting the flute down and doing my best to look not at all unsettled by the conversation. "Not as good as this, though. I'm sorry—I don't like to talk much about my past. It's not the happiest story."

There's a beat where I wonder if he'll push, if he'll try to pry apart the cracks in my story. His icy eyes hold mine, the flute still held gingerly between his fingertips, and I can feel the beat of my heart in my chest like never before.

And then he gives me a pleasant smile, his face softening. "Well, I want this to be a good night for you. That was the point of it all, wasn't it? To spend an evening together away from all the depravity of that club." He gives a light shudder as if just thinking about it makes him feel slightly dirty. "We don't have to talk about anything that you don't want to."

"Thank you." I take another sip of my champagne as he sips from his, but it's hard to take the same pleasure from it that I might have before. The conversation was a reminder of the fine line I'm walking, how quickly I could give away the truth of who I am, if I'm not careful.

The server comes to the table then, giving me a moment to escape any further conversation, as Mikhail orders caviar for an appetizer. "Something new for you to try," he says, a glint in his eyes, and I have a sudden feeling that it's a test.

I've had caviar before. Of course, I have. But I force a smile onto my face, twirling my champagne flute. "What if I don't like it? I hope you won't be disappointed."

An expression that I can't quite read slides over his face. "Not every new experience is a good one. But you should be willing to try anything–at least once."

That shivery, icy feeling in the pit of my stomach makes a reappearance. I can't help feeling that there's a hint of a threat to his words, and I try to calm myself down, before my paranoia rears its head. *There's no reason to think that. He's just being playful. Flirtatious. You're reading too much into all of this.*

I'm a dancer, not an actress, but I do my best to come across as if I'm tasting caviar for the first time when it comes to the table. I don't have to fake how much I enjoy it, at least–I've always liked it, and it's just another pleasure of being back in a world that I've missed…at least parts of it, anyway.

"Would you like to place your dinner order?" the server asks, and Mikhail glances upwards at him.

"We'll do the tasting menu," he says firmly, handing over the leather-backed menus to the man. "For both of us, with wine pairings."

"I hope you don't mind my ordering for you," Mikhail adds as the server walks away, his gaze sliding over my face, down to my slight cleavage in the low-cut dress. I can see that glint of possessiveness again, the heat in his face, and I try to recollect myself. *This I can handle. This, I'm familiar with.* "I just enjoy spoiling beautiful women, and I think you'll enjoy what I've chosen. The chef's menu here really is delightful, and it changes frequently."

In reality, I'm irritated by the high-handedness of it all. I would never have allowed a man to order for me in my old life. But I push it aside, forcing that same smile. "I'm happy to try whatever you think I'll like," I say softly, and that strange expression flickers across his face again.

I can't quite figure out what it is that he wants—if he *likes* it when I snap back at him, if my fire and feistiness are part of what attracts him to me, or if he wants me sweet and compliant, thankful for being plucked out of my usual dingy environment. *I would be so bad at doing this regularly,* I think to myself as the first course, and the wine arrives, glancing across the table at Mikhail. *I could never do what Ruby does.*

"What do you think?" Mikhail watches as I take my first bite of the soup course, and it takes me a moment to speak. It's delicious, rich and velvety, and it's easy for me to look as astonished as I know I should at how good it is.

"This might be the best meal I've ever had so far." It's a simple lie to tell—right now, it feels like it is. I had forgotten what it was like to eat food like this, to not be getting by on cheap groceries, something that not all that long ago I would never have imagined I'd need to do.

"I'm glad to hear it." There's a satisfied look on Mikhail's face as he watches me, as if he's enjoying the sight of me eating.

I glance at him as I set my spoon down, feeling the urge to prod at him a little, to see what I can make him tell me. "Why are you doing this? I've never understood it, really. Someone like you–wealthy, decent enough manners when you need them, handsome–why would you need to pay a woman to go on a date with you? It's never added up for me, really."

Mikhail grins, taking a sip of his soup. "So you do think I'm handsome."

It's all I can do not to roll my eyes. "It was a serious question. Really, why?"

He shrugs, but I can see that familiar flicker of heat in his eyes. "Honestly? You're right. I wouldn't need to pay a woman to get a date with her. But you–you come with a price. And I didn't want a date with just any woman, Ekaterina. I wanted an evening with *you*."

I remind myself, yet again, that I can't fall for his flattery. That this man might be dangerous, and letting my guard down in the slightest bit is a bad idea. This is a business deal, and nothing that happens here is real. I shouldn't feel anything.

It's hard to feel nothing, though, when he seems so sincere. I've always thought I was decent at reading others, and looking at him, he seems earnest.

Or he's just very good at coming off that way, so he can get what he wants from you.

"I know what you're doing." I wave my spoon at him. "You're just trying to sweeten me up. You've seen where I work; don't you think I've heard it all before?"

"Is it working?" Mikhail raises an eyebrow. "Ekaterina, you said it yourself. I would have no trouble going out and finding a date for the evening. The difference is that I saw you, and I haven't been able to think of anyone else since."

He takes the last sip of his soup, pushing the bowl aside for the server. "I'm aware that this is a transaction. But I'd like to enjoy the fantasy. And right now–" his eyes slide over me again, and I feel my pulse quicken. "This is exactly as I hoped."

As the night goes on, I keep reminding myself of the same thing I told myself before. *This is a job. A shift like any other. It means nothing. You should feel nothing.* But as we sit there through course after course, I can feel myself relaxing by degrees. Everything we talk about is meaningless–I'm not about to make up lies about my past that I'll have to keep track of later unless strictly necessary, and I have a feeling that Mikhail isn't the type to be overly forthcoming–but I don't mind it. It feels normal, easy, and his light, continued flirtation feels like a familiar dance that I know all too well.

I know I'm being lulled by the charm of good food, better wine, and simple conversation, but it's hard to shake myself out of it. As we take bites from a dessert plate of tiny artistic confections, I find myself wondering whether Ruby has to remind herself of these things or if it comes more naturally to her.

"It's a shame the evening has to end," Mikhail says regretfully as he pays the bill, standing up as I do. "But it's been a pleasure."

His hand rests on my back again as we step away from the table. "And of course," he murmurs quietly as we walk, "I know where you work, if I want to see you again."

It's a joke. I know it is, but I feel a shiver go down my spine at the implications of it. Fear flickers through me, mingled with the pleasurable feeling of his hand on my back. It's a confusing mixture of emotions that makes me feel off balance, as if I'm stumbling on the steps all over again.

Just as we reach the valet, I feel his hand on my back press more firmly, turning me before I can respond away from the stairs and around the other side of the tall white-stone building. We are, for all intents and purposes, in an alleyway, but in this part of the city, it's clean and well-kept, just the space between the restaurant and some other luxury establishment.

My heart leaps into my throat, fear flooding me in an instant. "What are you doing?" I whisper, keeping my voice low. I'm under no delusions that if I scream out here, that anyone will care. A man like Mikhail can have what he wants, and if that's me, there's very little that can be done to stop him. I'll do my best, though, before I let him hurt me—even if I can only rely on myself.

"I know I said I only wanted a date." He doesn't touch me, only the muscled length of his body keeping me in place—doing so without touching. I could try to slip past him, under the arm beside my head, the hand planted against the stone, but I don't move. I can see it all too clearly—the moment when I try to dart away, his hand closing around my arm and pulling me back, and then all my negotiating power is lost.

"Then why are we standing here?" I know my voice sounds more breathless than it should be, that I hardly sound as if I'm prepared to fight back. "The car is waiting."

"I changed my mind." His eyes flick over my face, down to my lips, and I feel my heart start to beat faster. "I said we could wait until after dinner to negotiate. So now—" His gaze lingers on my mouth, heating, and I feel an answering throb of warmth pulse through my veins.

Not now! I don't want to think of what it would feel like for him to kiss me, of how long it's been since someone has, of how many times I've fantasized about that, and so much more. It's a boundary that, once crossed, will open the door to so much more. I've only fought my own disturbed desires by keeping it firmly closed and locked, and I can feel myself faltering.

But I want it. More even than just the lack of physical pleasure, I've felt so lonely. The thought of hands sliding over my body eagerly, of another body's heat against mine, of soft lips parting mine, and a tongue slipping into my mouth makes me feel an almost visceral craving, a need that feels nearly unbearable.

I could feel less lonely, just for a moment. Just a kiss.

"How much to kiss you, Ekaterina?" He says the false name without missing a beat, and somehow that makes me feel slightly better, weakening my defenses that much more. *If he were the stalker, if he were a threat, would he believe you so easily? Wouldn't he say it the same way he used to say, Athena, as if he were in on the secret?* "Just one kiss. Tell me the price, and I'll pay it."

He leans closer still, his mouth hovering so close to mine that I can nearly feel it. The ache pulses through me, a need like I've never felt before, a longing that's almost painful. *Let him pay*, I hear the voice in my head whisper, insisting. *Take the money and give yourself something, too. It's been a good night. Make it better, and end it like this.*

"Or—" His mouth is so close, the warmth of his breath caressing my lips like a kiss in and of itself, and I feel a shudder of desire ripple through me that he *must* be able to feel, too. "Or, you could just let me. Would you let me kiss you, Ekaterina? It's all I've thought about, night after night—how your lips would feel under mine. And now—all I want is a taste. We can negotiate later, if you want—"

I'm lost. His words slide over me like the silk of the dress, and I know none of it can possibly be true, that he's been thinking about *much* more than just kissing me. I know that from things he's said to me in the champagne room. I know this is all just a way to steal a kiss, but somehow at this moment, it seems so terribly romantic, so arousing, that I can't find the words to stop him. My mind feels foggy, muddled with desire and that aching, painful longing just to be *touched*, and I find myself tilting my chin upwards, my eyes meeting his.

"Yes," I hear myself breathe, before I've even consciously made a decision. My body feels as if there's a second heartbeat in my veins, pulsing through me, the entire world narrowed down to the handsome man a breath away from me, his eyes gazing down at me with a hunger that lights something on fire in me that I can't control.

Somewhere, in the back of my head, there's an alarm going off. There's a voice screaming at me to be careful, not to be tricked, not to give anything away for free, but it's drowned out by the blood beating in my ears, by the need flooding through me and making my knees weak, by the way he's looking at me as his other hand comes up to cup my jaw so delicately that I don't even realize he's touching me at first—and then his lips are on mine.

It's a brush at first, a kiss so soft that it takes my breath away from the sheer gentleness of it. I can feel him holding himself back, tasting my lips as if he's sampling fine wine, caressing my mouth with his. I hear myself gasp, a sharp indrawn breath, my lips parting under his—and that's the moment when he deepens it.

I feel him step forward, his body making full contact with mine against the wall of the restaurant, every line of it touching mine, as if that last thread of his control snapped with the opening of my mouth beneath his. I feel his hand sliding into my hair, his tongue sliding over my lower lip, and the hard line of his cock pressing against my thigh. It sends a thrill through me, the feeling of that rigid arousal, and my hips arch upwards despite myself, pressing into him.

I'd almost forgotten what it felt like to *want* like this, to crave someone this way. At this moment, the strength of it makes me wonder if I've ever really felt it before, if this is something new and entirely different. My hands come up, reaching up to brush against his chest, my fingers curling around his tie to pull him closer. The kiss feels good, *real*, better than any kiss I've had in a long time. His tongue slides slowly into my mouth, tangling, caressing, his lips still moving over mine. He kisses with a heated expertise that's part skill and part lustful desire, treading that line in a way I've never experienced before.

I feel as if I'm losing myself in it, as if I'm treading water and about to slip beneath the surface. I hear his deep groan of pleasure, feel the way his hips lean into mine, pinning me against the wall. There's a burst of fear somewhere inside of me, the feeling of being trapped setting some reminder off that this could be so very, very bad—and then it's lost in desire, my heart beating wildly in my chest like a caged bird at the very same feeling that frightened me.

It's the dichotomy that I've felt with him all along, fear and desire mixing into a sweet, intoxicating cocktail that dulls all my better senses and makes me forget why I should want to push him away, why I should want to escape. I hear my soft, breathy moan as his hand leaves the wall to slide up my waist, cupping my breast through the soft silk, and when his thumb flicks over my nipple, I gasp.

"I–" For a moment, I almost don't stop him. I know where this is going. I can feel the heavy pressure of his erection against my thigh, can feel the insistent circling of his thumb against my nipple. I know before long, I'll feel his other hand on my leg, his fingers slipping beneath my skirt, and I can see the future where he makes me come up against this wall, taking so much more than a kiss because I let him go this far.

I can't let him have that much. Not without negotiating it. Not without him paying. That's what this is about. This is about escaping, not falling into a new trap, no matter how sweet the bait is.

I twist my head away from his mouth, breathless, gasping as my heart gallops in my chest. "Mikhail–"

His mouth finds my neck, his hand closing around my breast, and the spike of sudden fear that I feel is enough to propel me out of the sinking quicksand of lust.

I reach up, shoving both of my hands against his chest, hard. He stumbles back a little, startled, giving me enough space to dart to one side, my chest heaving as I try to catch my breath. I press one hand against the galloping pulse of my heart, the other warding him off, as I glare at him

"No more negotiating *later*," I snap, glaring at him. "I let this go too far already. I shouldn't have even let you kiss me at all, but–"

"But you enjoyed it." He doesn't look as angry as I expected. If anything, he looks overly satisfied, like a cat with a dish of cream. "You can't pretend that you didn't, Ekaterina. I know when a woman is enjoying herself."

I laugh. I can't help it, even though I know it can be a dangerous thing to laugh at a man like Mikhail. "Men like you never know when a woman is enjoying herself."

His eyes narrow, and I know instantly that I might have taken it a step too far. "I do," he says silkily, taking a step closer, and I feel that small burst of heat through my veins again. The memory of how much I *did* enjoy it is much too close, and I swallow hard as I step back, keeping my hand up to warn him off.

"If you want more, we'll talk about it," I say as evenly as I can. "But not now, and not here. I'll hail a cab–I think our date is finished."

"I can take you back home." Mikhail doesn't move, but I can still see that predatory lust in his eyes, that look that both arouses and terrifies me. "You shouldn't be left to find your own way home. That wouldn't be very *gentlemanly* of me–"

"Neither was what you just did. I can find my own way back." I step away from him a little further, trying to calm my racing pulse. "Goodnight, Mikhail. Thank you for dinner."

"Wait." He calls after me as I start to turn, and god help me, I don't know why I stop. I tell myself it's fear of angering him further, that he knows where I work–maybe even where I live–but in truth, I feel that magnetic pull again, that draw that I've never felt before and can't seem to resist, and I find myself turning back to look at him.

"What?" The snappish fire is back in my tone, and from the way his mouth twitches at the corners, I think I was right in wondering if he likes it when I fight him. "I need to be going–"

"I want to see you again." Mikhail spreads his hands open in an innocent gesture, looking at me with something that almost looks like pleading on his face. "I'm sorry for overstepping. I want to take you on another date, Ekaterina. To make up for–this."

Tell him no. I should; I know it. But I can feel the weight of the envelope in my clutch. I tell myself that's what makes me say something different, and not a desire to have him pressing me up against another wall, his mouth hot and hungry on mine.

"We can negotiate that *later*," I tell him, letting a little haughty disdain thread through my words, that hint of arrogance that I think he likes. "But not here and now."

"When?" There's something else in his voice, a slight desperation, and it sparks something in me. I like the way it makes me feel, as if I have a power over him that I hadn't expected.

I toss my head, raising an eyebrow at him. "You can come back to the club, and we'll talk then."

And then, I turn and walk away without a backward glance, my hand outstretched for a cab.

Natalia

"So? How was it?"

Ruby is, quite literally, on the edge of her seat as I walk into the dressing room. I half expect her to bounce up and down as I drop my bag next to my desk, glad that tonight I *know* I have my own things with me.

I'd gone back and forth about how much to actually tell Ruby. I know very well that I shouldn't have let Mikhail kiss me without negotiating for it first, and I don't want her to be disappointed in me. It's a strange feeling–I can't recall ever having a friend that I cared about disappointing before. In the end, though, if there's anyone who *wouldn't* judge me for any choices I made, it's Ruby.

"I don't know," I admit as I sit down. "I really don't."

"Did he not want to see you again after?" The outrage on Ruby's face makes me want to laugh. She's clearly horrified at the idea that *Mikhail* might be the one who doesn't want to see me again, and is ready to fight someone on my behalf.

"No, he does. It's me that isn't sure if I want to." *That's not exactly true.* I've been wondering all day if he'd come to the club tonight and buy time with me, hoping that he will, even if I've been doing my best to pretend otherwise. "I'm not sure if it's a good idea." *There, that's closer to the truth.*

"Why not?" Ruby looks at me with clear confusion. "Did something happen?"

"It's—it's complicated." I run my hand through my hair as I pull it down from the messy bun I had atop my head, trying to think of how to explain. "He was a perfect gentleman at first. He paid upfront—"

"He *what?*" Ruby stares at me. "Girl, hang onto that one. They usually don't pay until the end, like they want to keep you thinking about that paycheck the whole time."

"To be fair, it was something I insisted on when I agreed to the date in the first place. But I wasn't necessarily expecting him to do it. I was a little surprised when he kept his word about that."

"Well, that's a good start." Ruby leans forward, gluing on an eyelash. "I don't see what the problem is so far?"

"He took me to a nice restaurant and started pushing boundaries just a little. He put his hand on my back—"

"*Athena.*" Ruby shakes her head. "Don't tell me you got upset at him for that? He paid you a fortune for a date. It's not like the champagne room. You can't expect them to be totally hands-off—"

"Well, I didn't know that! He said he paid for my time." I frown at her, irritation bubbling up. "I didn't know how I was supposed to react."

"Did you like it?" Ruby grins at me, wiggling her eyebrows. "He's a lot more handsome than my guy, that's for sure."

"I—" The words to deny it stick in my throat, and Ruby giggles.

"You did like it!"

"I'm not supposed to, though." I dump my makeup tools out on the top of the table, feeling more and more frustrated by the minute. "It's a job."

"That doesn't mean you can't like it a *little*." Ruby shakes her head at me. "I'd kill for a rich, handsome guy that I actually *liked* touching me. Doesn't make it less of a job if you get some enjoyment out of it."

"I suppose that's true." *I liked being a ballerina, and that was a job.* I'm struck by a sudden, aching wish that I could tell Ruby about that, about what I used to do. I can imagine how thrilled she would be by it, all of the questions she would ask, and I wish I could share that part of myself.

I hadn't expected, when I came here, to find an actual friend–much less the best friend I've ever had.

"Tell me the rest because I still don't see what the problem is," Ruby insists, uncapping her mascara. "I need to know."

"He just–there were little things that were weird. Like for instance, I asked him why he paid to take me out on a date, when he could easily get anyone he wanted to go for free–he's handsome and rich. And he said it was because he specifically wanted *me*. Like he wandered into this club and happened to see me and be so infatuated that he's spending an *insane* amount of money just for time with me." I pause for breath, feeling my pulse speed up as all of my anxieties and nerves come rushing back, threatening to strangle me. "And then, as we were leaving, he said something about knowing where I work, if he wanted to see me again."

"I mean, that's maybe not the best phrasing," Ruby admits. "But it sounds like a bad joke. This is how guys like that behave, Athena. They're used to getting what they want, and they have enough money that they don't care if they have to pay for it. Sometimes they *like* paying for it, because it makes them feel powerful, that they can just buy any woman they want. So it might seem implausible to you that he'd walk in here and just happen to see you and decide that he *had* to have your time, or whatever else, because you or I wouldn't do that. But for guys like that, it's normal."

She sounds so sure that it can't help but calm my anxieties, at least partially. *I'm new to all this*, I remind myself as I lean forward, working on my makeup to give myself a moment to think. *This isn't my world. That's why I chose to hide out here, remember? Because it's so far removed from who I used to be that no one would think to look for me here.*

It's entirely plausible that I'm just overreacting and that Ruby is right. That Mikhail is just a man with too much ego and too much money, who happened to slum it here one night and fixated on me. That the things he's saying are technically true, even if they're just meant to get me to allow him to do more and more, so long as he pays me for it.

If he was the person stalking you, the one leaving threatening notes and strange gifts, would he have left you clothes and shoes and jewelry that cost thousands of dollars? That's not how stalkers behave.

"Is that all?" Ruby prods, narrowing her eyes playfully at me. "Anything else you want to tell me?"

It's on the tip of my tongue to say no, that we just left the restaurant and nothing else. But a part of me wants to tell her. I want to see what her reaction is, if she could somehow make me feel better about not just letting Mikhail kiss me, but *enjoying* the kiss.

"He kissed me," I mutter, still not entirely sure that I want to admit it. "After we left the restaurant."

"After you talked about how much he'd pay you?" Ruby sees the look on my face, and lets out an indignant squawk. "Athena! You were so worried about his hand on your back, but you let him *kiss* you! That you *should* get paid for!"

"I know." I toss my makeup brushes down, resisting the urge to rub my hands across my face. "It just—he got me on the other side of the restaurant, up against the wall, and it happened so fast. He said something about how we'd talked about negotiating for touching later, and that he wanted to add a kiss to that—or something like that. It was hard to think. He was so close, and—"

"*Athena.*" Ruby shakes her head at me. "You're not supposed to enjoy it *that* much. Not so much that you can't think straight. You have to be able to keep your head. But—" she bites her lower lip, grinning slyly at me. "Was it good?"

"It was." I run my hands through my hair, frustrated. "It was *too* good. I was supposed to tell him not to kiss me unless he paid more upfront or something—I don't know, drag it out somehow. I *know* that's what I was supposed to do. But he was so close, and he smelled good, and I wanted him to kiss me, like it was a fucking actual date, and—oh fuck, I'm so stupid."

"You're not!" Ruby leans over, patting my arm comfortingly. "You're not stupid at all. It happens. There was a guy last year that was hotter than anyone who usually comes in here, and he kept buying dances with me. I couldn't help but fantasize a little that he'd fall madly in love with me and sweep me away from all this. It's normal. You just have to remember that it's just that—a fantasy. He got bored, like they always do, and then he drifted off. It's always going to be a fantasy. And make sure it doesn't get in the way of you getting paid," she emphasizes, reaching for the heated curling iron. "That's the important part."

"He said he wanted to see me again. I didn't let him give me a ride home—he didn't want to stop when I pulled away, and I felt uncomfortable."

"Good choice. I would have made him pay for my cab, but it was your first time. I think you did just fine," Ruby adds encouragingly. "So what did you tell him? About seeing you again? Is that what you're all in knots about?"

I nod. "I told him to come by the club, and we'd talk about it. And now–I feel like maybe I should have just told him no, full stop. Maybe this was enough."

"No! You did exactly what you should have done. He'll buy time in the champagne room, and then you can negotiate your next date, here where it's safe. That's perfect." Ruby grins at me. "See? You know what you're doing."

The encouragement feels good, but it's hard for me to calm down. I know as well as Ruby does that I'm crossing lines I've never crossed before. I'm doing things I swore I wouldn't, in uncertain terrain, and it's made worse by the fact that I'm actually attracted to him. If I wasn't, it would be so much easier to stick to the rules and boundaries and so much easier not to worry that I might lose my head.

Especially when I feel such a strange, magnetic draw to him, something so different from anything I've felt before.

I wish I could enjoy it. The thought comes out of nowhere, but as soon as it crosses my mind, I know it's true. I know, if I'm being honest with myself, that I'm developing an infatuation. If it were with anyone else, there would be nothing wrong with that. I could throw myself into it and enjoy it until it burned out.

I've done it before and enjoyed every second of it. I can think back to a dozen of them–handsome men who were not good enough for a real relationship, not good enough for my father to agree to my marrying them, but who were more than good enough for a wild fling. I loved it, enjoying their company with no strings, no pressure, only fun and pleasure until I cut them loose. It had been thrilling, exciting, and I miss it. I miss men like Adrian Drakos, who were never right for me, but who were perfect for a little while.

Could I just have fun with it? Just for a little while? I try to think what would be the harm in it. For all my worries and paranoia that Ruby is constantly soothing, I haven't seen any actual proof that he wants to hurt me, just what is, apparently, a normal kind of fixation for a man with more money than sense. It's all a transaction at the end of the day, but—

It could still be pleasurable and exciting. I live my life without much of that now. If anything, I have a feeling that the draw I feel towards him is because of exactly that—because being with him is both of those things. It makes me feel things that I'd been forced to shove away and bury in order to survive here.

Whatever he asks for, if he comes in tonight, just keep an open mind, I tell myself as I take the curling iron from Ruby, quickly doing my hair in the little time left before my set. As I get dressed, I feel a bubble of excitement, slipping into my silver lingerie and painting my lips red, wondering if I'll see him.

If I'll get a chance to keep an open mind at all, or if he's changed his.

I don't have long to wait. By the time I'm walking down from the stage at the end of my set, I see him coming towards me, that gleam in his ice-blue eyes that I'm coming to know very well. It ignites something in the pit of my stomach, an excitement I'm not sure I should allow myself to feel.

Is it so bad if I want to enjoy this? I don't even really like Mikhail—sometimes I think I might actually hate him—but that's thrilling in its own way. There's the push and pull, the banter, the passionate sex with someone that you're not sure if you want to fuck or strangle or both at once, and I could have that with him. It would be hot and wild, and it would flame out eventually—but in the meantime, it would feel so good.

Or, you could be wrong about all of this, and you end up getting caught, or worse.

It's so frustrating I could scream. All I want is to enjoy something, instead of living in fear constantly. I never knew how awful it could be to live every moment looking over my shoulder, wondering when the hammer will fall, when I'll slip up, when I'll get myself or someone else hurt.

"You seem like something's on your mind," Mikhail says as I lead him back to the champagne room. "Bad night?"

"No—just tired." I smile at him, forcing myself to silence the stream of consciousness running through my head and focus on this, now. "What do you want tonight?"

Mikhail laughs. "Right to the point, I see." He waits as I hit the pink-hued lights and turn on the music, his gaze lingering on me hungrily. "I can appreciate that. After all, we didn't leave on the best terms—and that's my fault. I apologize."

The apology catches me off guard, but I do my best not to show it, keeping my face as blank as I can as I swing up onto the stage. "You still didn't answer my question."

"Just a dance, while we talk." He smiles affably at me, striding to the couch. "I've rarely seen anything as beautiful as the sight of you dancing."

"There are those compliments again." I spin around the pole, arching and swaying against it. "So, what do you want to talk about?"

"An—arrangement." He watches me for a long moment, and I can see his hands twitch on the couch, as if he's itching to touch me. "I'd like to get the basics out of the way. I want your time and your attention, Athena—or Ekaterina, whichever you prefer—when you can give it to me. I know there's other things that might need to be negotiated for, but I'd like to give you a baseline allowance for that. Your time, your full attention on me when we're together, and—" he holds up a finger before I can speak. "Before you ask, it doesn't have to be more sexual than you want it to be. You can draw your own lines there—"

"Athena, while we're in here," I tell him firmly, as I slide down into a split on the stage. "Ekaterina outside." *Fucking aliases. It's hard to keep track of.*

"Fair enough." He smiles at me, that slow, seductive smile that makes me start to forget what we're actually doing here. I remind myself as I move across the stage to pay attention, to make sure I actually get what I want–what I *need*–out of this.

"My question from the other night still stands," I tell him as I slide towards him. "Why would you go to this much trouble and so much money? You don't need to do this."

Mikhail shrugs. "And my answer stands, as well. I want *you*, Athena. And since I can't have you for free, I'm prepared to pay what's necessary."

There's a ring of truth to his words that brings me up short. I could swear that he's telling the truth, that he means what he's saying–or *thinks* he does, at least.

"You really want me to believe that you walked into this place, for no specific reason, and you want *me* so much that you're going to go to these lengths?"

"Have you looked in a mirror?" Mikhail laughs. "You're stunningly beautiful and a talented dancer, more so than anyone else here. You drive me insane, Athena, so yes. If I have to pay, I will. You'll excuse any fantasies I might have that one day you might want me for myself–but as long as it takes a fee to buy your time, I'll happily pay it."

"My time. That's it?"

"If that's what you want."

"What do *you* want?"

He grins, sprawling lazily on the couch as he watches me. "I want you, like I said. I want to spoil you, take you out, make you a little happier than you are now–and I'm prepared to pay you for all of it." He reaches into his pocket as he speaks, pulling out a small box, and leans forward at the edge of the couch, pushing it forward onto the stage.

I glance at him confusedly, caught off guard. "What is this?"

Mikhail shrugs. "Open it."

I do, cautiously. To my surprise, glittering under the pink lights, is a pair of gold thread earrings with teardrop-shaped diamonds dangling at the end of each. They're beautiful, and under other circumstances, I would have been thrilled to receive a gift like this, but I can't help but feel suspicious.

"This is too much. An allowance, the gifts from before, these earrings–" I snap the box shut, narrowing my eyes at him. "What else do you want? There *has* to be something else."

Mikhail shakes his head slowly. "Nothing else, except what I've already told you. I want more of *you*, of course, but we'll talk about that when the time comes. For now, if you agree, I want to take you out again tomorrow night."

I shake my head. "I'm supposed to dance tomorrow night. I'm on the schedule–"

"I'll handle it." Mikhail looks at me coolly, his expression one of absolute certainty that something as small and insignificant as my work schedule can't possibly get in the way of his plans. "If you need me to compensate you for the missed work as well–"

"No–that's fine. Depending on the allowance–"

When he names an amount, I nearly choke. It's more than I could expect to make in a week or more of dancing. "You don't have to do that," I tell him quickly. "We can meet tomorrow. Wherever you'd like to go."

Mikhail smiles, a pleased expression on his face. "Good. I'll send you something to wear again."

"You don't have to–"

"I insist." His tone flattens, brooking no argument. "I want to see you in the things *I* choose for you."

Fair enough. I start to dance again, finding the rhythm of the music, but all I can think about is tomorrow night, and what else might come after that.

If this continues for long, I'll soon have everything I need to be free of this place—and I won't have to think about Moscow, the Cat's Meow, or Mikhail ever again.

I'll be somewhere else, far away.

Mikhail

The next morning, it's difficult to remind myself, that I have another job to do.

Valeria isn't known for being a patient woman, and I can't afford to let my own personal mission get in the way of a contract. *Just as I can't allow my own unusual feelings to get in the way of my personal revenge.*

I sit on the edge of the bed in the late morning light–still earlier than I would prefer, given how late I was at the club last night, and how long I stayed up after thinking of her here in this bed–and reach for the wallet on my side table. I need to remember why I'm doing this, the purpose that I have. It's not to fall into wild lust with a woman who was once above me and is now far beneath, and it would do me well to remember that.

It's been days since I looked at the photograph. It was once a near-daily ritual, a means to rub salt in the wound and remind myself of why I'm still here, to grind the hate and anger that I feel deeper, until it's a part of my blood and my bones and my very soul.

I unfold the well-worn photo, running my fingers over the slightly faded surface. And I realize, as I touch the faces of the woman and the small boy in the picture, that at some point, I've forgotten the sound of her voice.

I've forgotten the sound of his laugh.

My hand flexes around the photo, nearly crumpling it as a burst of rage washes over me, tightening my gut in a painful cramp. *I've forgotten.* I can still hear the imagined sounds of her screams and his cries in my nightmares, but I've forgotten the sound of their joy.

In that instant, I hate myself for every moment of pleasure I found with Natalia. Every moment when I wanted *her*, and not just to sow the seeds of a future revenge, to draw her in and wind the rope tighter and tighter until she hangs herself with it. I think of the moments when I've simply enjoyed her company, her sharp tongue, and her beauty, and I feel myself grinding my teeth until I can hear my jaw pop.

She is nothing but a means to an end. Nothing except a vessel for your revenge, and a path back to your life. When that's done, she should mean nothing to you at all.

"The Obelensky family name will be wiped from the earth when I'm finished," I murmur under my breath, flattening the photo out again. "I'll make sure they pay for every drop of your blood they spilled, for every scream and every tear, and when I'm finished, I'll make certain she knows what it feels like to fear."

That's the point of all of this, isn't it?

I refold the picture, slipping it back into my wallet as I stand. I have a job to do, and when it's done, I can focus on tightening the noose around Natalia, until she has no escape. But I want to be sure that she won't see it coming.

I want her to trust me, so I can see the horror on her face when she realizes what's happened.

I could tell that she enjoyed the date, that the dinner I treated her to was a rare luxury for her now. She was an impressive actress–if I hadn't gotten the information from Jakov that made me so certain that "Ekaterina" really is Natalia in disguise, I might have continued to doubt myself. She'd done an excellent job of pretending to be stunned at the embarrassment of riches I treated her to–the clothes, the earrings, the dinner out. If I hadn't known better, I might have thought it was her first time experiencing all of that, instead of a reminder of a life that, once upon a time, was her everyday existence.

She'd almost slipped up with her comment about the champagne. I had a hard time hiding my own reaction to that, how closely she'd come to making a mistake. But she'd caught herself nicely.

I'm enjoying this game too much. Watching how hard she works to pretend to be someone else, to keep me from being suspicious, when I already know who she is–and me, pretending to buy all of it, because I'm so desperate for her company and her body, so infatuated with her.

Isn't the obsession you feel just infatuation packaged in a different box?

I grit my teeth as I finish dressing and slip my gun into my waistband, ignoring the small echoing voice in the back of my head that refuses to leave me alone entirely. *I'm driving the knife deeper, so it will hurt all the more when I twist it. That's all that this is. Who knows? Maybe I'll even get her to fall for me, and the revenge will be even sweeter. When she wants me, at the very least, it will be that much more delicious.*

It's not hard to track Yuri down. I know his movements fairly well already from working with him. He's a creature of the evening, however, a night owl, and it's hours before I see him emerge and head towards the dingy bar where I often meet him, probably to meet with someone else.

I check my watch, wondering if I should make a move tonight. I know that meeting or no, he'll take a smoke break about every hour, and that would be the easiest time to grab him. But–

Fuck. I'm meant to meet Natalia. I hoped I could catch Yuri earlier than this, that he might go out for errands, somewhere that I could grab him from an alley. I might have enough time to catch and stow him before I need to be ready to go and meet her, but that would mean leaving him in the warehouse overnight before I could finish the job.

It's long been a policy of mine to finish a job on the same night that I grab a mark, unless they're meant to be delivered to someone else. There's too much risk in leaving them in the warehouse overnight alive, even drugged, too much risk in waiting so long. For as long as I've been doing this kind of work, I've followed specific rules for myself—and neat and tidy jobs are part of that.

If there's no one else to take them to—catch, question, dispatch.

I could reschedule the date.

I don't have any way to reach her, though. *She needs a phone.* If I ghost her, it will undo all the hard work I've done. *That's the only reason I care. Not because I'm looking forward to seeing her, not because I crave the possibility of what she might let me do to her tonight.*

I can't jeopardize this chance. That's all.

I can make the hit on Yuri tomorrow. Valeria will wait a little longer.

I hesitate, knowing I'm crossing a personal line, doing something I've never done before. I've never prioritized my own desires over work. I've never put off a job I was on to pursue something for myself. But the thought of losing the progress I've made with Natalia, of having her throw up the walls that I've only barely begun to breach, gives me a visceral feeling of something almost like panic.

Doesn't that mean this has gone too far?

I'm already slipping away from the bar, though, heading back to my car, the decision made before I can even really decide it for myself.

I have a date that I can't afford to miss.

—

The majority of what I need for tonight is already arranged. I have no intention of bringing her back to the apartment I've been staying in—it's nowhere near nice enough for the game I'm playing with her, that of being a rich man who wants a beautiful woman to spoil.

The first half of that is true, at least. I don't want for money, but without the cash flow that I used to have working for Viktor, I've been careful to save what I made in the past by living as frugally as I can while in Moscow—not to mention the need to stay as under the radar as possible, up until now. I had no need for a luxury apartment or five-star dinners while I was biding my time, but now I need the facade of it all—of a man in power, living large and spending without thought—the kind of man I used to be, and what I will very soon be again, if all goes to plan.

Standing in the doorway of the rented penthouse that I hope to bring her back to very soon, I feel a fresh sense of calm wash over me. I want two things—my revenge, and an offer of my place back in Viktor's Bratva, with his apology for ever mistrusting me. Wiping out all traces of Obelensky's family, bringing Natalia to him as my proof and for whatever revenge he wants to take, will accomplish that.

I feel certain of it, and at this moment, looking out over the luxurious, minimally decorated space that's meant to be mine, I feel as if my plan is settling into place. After what happened on our first date and her acceptance of my proposal for a more secure arrangement, I don't doubt that it won't be long before I have her back here.

Just be careful of your feelings. Don't get lost in the pleasure of it. It's a set-up, a ruse to gain her trust. This is not your home, and she is nothing to you beyond what you can take from her.

I repeat it like a mantra, over and over again as I walk into the elegant bedroom, where I stowed enough changes of clothes for it to look as if someone really does live here. I take what I planned to wear tonight out of the closet, shedding my clothes from the day and tossing them into a laundry hamper, just to add a little to the lived-in feeling.

What if it's tonight?

Just looking at the bed, imagining Natalia spread across it, has me half-hard in an instant. I grit my teeth, trying to shove the desire back, to focus on the purpose of what I'm doing. Still, the vision of her naked and open for me is solidly planted in my mind, sending shudders of need down my spine.

I want to fuck her so badly it hurts—my cock is so hard that it aches, and all I've done is think about her. I can't recall ever wanting a woman this badly, ever being so consumed with thoughts of any other woman I've desired or gone to bed with. My hand goes around my cock before I can stop myself.

This will make sure I'm clear-headed before the date. I justify it to myself as I start to stroke, hard and fast, my mind full of her imaginary cries of pleasure, the way her body would feel pinned under mine, held down as I thrust inside of her. A dozen images, each more lewd and vicious than the last, rush through my mind as I run my hand up and down my cock, aching to come.

The sound that comes from my mouth as I cup my hand over the head of my cock, spurting against my palm as I come, is something between a moan and a growl. It's primal, animal, the sound of a craving that I can't satisfy, a need that still throbs through me even as I grab the foot of the bed and thrust into my palm, shuddering as I picture Natalia coming too, in spite of herself, underneath me as I fill her up.

When I've cleaned up, I do feel a little better. *Now maybe the attraction I feel won't get out of hand,* I tell myself, dressing quickly. *I'll be able to think.*

She'd said after we agreed on our new arrangement to pick her up near the club, and I can't help but laugh at what, to me, is so clearly an attempt to keep me from being so close to her apartment. *If only she knew, I've watched her from the window.*

She's there waiting when I pull up, dressed in what I arranged to have sent to her. A black dress with a tight, bustier-style bodice that shows off what little cleavage she has, and a black chiffon skirt that reminds me faintly of a ballerina's tulle, although it lies closer to her body. As I step out to open her door for her, I can see that she's wearing the gold and diamond earrings I gave her last night. I feel a flood of possessive satisfaction at seeing her entirely wreathed in things *I* gave her, like a particularly beautifully dressed doll.

My doll. *My* toy. Mine to dress, manipulate–soon, fuck–and eventually, break.

I can't help the satisfied smile that spreads over my face as I slide back into the car, and she catches sight of it.

"You look pleased," she says with a laugh that sounds the slightest bit nervous, smoothing her skirt over her knees. "Did something good happen?"

"You're here with me." The words flow out as naturally as if I mean them–and in a way, I do. It pleases me that she's here, that my plan is unfolding as I hoped it would. "And you look beautiful. I'm glad that you like my gifts enough to wear them."

"You asked me to." She shrugs lightly, smiling at me. "How could I refuse?"

"I enjoy seeing you in what I choose." I can feel my hand on my thigh twitching, aching to reach out and touch her.

"Men like you do love that kind of power, don't you?" Her black hair is loose and falling over her shoulders in thick curls, and she tosses it back, raising an eyebrow at me.

"What do you mean, men like me?" I turn down a back street, and I have a sudden, visceral desire to skip ahead. To pass up the date, the night out, the slow build to her giving me her trust so that I can snatch it out from under her and go back to the penthouse. I still have the drugs meant for Yuri in the trunk of the car–it would be easy enough to get it into her. I could end it all now.

It wouldn't be as pleasant. It wouldn't be as good. You know it wouldn't. Draw it out, and make it better in the end. Patience, Mikhail. Patience.

"Rich men. Men who know they can use their money to get what they want." There's a teasing note in her voice, so it's not as cutting as it might have been otherwise, and I'm not exactly surprised to hear her speak to me like that. Her sharp tongue is, despite how I might try to tell myself otherwise, part of my attraction to her. I've so rarely met women who challenged me the way she does.

"Well, I've done that, haven't I?" I glance over at her. "Here you are. Of course, if it's not what you want–"

"That's not what I meant, and you know it." Her voice tenses slightly, and I can feel the air in the car thicken, a heaviness surrounding us as the tone of the conversation changes. "I'm glad to be here. But you can't deny that you like the power of this, as much as you say you want *me*, specifically."

I shrug. "Is it so wrong to enjoy having power?" As I stop the car, I look over at her, letting her see the growing heat in my gaze as I take in how beautiful she looks in the gifted clothes and jewelry. "Is it wrong to enjoy what I have right now?"

"And what is that?" Her voice goes softer, breathier, and from the look in her eyes, I don't think she meant for it to. I can see a new tension running through her body, like a faint vibration. I feel myself responding to it instinctively. I want to reach for her, to crush her back against the seat as I devour her mouth with mine, to muffle her cries–whether they're pleas or pleasure–as I push that skirt up and find out just how wet she can get for me.

A surge of lust grips me, almost uncontrollably, and I grit my teeth as I try to hold it back. *I have to be able to control myself around her. No woman should have this kind of power over me.*

"Are you alright?" Her voice is still breathy, as if it's caught in her throat, and I nod.

"You know what I have," I murmur, leaning the slightest bit closer. "I have you, here, in my car alone. Wearing clothes I gave you, diamonds I gifted you. There's an envelope of cash in the center console, waiting for you to take it. I have power, Ekaterina, and you *like* it. You want to take some of it for yourself. But I think, the truth is, that if I kissed you right now, you'd let me before you ever took the money. Am I wrong?"

For the briefest second, I think I've gone too far. I see a hesitation on her face, a tension that tells me that she's thinking of running. For a moment, I think I've fucked it all up anyway.

And then, her mouth twitches, and she tilts her chin up with playful defiance.

"I'd let you kiss me if I had the money first," she says, the gasping note gone from her voice and replaced with something else, something I like much less. "You know the arrangement we have, Mikhail. So doesn't that mean that the power is in *my* hands?"

I have a sudden flash of the image of my hand around her throat, tightening as I press her head back against the seat, her delicate flesh bruising like ripe fruit under my fingertips. *You'll see who has the power then. You'll find out that sharp tongue will only stay in your mouth so long as it makes me hard, or you're willing to use it on my cock.*

Instead, I force myself to pull back, raising an eyebrow at her. "That's the game of it all, isn't it?" I say lightly, letting her see only desire in my gaze. "That's what makes this so enjoyable—and why I can't get you out of my head, Ekaterina."

The words are more accurate than she knows, just not in the way she thinks. And as I step out of the car and walk around to open her door, all I can think is that I can't wait for the moment when she finds out what I really mean by it.

By then, it will be far too late for her.

Natalia

I'd known this would happen, at some point. No man does all of this–dinners and dates and endless money spent in the champagne room and taking me out, without wanting more. I know that a drink at his apartment isn't just a drink, that it will come with other strings. Other things that he wants, for more money.

"It'll cost you," I say as playfully as I can, leaning in slightly as we stand outside of the bar he'd taken me to at the end of our date. I feel his fingertips brush against my arm, sliding upwards, raising the hairs as my skin prickles under his touch. It's a liberty, but one I'm willing to let him take, in exchange for the possibility that he might pay a good deal more for whatever it is that he wants from me tonight. "And we're not going all the way yet." I reach up, tracing his chest in the open v of his shirt. "I'll have to get to know you a little better first."

"Get to know my bank account, you mean?" Mikhail asks, but there's no accusation to the words, only the same teasing playfulness that I tried to keep in my voice. "What if I offer the same amount that I gave you for tonight, again? For drinks, and–" his eyes slide down my body, resting on the scooped neckline of the dress as his gaze heats. "Whatever else I want to do to you–so long as we don't go as far as intercourse?"

No one should ever be able to make the word 'intercourse' sound that hot. The silky, smoky sound of his voice wraps around me, making my heart beat a little harder in my chest, making it hard to think. I feel that ache again, the desire to be touched, pleasured, to have someone other than myself touching me.

It's just business, I tell myself. *He paid me at the beginning of the date, a huge sum. He's willing to give me that again. If he keeps paying me like that–well, he's going to run out of spare cash or get bored at some point. And by then, I will have accumulated enough to get out of Moscow, get new documents, and set myself up somewhere new.*

If it keeps going like this, Ruby will have been right. Mikhail could change my life faster than I've been able to change it myself. All I have to do is let him enjoy me, a little at a time, dragging it out so that he keeps chasing the next boundary until I've gotten all I can. I've set the line for tonight–no actual sex–and so long as I don't let him cross that, I'll be able to keep him on the hook a little for longer.

"Well, with that kind of offer, how can I say no?" I smile up at him, soft and sultry, stepping back a little so that he can open the door to the passenger's side. "I'd love to see your place."

My heart is racing as I slide into the car. I'm about to go to his home, alone with him in private, and every woman knows the risks inherent in that. Natalia Obelensky would never have worried about it–she had security and protection. No man would have dared lay a finger on me when I was her. But Athena, Ekaterina, those names have no such protection. All I have is myself, and I know already that Mikhail is a man who likes to test my boundaries.

But he's also shown himself willing to stop and make up for those moments when he's pushed too far.

I've already made the choice. Now all I have to do is make sure I don't lose myself in it.

He takes me to a part of the city that I know very well—one of the most expensive residential areas, not far from where I once rented my own secret apartment. The building is a high-rise that I know very well is one of the most expensive. I feel a small thrill as he drives into the parking garage at the idea of being in such a luxurious place again, instead of my own small and shabby apartment.

"I hope you're impressed," Mikhail says with a grin as he opens my door, offering me a hand. "I'm partial to it, and to the views, but I'm interested to see what you think."

"How could I not be?" I flash him a smile. "I'm sure I've never seen anything like it before."

It almost makes me hate him a little more, how eager he is to play Prince Charming, to show off his wealth to the poverty-stricken escort he hired. *Idiot, I used to rent a place every bit as nice as this. If you knew who I was, you wouldn't be so fucking patronizing.*

I follow him into the elevator, and he hits a button for the penthouse. He raises an eyebrow, waiting for my reaction. I give him appropriately wide eyes, as a warm satisfaction ripples through me.

He has every bit as much money as you hoped. If you play your cards right, you'll come out of this better than you could have imagined.

We step out of the elevator into a hallway, and Mikhail slips a matte black keycard out of his pocket, holding it up to the door. It unlocks, and he ushers me in first, stepping in behind me and locking the door.

I feel a shiver go down my spine at the sound of the lock clicking behind me, but I'm momentarily distracted by the beauty of the penthouse in front of me.

It's an expansive, open-floor, loft-like space. The kitchen, dining area, and living room are all open, done in a very masculine, minimalistic black, white, and grey color scheme, with three of the four walls floor-to-ceiling windows. I see a door on one side that I imagine must go to a bathroom, and a twisting staircase leading up to the upper level. The view is, in fact, incredible, and I find myself walking toward one of the windowed walls despite myself, looking out over the city beyond. It's been a long time since I've seen a view like this, and I let myself relax a fraction, looking out over the lights beyond the apartment.

I feel Mikhail walk up behind me, his hand reaching for my clutch. He takes it out of my hand, opening it, and slides another envelope inside, before setting it aside on the table next to where I'm standing. "Beautiful, isn't it?" he murmurs, his hands resting gently on my waist. Something about the fact that he paid before touching me makes me relax a little more, leaning into his touch the slightest bit.

"It's lovely," I breathe, stepping back just a little, so that I'm almost brushing against the warm, hard line of his body. "I can't imagine having a view like this every day. Don't you ever get tired of it?"

"Never." His head dips, and I feel his lips brushing along the edge of my ear. "Just as I could never get tired of looking at you."

The compliments are as heavy-handed as his insistence on buying my time, and it should irritate me just as much—but I can feel myself softening, just a little. It feels good to be touched, complimented, to have someone want me in the way that used to be so commonplace that I expected it.

"What do you like to drink?" His lips are still against my ear, his fingers sliding up my waist, caressing just beneath my breasts. "I have the makings of just about anything here."

Slowly, I turn in his embrace, arching the tiniest bit, so I'm brushing against him, teasing. "Make me whatever you think I'd like. I haven't tried that many different things."

There's a slight innuendo to my words that I know he'll pick up on. A smile twitches at the edge of his mouth, and he steps back, his hand sliding down my arm to take my hand and lead me towards the long black leather couch that's the centerpiece of the living room.

"Wait here," he says, a touch of authority to his voice that I know he expects me to be turned on by. I've never in my life been turned on by a man telling me what to do, but I let my expression soften, my fingers lingering against his as I sit, watching him walk towards the bar cart in the dining area of the open loft.

I focus on the view while I wait for him to come back, trying to slow the beat of my racing heart. I almost don't hear him when he walks back up to the sofa, jumping a little as he holds out a glass with a large round ice cube clinking in it.

"What's this?" I take the glass from him, looking curiously at the amber liquid inside.

"An old-fashioned." His glass looks as if it contains the same thing, and he sits down next to me, a hand's space between us. "Have you had one before?"

"No." It's the truth for once. I'd never been a whiskey drinker. "But like you said–anything is worth trying once, right?"

A slow smile spreads over Mikhail's face. "Absolutely."

I take a small, gingerly sip of it, wincing a little at the bite. It's hot as it spreads over my tongue and down my throat, but not in an entirely unpleasant way. I can taste the bitter and the sweet, the burn of the alcohol, and as I take another, second sip, I decide that I might actually like this.

"What do you have?" I glance at his drink, and he grins.

"A Manhattan. It's very similar. Here, would you like to try it?"

I hesitate. "Sure," I say finally, reaching out, but instead of handing me the glass, he extends it instead, tipping it against my lips.

I can feel his eyes on my mouth as the liquid touches it, feel the tension thickening in the air. It tastes very similar, and I swallow hard, feeling the alcohol swimming through my bloodstream.

"How was that?" Mikhail murmurs, and I smile a little shakily, reaching for my own drink again.

"It was good. Similar to mine—" I hear my voice trail off as his eyes linger on my mouth, and I can feel him moving towards me.

"This is what I meant," he says softly, his voice thick with desire already. "When I said I would do what I needed to, because I want *you*. There's no other woman I want sitting here right now, Ekaterina. Only you."

"It's hard for me to believe that's all you want. You can understand why—"

He's sitting very close to me now, his knee brushing mine, and I can see the heat in his gaze as he looks at me. "If you keep teasing me like this," he murmurs, his eyes lingering on the edge of his glass where my lips were, "you'll find out sooner than you might expect what I really want from you tonight."

I half-hoped he might get drunk enough to not be able to follow through on that part of the night, that I could take the money and go home without having to let him make good on what we'd negotiated for. It would have been better that way. I wouldn't have had to fight my own desires, then, my own reaction to the way he's looking at me, the way his touch makes me feel—the way he makes me ache for a pleasure that I feel like I've almost forgotten, it seems so far away.

"What's that?" I breathe, taking another sip from my own glass. The whiskey is warm and sharp on my tongue, only adding to the heat in my blood, and I swallow hard as Mikhail's hand touches my thigh, pushing up the soft chiffon skirt of my dress.

"I want to taste you," he murmurs, and suddenly his other hand is on mine, taking the glass out of my fingers and setting it aside. "I've wanted that since that night I watched you touch yourself for me, in the champagne room. It's all I've thought about."

"I thought all you'd been thinking about was kissing me," I say innocently, giving him a small, sly smile. "And you've kissed me already. So you know—"

"It's not your mouth I've been thinking about kissing." His voice is hoarse and rough with lust, and an answering jolt of desire sparks over my skin as he grabs my waist and my thigh suddenly with hard, demanding hands, pushing me onto my back on the couch as the hand on my waist slides down to push up my skirt.

"I've been wondering all night what you had on beneath this–ah." He lets out a satisfied groan as he pushes the chiffon up to my hips, revealing the black lace panties beneath. "You never disappoint me, Ekaterina."

The name is a breath on his lips, full of need as he tucks my skirt beneath me, his fingers hooking in the edge of my panties. For one brief, wild moment, as I feel desire pool between my thighs at his fierce urgency, I want to tell him no. I want to push him away, get up and flee this place, because the way this makes me feel is more dangerous than anything that's happened up until this point.

The way I'm aching for his tongue between my thighs, for the fantasy of his ice-blue eyes looking up at me as he licks me to a shattering orgasm, is dangerous.

But it would mean leaving the money behind. It would mean angering a man who could be my ticket out.

And it would mean never, ever finding out what it would feel like to have Mikhail's face between my thighs.

He drags my panties down my legs, tossing them aside on the hardwood floor as his hands slide upwards again, over my calves, my inner thighs, spreading me wide as he looks at me with a hunger that startles me. His lips brush against the soft skin of the top of my thigh, his tongue tracing the edge of the crease there, and I hear him breathe in deeply, a sound that makes me flush pink at the implications.

"You smell so sweet," he groans, his hands tightening on my thighs, holding me open for him. "I can't wait to find out how you taste."

His fingers brush against the folds of my pussy, parting me for his tongue, and I hear the soft, wicked chuckle as his fingertips find how slick and wet I am. "So eager for me," he murmurs, his voice thick with lust. "How quickly will you come for me, I wonder?"

I want to tell him he'll have to try harder than that, that it won't be as easy as he expects, but I'm certain by this point that isn't true. I can feel myself dripping with arousal, soaked and every bit as eager as he said. When I feel his warm breath against my swollen and aching pussy, it's all I can do not to give myself away even more and arch up against his mouth.

When his tongue slides against me, tracing a slow path from my entrance all the way up to my throbbing clit, I cry out. I can't stop myself. It feels so fucking good, warm and hot against my needy flesh, every bit of what I fantasized about. I can feel him teasing me, flicking his tongue along the edges of my inner folds, sliding down to trace my entrance, pushing inside of me the tiniest bit as he laps up my arousal, groaning with pleasure at the taste of me.

All it does is drive my arousal even higher. I twitch beneath him, unable to stay still, arching against his mouth, and I hear him chuckle.

"So impatient." His fingers brush against my inner thighs, as if trying to soothe me, to keep me still. "So needy. Is this what you want?"

His tongue flicks upwards, circling my clit, and I cry out again at the jolt of pleasure that bursts through me. "Ah, there it is. You like it when I lick you like this, don't you? When I run my tongue over your clit?" He flicks it again, pushing his tongue against the swollen flesh, and I let out another gasping moan.

"I could tease you like this all night." Another flick, circling this time, making me gasp. "I could push you to the very edge, again and again, until you begged me to come." He makes another slow, lazy circle, and I struggle against his hold on my thighs, wanting more. "It could be so much fun–for us both."

Oh god. I don't think I can stand it. Under other circumstances, the idea of being edged to multiple denied orgasms before finally being allowed to come might have been a fantasy I'd be willing to entertain, but at this precise moment, I'm so desperate for a climax that the idea makes me feel as if I might go insane. I want to come, but I'll be damned if I'm going to beg him for it, and I feel a growing fear that it's what he wants.

I'll have to do it, in the end, if he insists on it. *And if he keeps this up, I won't be able to stop myself.*

It's fucking torture. His tongue slides over my clit in slow, lazy circles that feel so fucking good, and yet not enough to bring me to the edge. I hear him chuckle again, his tongue tracing over my inner folds once more. Then I see his icy eyes roll upwards, fixed on mine exactly as I'd once fantasized, alone in my own bed.

"I think," he says slowly, running his tongue over his lips as if to savor the taste of me. "We'll save that for another time. I want to see how hard I can make you come now–and I don't think I want to wait."

Oh, thank fuck. It's the last thought I have before Mikhail presses his mouth tightly against my pussy, his tongue attacking my clit as if he's determined to race to the finish, lashing it over the sensitive flesh until all I can do is writhe and moan, my fingers grasping at his hair in an effort to anchor myself. He holds me open wide, unable to close my thighs around his head, and I feel his lips press against my clit, sucking it into his mouth.

"Oh god–oh–*fuck!*" I scream so loudly that I'm sure everyone else in the building, from the penthouse to the first floor, must be able to hear me. The pleasure crashes over me like a tidal wave, the orgasm hitting me hard and fast, bursting through me until I feel as if I'm no longer in control. I can feel my arousal flooding his mouth, drenching his face, but he doesn't stop. He's still licking, sucking, stimulating my clit until I can feel the waves of pleasure peak and keep crashing, as if I'll never stop coming.

I've never felt anything like it. I can feel my pussy clenching, hollow and aching to be filled. I'm grateful I can't speak because if I could, I'm certain I'd beg him to fill me with his fingers, his cock, anything he could. The pleasure feels as if it doesn't stop, going on and on until I'm finally collapsed on the couch, loose-limbed, and lost in a fog of satisfaction and desire. I feel him drag his tongue over my throbbing pussy in one last, long lick before he pulls back, wiping his mouth.

I see him reach for his glass through hazy vision, watch as he takes a long drink of his Manhattan, and then slowly, he sits to one side.

"Well, now, look what you've done." His hand rubs over his thigh, pressing down on the fabric of his trousers, outlining the hard ridge of his cock. "I've never tasted anything as delicious as your sweet pussy, Ekaterina. And now, I need to come very badly."

I don't need him to explain further to know what he's insinuating. A very small part of me wants to push, to make him explain, ask, *beg*, even–but something tells me that Mikhail isn't the begging type. I can't quite think of the kind of witty comment that might turn it into that sort of banter. I can't seem to think at all, but I can feel the weight of his icy-blue gaze, the expectation of what comes next, and I slowly push myself up to a sitting position.

Mikhail spreads his legs, nodding to the space between them on the floor. "On your knees, *dorogoy*," he murmurs, his accent thick and rich, and I nod, swallowing hard. I know what's expected of me, what he's paid for, and I remind myself that this is a job, business, that if I please him now, that he'll want more later.

That this is my ticket to freedom.

That it has nothing, *nothing* to do with wanting to see what his cock looks like, how thick and hard and long he might be, how much I might want to taste *him*, after what he just did to me.

Nothing at all.

Natalia

His hand strokes over my hair, and I feel myself leaning into the caress, my hands sliding up his thighs as his other hand goes to his belt. "Open your mouth for me, *malen'kiy*," he murmurs, his fingers twitching at his zipper. "I want to see where I'm going to put my cock."

He's gone, in a moment, from devouring me to demanding things of me, but I'm not sure that I mind it. There's something impossibly hot about what's happening right now, me on my knees in my rumpled black chiffon dress, my lipstick a little smeared, and my thighs sticky with my release, this gorgeous and demanding man on the verge of getting his cock out as he orders me to suck it. Faintly, in the back of my mind, I can't help but wonder what's come over me—I would never have thought this would turn me on. But I can still feel my clit pulsing from the overwhelming orgasm, my body still humming with pleasure, and I know I'm looking at him with the same hunger that he looked at me with earlier.

"That's right, *sladkiy*," Mikhail groans as he tugs his zipper down, and I catch a glimpse of bare flesh as the fabric parts. "You want my cock, don't you? I've been waiting for this moment, to see you wrap your pretty lips around it—"

His cock slips free, his fist wrapping around it as he watches my expression, stroking slowly, his fingertips teasing the sensitive flesh just beneath the tip, already pearling with pre-cum. "Is it bigger than you thought it would be?"

I nod, speechless, and it's not a lie. He's *huge*, both long and thick, big enough that I know it will be an effort to fit him into my mouth, much less down my throat. He might be the biggest I've seen, and I know he can see it on my face, from the satisfied smile that spreads over his.

"Open your mouth for me," he murmurs, his voice low and rough, and I obey, still not entirely understanding how this is turning me on. Something about the soft, firm demands strikes a chord in me, making me press my thighs together and shift as I lean forward, opening my mouth as he'd asked.

"God, yes. Warm and wet—" He strokes his hand down the length of his cock, spreading his legs a little wider so that I can kneel comfortably between them. "You can go slow, *dorogoy*. Learn to take it. But I want to feel your tongue on my cock, now."

His voice is firm, sharper now, and I feel as if it's tugging me forward, urging me to obey. I see a drop of pre-cum sliding down his shaft as he watches me, and without thinking, I lean forward, lapping it up with the tip of my tongue.

Mikhail shudders, his hand flexing as he pushes his cock down against my tongue. "*Yes*, just like that. You know how to suck cock, don't you, *krasotka?* Show me how well you can suck this big cock."

I lean forward, pressing my lips against the head of it. He tastes salty, and I flick my tongue out, catching another drop of his pre-cum as I roll my tongue against the soft flesh at the edge of the head, pressing it firmly there. I feel him shudder again, and when he lets go of his cock, reaching for my hand to replace it with his… I let him.

My fingers barely touch as I wrap them around him, feeling the hot, velvety flesh quiver under my touch. He leans back, his head tilted back against the couch, as I start to stroke him slowly, still swirling my tongue around his cockhead.

"Ah, yes, *krasotka*. So fucking good. This is what I wanted when you rubbed that pretty pussy for me in the champagne room. I was so fucking hard. I wanted your mouth, just like this—"

I used to hate dirty talk, more because men were bad at it than anything else, but something about the way Mikhail speaks, rough and filthy, his words rolling over me as I start to push my lips around his cockhead, floods me with lust all over again. I can feel the heat between my thighs, wet and insistent, and as I take the first inch of his cock in my mouth, I reach down with my other hand between my thighs.

"I should make you ask for permission," he rasps, his hips jerking as I take a little more, deeper, sliding my tongue down the underside of his shaft. "But right now, I don't think I will. I like the idea of you touching yourself, rubbing that little clit while you suck my cock. I want you to come with my cock in your mouth, *krasotka*—"

He groans, his hips arching again as I grip the base of his shaft, forcing my lips further down, feeling him stretch my mouth wide as I try to take as much as I can. I can feel how hard he is, straining against my lips, and I slide my hand further down, reaching to cup his tight balls inside his boxers.

"Oh, *fuck*—" His deep, throaty groan sends another bolt of heat through me, and I roll my fingers over my clit, feeling them slip in my slick arousal, wetter than I've ever been before. All I can taste and smell is him—warm and smoky and musky and salty, flooding my senses. I grind down onto my hand, wanting desperately to come again as I force my mouth further down, feeling his cockhead bump against the back of my throat.

"Fuck yes, just like that—" Mikhail's hand wraps in my hair, holding me there so I can't move, his swollen cock pushing deeper. "I'm going to fuck your throat, *malen'kiy*. I'm going to fuck your throat and fill your mouth with my cum—"

His hips jerk upwards, pushing his cock deeper, and I feel myself choke, my eyes watering as he cuts off my air with his thick, hard length. His hand tightens, fisting my hair in his grasp as he pushes my head down, and to my horror, I feel a flood of pleasure wash over me, my clit throbbing under my fingertips as my nose brushes against his abs and his cock fills my throat, every impossible inch of it.

I can't be about to—but I am. I choke on Mikhail's cock, gagging as he forces me down to the very base. I feel my entire body clench as an orgasm that I hadn't expected tears through me, making me cry out with a muffled, choked sound as I arch my back and ride my fingers through the powerful climax.

"Oh *fuck*—" he groans above me, and as I roll my teary eyes upwards, I see a look of pure and utter lust wreathing his features. "Fuck, you're coming while you choke on my cock, *fuck*—"

I feel his cock throb, swelling in my mouth, and I can't breathe. I can't think. The orgasm is still pulsing through me, my fingers sliding lower, pushing into my clenching pussy in pursuit of more pleasure, even as I suffocate on the biggest cock I've ever sucked. *Is this how I'm going to go?* I think dimly, my vision blurring as another wave of pleasure tears through me. Then suddenly, Mikhail is dragging my mouth off his cock, his other hand fisting his shaft hard and fast as I stare at him, his cockhead still pressed against my tongue.

"Fuck, I'm going to come—keep your fingers in your pussy, *krasotka*, finger yourself while I come on your fucking tongue, your fucking face, *fuck, fuck*—"

I hear him cursing like a chant as his cock swells on my tongue, and I feel the first hot burst of his cum, thick and flooding over my tongue. His hips jerk upwards as I ride my fingers through another wave of pleasure and another, keeping them buried inside of me just as he said, as I feel my mouth fill up with his hot cum. I swallow, but not fast enough, as some of it drips down my chin and onto my breasts—somehow, that only makes my pussy clench harder around my fingers, my entire body lost in a fog of arousal and pleasure.

"God, you're so fucking beautiful. I want to cover you in my fucking cum—" Mikhail is still stroking, his blue eyes fixed hotly on my face. He shoots another thick stream of cum into my mouth, until I'm not sure if he'll ever stop coming.

I feel him tap his cockhead against my tongue, pulling it out of my mouth and wiping it against my cheek. Then suddenly, his hand is on my arm, the other reaching to wipe away the cum on my cheek and chin.

"Stand up, *malen'kiy*," he growls. I unsteadily get to my feet, feeling shaky and uncertain, still in a fog of pleasure, my hand sliding out from between my thighs.

But I don't expect what comes next.

He reaches up, his half-softened cock still outside of his trousers, and runs his cum-covered fingers over my breasts, scooping up the thick liquid there. And then, before I can react, he shoves his hand under my skirt with his other hand hard on my hip, holding me in place as he pushes his fingers, coated in his cum, inside of me.

I'm so shocked that I can't move. I clench reflexively around him, my sensitive flesh reacting to the invasion. Mikhail laughs, his arm going around my waist. He yanks me forward, suddenly, bringing me into his lap as I tumble forward. I let out a yelp of dismay as I feel his cock against my thigh, starting to harden again.

"We said no—"

"I'm not going to fuck you, *krasotka*," he murmurs, his arm around my waist, holding me tightly against him as his fingers work deeply into my pussy, curling as he thrusts. "I'm going to make you come again just like this, with my cum inside of you, while you ride my fingers. I want to feel you come, all slick and wet—"

Oh god. Fuck—

His fingers feel good, thick and curling inside of me, pressing against my most sensitive inner spots as his thumb finds my clit. *This shouldn't turn me on,* I realize dimly, fear spiking in me at the realization of what he's doing, but I can feel how wet I am, flooding his hand as he fucks me harder with his fingers, rolling the pad of his thumb against my clit. All I can think about is his cock filling my mouth up with his cum, dripping down my cheek, and that he's pushing it inside of me now, deeper and deeper as I clench around him, my hips riding his hand—

My head drops forward, my forehead pressed against the back of the couch as my hips jerk and spasm, coming for a third time as pleasure floods me. It feels better than it should, better than I want it to, but I can't help it. I let out a long moan, muffled by the couch, my entire body shuddering as he thrusts his fingers into me hard and deep, and I climax helplessly around them.

I feel him pull them free, and as I sit back dazedly, I see him lift his fingers to his mouth, grinning wickedly as he licks them clean, his gaze never leaving my flushed face.

When he's finished, as I sit there stunned, he takes me by the waist and moves me aside, reaching for my glass and handing it to me. "Finish your drink, Ekaterina, and I'll call you a cab. I have an early morning tomorrow."

He tucks himself neatly back into his pants, his face as clear and smooth as if nothing happened, and he stands up gracefully, leaving me sitting there as I look at my drink.

What the hell just happened?

Natalia

I wake in the morning with my jaw sore and the rest of me more relaxed than I have been in a long time, my body still faintly humming with remembered pleasure. I slept hard and dreamless, falling into bed the moment the cab dropped me off, completely worn out.

Now, I lie in bed as I blink awake, recalling the events of the night before. It had been good—*so* good that it scares me more than a little. I enjoyed myself more than I have in a long time, and I can't pretend that I don't want to do it again, see him again. Even, maybe—

I sit upright in bed suddenly, remembering *all* of it. What he did at the end—

"Fuck," I whisper aloud to the empty room, my mind racing.

What am I going to do? I haven't been on birth control in a long time, far too long to let a man put his cum-covered fingers inside of me. I'd been too lost in a daze to entirely process what was happening, and it hadn't seemed like Mikhail was going to take no for an answer anyway, but now—

The worst part of it is that I fucking liked *it.* I feel my face flame hot at the memory of how hard I'd come, the way my body had responded to his filthy words in my ear, telling me to come for him while he fucked his cum inside of me. I've never done anything that reckless or lewd. Still, even now, it's all I can do to ignore how my body tightens with arousal at the memory of it.

I could get plan B. I bite my lower lip, considering. It's not difficult to get, but the thought of spending any of the money I've carefully tucked away on anything except my escape makes me feel faintly sick.

It was just one time.

What if he does it again?

After last night, I feel convinced of what Ruby's been trying to tell me all along, that he's just a sugar daddy, someone I can use as a means of getting out of here. He wants me; that much is clear, and if I can string things out a bit longer, I'll be able to do just that.

It's for money, that's all—but after last night, it's clear that I can enjoy it, too. So why not?

Just don't let him do that again.

I go back and forth, trying to decide if I should go to the pharmacy. I know Ruby would say it's better to be safe than sorry, if I have the money for it, but what if I don't really need it, and it's all a waste?

It was just one time. You're not even near the part of your cycle where you're really risking anything. Just stop him if he tries it again. He clearly has some kind of kink, so find some other way to satisfy it. Especially if—

Am I going to fuck him, if he wants it?

I want to, I can't deny that. Seeing him last night sealed that. I wanted to find out what that cock would feel like inside of me—*but I'm going to make him pay for it,* I remind myself. And if I play my cards right, he'll want me badly enough that he'll pay handsomely for it.

I just have to not let myself lose sight of the reason I'm doing this. I made that mistake with Adrian, letting myself be overwhelmed by how good the sex was, how romantic and exciting it was to be having a fling with a gorgeous man on a Greek island. I got caught up in the fantasy. There, it was just a mistake, a whirlwind relationship that ended in yelling and anger when I realized he wanted me to rely on him more than I was willing to, that he wanted control I wasn't willing to cede.

Here, it's dangerous. I don't know who Mikhail is, not really. I feel confident that he's not someone trying to entrap me, but that doesn't mean that couldn't change if he ever discovered who I really was. I don't know what contacts he has or what connections.

I have to keep him at arm's length, enjoy this for what it is, and then get out as soon as I have enough to escape.

Slowly, I get out of bed, making my way to the shower to clean up, something I hadn't had enough energy to do last night before falling into bed. The hot water helps loosen my muscles and clear my head. I reason away any thoughts of going to the pharmacy, telling myself that it's not enough of a risk to be worth it.

It's not like he came inside of me. It won't matter.

I have to work tonight, and Mikhail didn't say anything about meeting tonight, so I expect I'll have to go. It feels like not enough, after what I've been able to make with him, but every little bit counts–and besides, I want to see Ruby. I haven't decided how much I'm going to tell her, but I know I'm going to have to tell her *something*.

And then I step into my kitchen.

There's a piece of paper under my door. I feel my pulse spike, the world slowing around me as I stare down at it. *It can't be Mikhail. When would he have done it?* But still, I hear my heartbeat pounding in my ears, beating wildly as I reach for the piece of paper.

We see you, malen'kaya shlyukha. We are coming for you.

I crumple it in my fist, sinking into one of my unsteady chairs as I struggle not to be sick. *We? Who is* we? I feel dizzy and faint, and I grab the edge of the table, struggling not to collapse into tears.

I don't know how much more of this I can take. I have to get out.

Mikhail is your way out. Whatever he wants, do it, and make sure he pays you for it.

I stand up abruptly, stalking to my garbage can and shoving the letter elbow-deep into it, my entire body shaking. I feel cold, shivery, and I close my eyes as I wash my hands and arm at the sink, feeling as if I might fold into myself, curl up into a ball, and never come out.

It's not so much that I want my old life back, exactly. I don't want my fake friends, my brutal and unfeeling father, or the promise of an unwanted marriage hanging over my head. But I don't want *this*, either.

I don't want to spend the rest of my life afraid, looking over my shoulder, waiting for the blow to come. I want to be *free*.

I want to live as I choose, as Natalia. Not Natalia Obelensky—just as myself. Without fear.

The possibility seems closer than ever—and still somehow too far away.

It's hard to shake the feeling by the time I get to the club. I know I'm not at my best, and I feel Igor's eyes on me as I walk past his office to the dressing room.

"*Devochka.* Athena." His rough voice stops me in my tracks, and I turn slowly, feeling a knot in the pit of my stomach as I swallow hard and step into his office.

"Yes?" I plaster a smile on my face, forcing myself not to look as worried as I feel. "Is something wrong?"

"I'm not sure." He steeples his fingers in front of him on the desk, his eyes narrowed. "That man came to my office two nights ago, after buying time with you. The one who took a fancy to you the night I almost fired you. I'm sure you know who I'm talking about."

I feel my mouth go dry, but I manage to nod. "Yes–of course. I do."

"Well, he informed me that you wouldn't be working last night. I told him that wouldn't do, since I get a cut of your earnings, and if you're on the schedule, you're on the schedule. Sick is one thing, but getting money that I don't get a cut of, well–"

He trails off, and I feel the knot tighten, a sick feeling spreading through me. "I assumed he paid you for my time," I say faintly. It's the truth, it is what I assumed, but I have a feeling this isn't going to go the way I want it to.

"Maybe he did, maybe he didn't." Igor shrugs. "That doesn't change what you owe me." He holds out his hand, his gaze flat and cold. "You don't make money unless I make money, Athena. I don't take kindly to my girls hiring out their services on the side. So if you want to keep reeling in this fish you've caught, you'll hand over your share."

I truly feel as if I'm going to be sick. I can feel myself going pale, thinking of how much he could take from me. "I don't see how that's fair–"

Igor stands up, suddenly, his bulk filling the space behind the desk as he slams his hands down onto it, making me jump and bite my lip to keep from bursting into frightened tears at the shock of it. "I don't give a fuck about *fair, devochka*. Do you think anyone cares about a girl like you?" He sneers at me, his upper lip curling. "Do you think anyone will miss you, *shlyukha?* I could strangle you here and leave you in the dumpster out back, and no one would think twice about it. That is your choice. You pay up what you owe, or I take it out of your flesh."

He leers at me, licking his lips as his eyes rake down my body. "I know what's under those ugly clothes, *devochka*. I know how pretty it is. If you want to give it away without cutting me in, then maybe my cock wants a taste, too."

"You—" I struggle for words, trying to think of some way out of this. Igor's hands on me are the last thing I want, but I don't want to lose my money, either. The memory of the letter I found today is far too vivid, and I can see my escape fading, further in the distance, if Igor is going to take a cut of what Mikhail gives me. I know it won't be cheap, either, what he takes from me.

Igor is around the desk faster than a man of his size ought to be able to move, his meaty hand on my face as he pushes me back into the door. He leans too close, his breath smelling of lunch and alcohol, and I feel myself instinctively shrinking away.

"Please—"

"Money or pussy," he rasps close to my ear. "I'll let you choose, *devochka*."

I feel my eyes welling up with hot tears, and with everything in me, I force them back. "Fine," I spit, pushing him away. "How much do you want?"

He grins toothily. "I knew you'd see it my way. I'd rather have the money anyway. Normally, I'd say thirty percent, but since you decided to try to keep it from me, we're going to go with sixty, this time."

"I don't have it *on* me." I glare at him. "I'm not an idiot. Do you think I'd walk around with that kind of cash on me?"

My mind is spinning as I'm speaking, trying to figure out what I'm going to do, if I'm really going to give him sixty percent. *So much of that, gone.* He has no idea how much Mikhail gave me—but I have a terrible feeling that he'll know if I shortchange him.

As if he can hear my thoughts, Igor grins wider. "I know what you're thinking, Athena. You're thinking how you can get away with getting me less, but I have those rooms bugged. I can find out exactly how much he promised you if you talked about it in there. And I'll check. If I find out you're cheating me—"

I feel my heart sink. "I can't get it to you tonight. Next shift—"

Igor crosses his arms over his chest. "I'll take half of your earnings tonight, against it. And then you bring the rest tomorrow."

I nod, feeling shaky and desperate to get out of the room. "Tomorrow. Of course."

I can't get out of there fast enough. As soon as the door closes behind me, I cover my mouth with my hand, trying desperately not to cry. I don't want Ruby to see me like this, and I know she's going to pick up on it. She always seems to know when I'm upset.

Sure enough, the moment I walk through the door, her eyes go wide.

"What happened? Something with Mikhail?"

I shake my head, teeth still gritted against the tears I'm trying so hard to hold back. "Not really." I sit down heavily in my chair, explaining to her what had just happened in Igor's office. I see her expression change, a mixture of sympathy and resignation, and she lets out a sigh.

"Did he do it to you, too?" I ask, staring at her, and she shrugs.

"I offered before he could. I know men like him—I knew he'd find out, and it would be worse if I didn't go to him first. This way, I got better terms. I—" She bites her lip. "I'm sorry. I should have said something to you. I just—I didn't want to scare you. You were already having such a hard time with it. And I thought Mikhail might be savvy enough to take care of it. He seemed to know his way around this type of place—you know, the type who knows how to grease palms. My guy isn't like that."

"I think he did." I squeeze my hands together, feeling my nails bite into my palms. "Igor just said I needed to pay him, too. He wasn't satisfied with whatever Mikhail gave him."

"That fucking—" Ruby seethes, gritting her teeth. She looks around quickly, her eyes narrowing. "We need to be careful what we say in here."

"He said he has the rooms bugged."

"I figured as much." Ruby sees the expression on my face and reaches out, grabbing my hands. "Oh, Athena. I'm sorry—"

"Is there anything else you want to tell me that you haven't?" I snatch my hands back, feeling suddenly betrayed. "I could have used all of that, you know."

Ruby has the good grace, at least, to look chagrined. "I'm so sorry," she says softly. "You're so new to all of this, you said. I didn't want to scare you. I was afraid you'd leave, honestly, and I—" She swallows hard. "It's no excuse, but you're the only real friend I've had in a while. I didn't want you to go."

Part of me wants to lash out, to stay angry, to take all of my complicated feelings out on Ruby. It would be easy to do it. I could sever our friendship with a few sharp, well-placed words, and before all of this, I might have.

But I don't have so many people left in the world that I can do that so easily. I know for a fact that what Igor said wasn't true—if I disappeared, Ruby would care. It would matter. And because of that, and because I don't want to hurt the one friend I have, I let it go.

"I understand," I say softly. "I really do. We're all just doing our best. I'm not mad at you."

I'm not. But the fear that Igor left me with sticks with me. It's hard to focus, and all I can think about is the money I'm losing and how much further I'm going to be now from my goal than I was before.

When I have a chance to slip away, I step outside into the rain and fish out the last thing Mikhail gave me last night before he put me into a cab—a phone with his number in it. I hadn't planned on using it so soon, but with my heart pounding in my chest, I pull it out and hit the call button, wanting to talk to the one other person who might actually care that I'm being extorted. Most of all, because he'd already tried to pay Igor off.

The phone picks up on the second ring, and I try to ignore the way a chill goes through me at the sound of his low, rough voice on the other end, or how much I mean it when I say quietly, under the dripping of the rain:

"I need to see you."

Mikhail

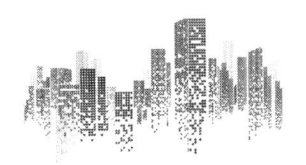

I'd woken up this morning with a sense of satisfaction that I haven't felt in a long time.

It had been so fucking long since I had my cock in a woman's mouth. Natalia's—or Ekaterina, as she's pretending to call herself—had been especially sweet. I'd been thinking of that moment for a long time, imagining what it would be like, and it had exceeded my every fantasy.

Last night, I wasn't sure if I'd get that far with her. I thought it might take longer, but the greedy little bitch wanted money, and I flashed it in front of her. My longer goal—to make her want me without the promise of cash, seems less likely. But either way, I can tell that Natalia Obelensky is beginning to trust me, to believe the story that I'm selling her, and it feels better even than I imagined.

I told her that she's worth every ruble I'm spending, and I meant it—just not in the way she thinks.

For the first time in weeks, when I woke up, I wasn't achingly hard. In fact, my cock barely twitched as I came back to consciousness.

However, I felt it start to pleasantly swell when I remembered how she'd come for me the night before, particularly that last one.

The memory of shoving my cum inside of Natalia Obelensky before she realized what was happening is one that will sustain me for a very, very long time.

My cock twitches, swelling even more at the memory, and I reach down to lazily run my fingers over the length of it, remembering with pleasure the look in her eyes when she'd seen exactly what I planned to shove down her throat. She choked on it deliciously, and I groan as I harden, stiffening at the memory of suffocating her with it.

That's only a taste of what you have to look forward to.

I have the urge to stay in bed a while longer, to indulge in a long, slow stroke as I play back the events of last night. I have to force myself to get up, reminding myself that I have a job to do today. In the rush of my fresh victory, I'd almost forgotten, but I've already put the job off once.

I can't do it again.

Careful, Kasilov, I caution myself. I'd been blown away by how well last night had gone, by how thoroughly she'd given in to what I demanded of her, and how she'd given herself over to her own pleasure. I prepared myself for the possibility of a cold fish, a woman who would only give as much as she had to in exchange for my money, but all it had taken was a flick of my tongue against her dripping pussy, and she'd come apart for me.

It's only going to get better. But you have to keep your head. Valeria won't give a shit about my game, and she wants Yuri dead and her proof in hand. I can feel my gut clench with disappointment at the thought of a trip to Novogrod, at least a full day without seeing Natalia, and I grit my teeth.

Get it together. You're going to fuck this up if you can't manage twenty-four hours without seeing her. She's a mark, not your fucking girlfriend, no matter how good she feels choking around your cock.

The last thing I want to do is spend my day staking out Yuri and waiting for a chance to grab him, but I know I've got to finish this. As much as I have no desire to spend a day away from Moscow and Natalia, I know that, too, is something I need. The space to clear my head, to remember that this game with her is almost finished as well.

Yuri proves to be easier than I thought. I park around the back of his shabby apartment building—fortunately, in a different part of town than Natalia's, so there's no risk of running into her so far as I can tell, but even if I did, I doubt that she'd recognize me. I have my usual disguise on, a short, shaggy dark brown wig with a baseball cap pulled low over my eyes, old jeans, and a t-shirt with a jacket thrown over it to disguise my tattoos. I keep to the shadows, waiting for Yuri to emerge, and to my relief, he comes out much earlier than he did the last time I was here.

As he walks down the sidewalk, I give him space before I step out after him, following at a pace that won't seem suspicious. I want to make sure that he's not meeting with anyone else who might pose a problem before I make a move—it would be unusual for Yuri to have a meeting during daylight hours, but there's always a chance. I'm good at my work because I'm cautious and patient, and I have no intention of changing that now.

When he walks into a grocery, I could shout with how pleased I am. *See? It worked out, after all. It'll be even easier today than it would have been the other night. Waiting was to your benefit.*

It's an excuse, and I know it. Still, I ignore the thought, walking casually across the street once Yuri has disappeared into the store. Formulating a plan comes as naturally as breathing. I slip into the alleyway next to the grocery, my fingers tapping against the syringe in my pocket as I wait in the shadows. The streets are mostly empty, and once he comes out, he won't see me, as long as I'm quick and careful.

I've spent years honing my ability to be both. When Yuri steps back out some time later, as he passes by the alley, I take one look to make sure there are no eyes looking our way as I reach out, grabbing him and pulling him back. He's not a large man, and my hand covers his mouth quickly before he can shout.

He struggles, but it's not much difficulty to restrain him. I have the needle in his neck before he can twist away, and as I drag him deeper into the darkness of the alley, I feel him sag against me.

"Sorry, Yuri," I mutter. "I wouldn't have chosen this end for you. But a job is a job, and no one tells Valeria no."

I know a path back to where I left my car through the alleys. I leave his bag of groceries there, potatoes and onions spilling out of the alley shadows into the sidewalk's sunlight, and disappear behind the buildings.

—

When I have him safely in the warehouse, still unconscious, I look down at him and consider. He hadn't seen my face in the alleyway, and I feel an unfamiliar twinge of guilt as I look down at the bound man.

He might have given Valeria bad information, but it's thanks to him that I found Natalia at all.

"Valeria didn't ask me to question him," I mutter to myself, considering what to do. She only asked for proof that I killed him. I'm not going to spare him, I'm not a fool, but it occurs to me that I could make this easier on him.

I could make his death kinder.

I planned to wait for him to wake up, to spend some time questioning him myself, verifying the truth of everything he'd given me. But I have no reason to believe he's ever led me astray.

"Just finish it." I shake my head as I mutter the words, reaching for my gun with the silencer already affixed. The last thing he'll ever know is being grabbed as he walks out of a grocery. Still, he won't wake up to feel the fear of knowing for certain he's going to die or endure the pain of a slow questioning. He won't know that I, someone he trusted as much as men like he and I can ever trust someone, was the architect of his end.

It's to salve my own twinge of guilt as much as out of mercy, I know that, but I focus on the part of it that *is* mercy, as I press the muzzle to his temple.

One shot, and it's finished, without Yuri ever awakening to know his fate. The body slumps, and I set the gun aside, already thinking ahead to what's next. Valeria will want to know the job is done, and I still have yet to speak to the Syndicate about Natalia, now that I feel certain it's her.

When Yuri is disposed of, a tattooed finger kept to deliver to Valeria along with the wallet I found in his pocket with his identification, I clean and reorganize my space. Only when there's no trace of what's happened, just as it was when I arrived earlier, do I pull out the two burner phones I'm carrying.

The job is done, I text Valeria on one. **Tell me when you want to meet.**

And then, on the other, I dial the number she gave me for the Syndicate.

She'd given me the password to speak when someone answered, and I deliver it smoothly, without a hint of the nerves that I feel knotting in my gut. "*Smert elo milost.*"

Contact with the Syndicate is not something to be taken lightly. In all the years I worked for Viktor, I never spoke to anyone there. I knew that Levin, his right hand, had once been one of their best assassins until he broke away from them after the murder of his wife. I'd been careful to give them, and everything associated with them, a wide berth. Once in, it's difficult to get out.

But I have no intention of staying for long.

"Who is this?" The voice on the other end says, low and coarse. "Your name or I hang up."

"Mikhail Kasilov."

"And how did you get this number, Mikhail Kasilov? Who gave you the password?"

"Valeria Belyaevna," I say smoothly. "I have information about Natalia Obelensky that your boss might be interested in."

"Wait on the line." The voice is curt, cold, and then all I hear is silence and the pounding of the blood in my ears.

They have my name, now. But I doubt Valeria, who has made an effort to put distance between herself and the Syndicate, would give me the contact and connect herself with this if she didn't think that Vladimir would want the information I have. I remind myself of that, to keep myself calm until the voice returns.

"Tonight. Come alone. Vladimir will see you."

The relief I feel is almost palpable. I open my mouth to speak, but the line goes dead, and I know that whatever else I might want to say or ask, I'll have to wait for tonight.

I just have to hope that once I go into the Syndicate compound, I'll come out again.

—

I'm so keyed up on the drive to the compound, which is located outside of the city proper, that the buzzing of my phone makes me jump, jerking the wheel to one side as I drive. When I've recovered, I reach for it, bracing myself for it to be the same cold voice I'd spoken to this afternoon.

Instead, to my surprise, I hear a feminine voice that takes me a brief moment to place. She sounds upset, and for a moment, I have a memory of a different woman's voice, before I realize that it's Natalia.

"Mikhail?" There's a soft, pleading quality to her voice that I've never heard from her before. "I hope it's alright that I called."

It takes me a second to steel myself against the momentary weakness I feel, the desire to ask her what's wrong. "I gave you the phone for that reason," I tell her instead. "I'm very busy, but if you need something—"

"I need to see you. If I can. I don't mean to push—I know this is a different kind of arrangement, but what I mean to say is—I'd like to see you tonight, if—"

For a moment, I have the wild and entirely inappropriate urge to turn the car around and drive back to Moscow. *She's vulnerable*, I think, my body tightening with anticipation at the idea of how that could be exploited for my own plans. *She clearly is upset to call you like this. This isn't like her.*

What if it's some kind of trap? What if she's figured something out?

As if she could do anything to me, even if she did.

Once upon a time, Natalia Obelensky discovering my plans for her might have been very bad indeed. The sort of things her father could, and certainly would, have inflicted on me are the sorts of things that make even me shiver with horror. But he's buried and rotting, and she has nothing and no one now. Even if she suspects me, the worst that can happen is that I have to take her by force, instead of enjoying the pleasure of her giving herself to me willingly.

On the other hand, not arriving at a meeting with the Syndicate has much more far-reaching consequences.

"Mikhail?" Her voice comes over the line again, small and hesitant. "I'm sorry if I shouldn't have called—"

Maybe after the meeting?

"I'll have to call you back," I tell her firmly. "I'm in the middle of something, but when I'm finished, we can talk. Of course, I want to see you again, but–"

"I understand," she says hastily. Something about the interruption makes me clench my teeth, a hot burst of anger replacing the softness I'd so momentarily felt. "I'm sorry, I–"

"I said it's fine. It's just a bad time. I'll call you back."

I hang up before I can say anything else that might make the situation worse. I shove the phone into the center console, fighting the surge of emotion that wells up in my chest.

On the one hand, this is good. She trusted me enough to call in a moment of weakness, and that means that things are unfolding just as I hoped they would.

On the other, what I felt at the sound of her soft voice is dangerous. It's wrong. And it's nothing I should ever feel for Obelensky's daughter.

She's not Mika. She's nothing like Mika. She's not a damsel in distress. She's a snake. A woman hiding from the truth of what she is. And I'm going to make her pay for it.

When I see the forbidding buildings and black iron gate of Obelensky's compound rising up in front of me as the car winds its way down the long drive, I force my thoughts away from her and the unexpected call.

I need to be at my best for this meeting.

"*Smert elo milost.*" I give the password again to the guard at the gate. "Mikhail Kasilov. Here to see Vladimir Babanin."

The guard raises an eyebrow and turns his head, speaking in sharp, rapid Russian into his earpiece. He waits for a moment and then nods.

"The Wolf will see you."

The gate opens, slowly, and I swallow hard as I put the car into gear, driving up to the front. Four more black-garbed guards are waiting for me when I get out, and one of them holds out his hand.

"Keys and weapons," he says sharply. "Or no entrance."

I'm more loathe to give up my gun than my keys, but I hand over both, and the knife I keep on me. In other circumstances, I might have tried to smuggle some weapon in, but not here.

Here, the crime is not worth the punishment. All men in my line of work know what happens if you cross the Syndicate.

I follow the other three guards into the huge building, their shoes slapping smartly against the black and white checkerboard tile that we cross, pass a fountain in the center of the large central room, up a mahogany staircase to a room with broad double doors. As we pause at the doorway, the guard raps on the door, speaking the password again.

"*Vkhodit!*" The word is barked from inside the office, and the guard pushes open the doors. As we stand there, I see a tall, sharply dressed man with his back turned to us, looking over a series of papers on a long desk.

"*Volk.*" One of the guards speaks. "A man named Kasilov. Says he is here to see you."

The man at the desk turns to face us. His hair is blond, neatly combed back, his eyes a flinty blue, his expression harsh and forbidding. His eyes rake over me appraisingly, and it's hard to tell if he approves of what he sees.

"Mikhail Kasilov." He says my name flatly, and I nod, stepping forward.

"Thank you for seeing me, Babanin."

"Only because of what you say you have." He raises an eyebrow. "Information on the Obelensky girl. I had heard she was dead, or long gone. How is it that you have uncovered information the Syndicate has not?"

It's on the tip of my tongue to say something smart-assed, but I'd likely leave without my tongue for it. It's not worth the momentary pleasure. "Luck, Babanin," I say smoothly. "And so I have brought you my luck, in hopes that it might be worth something to you."

Vladimir snorts. "You were one of Viktor's, *da*? Just like one of his men, to think of it in such a crass manner. What do you hope to get out of this? Favor with the Syndicate? Money?"

"I've looked for over a year for a way to get to Obelensky," I tell him plainly. "It has not exhausted my resources, but it has been costly. If you would be willing to pay for me to do the dirty work of removing this girl for you, I would be happy to do so."

"So you don't wish us to take over the task of dispatching her?"

"No," I say as firmly as I can, a small bolt of panic shooting through me at the thought of Vladimir taking my mark from me before I can finish my plan. As quickly and succinctly as I can, I tell him what I've been doing, the plan I've had in order to kidnap Natalia, in brief. "I have my own reasons for going after the Obelensky girl, and I wish to see them through to the end. But I will give you the information I get from her. And you will not have to expend any of your manpower on the task. All I ask is that, in addition to whatever you think this work might be worth, that you allow me to dispense of her as I see fit, when I'm finished questioning her."

"Mikhail Kasilov," Vladimir repeats my name, tapping his fingers against the desk as he leans back against it. "You are fortunate that your reputation precedes you, or else you might leave here with a few pieces missing for wasting my time. But I know your name well enough to know that you can question as well as the men I set to that sort of task. If it were her father—" he shrugs. "I would want him down here in my own territory, to see what I could extract from him personally. But as far as the daughter—" His shoulder lifts again and drops.

"I don't believe she knows as much as you might think she does," he continues, looking at me thoughtfully. "My concern with the girl is more that she is removed from the chessboard, so to speak. With her father dead, there is a power vacuum in Moscow, and I have my own ideas about who should fill it. It's not often that a woman rises to power among our kind, but I heard the girl was stubborn, and she was his only living and legitimate child. If she made a claim to his money and connections, it could complicate things. So as long as you can ensure that she will not survive whatever you have planned for her—*skhodit's uma*. Enjoy." He grins, a wolfish smile. "I will not pay you as much as I'm sure you hoped, but there will be a stipend."

Vladimir pauses then, considering. "Where is it you plan to take the girl?"

"I have a penthouse that I've been using as I work on gaining her trust. When I am finished with her, I plan to take her back to New York and give her to Viktor to finish off. Proof that I was not a part of Obelensky's plot against him."

Vladimir nods. "And Viktor will kill her, you think?"

"Her father had his wife kidnapped and raped and helped to organize a coup within his Bratva. I think he will enjoy taking his anger out on her flesh."

"As he should." Vladimir steeples his fingers, frowning. "I have heard, though, that the *Ussuri* is a changed man these days. What will you do if he does not take your gift in the spirit in which it is intended?"

"Then the girl will remain with me, to finish off as I please."

"A different deal, then." Vladimir smiles. "If your plans with Andreyev do not go as planned, then you will bring the girl back here. I will provide you with protection against him, if need be, in exchange for the pleasure of finishing off the Obelensky girl myself, as I please. You will be finished with her by then."

I consider it for a moment, wanting to be sure. But there's no flaw in it that I can see. "Agreed. If Viktor does not respond as I think he will, I will bring her back to you. I may need assistance in that."

"Of course. You will need a different place to take her to when you have decided it is time. You should not wait much longer. Come back tomorrow evening, and I will have you set up with a stipend and keys to a house where you can take her. A penthouse in a neighborhood like the one you are staying in—not good. Too many eyes. You will be more hidden where I will send you."

It's on the tip of my tongue to refuse, if I can. The idea of being beholden in any way to the Syndicate, of having Natalia in a place that Vladimir knows, feels like a dangerous one to me.

But I'm also reasonably certain that I don't have much of a choice. I'm not the only one pulling the strings now, and I wonder if taking Valeria up on her suggestion was the right one, even for the money and backup that I'll get out of it.

It's too late to question it now.

"Thank you, *volk*." I incline my head, showing respect. "I will come back the evening after next, then."

"You will receive a call. Come then." Vladimir straightens, and it's clear that the meeting is over. "Until then, Kasilov."

I'm not sure my pulse returns to a normal pace until I'm back in my car and driving away from the compound. *It's done,* I tell myself. *I've made the steps; now, I simply have to stay on the path. And in the end, this might be for the better.*

I can't allow my feelings, whatever they might be, to run away with me now. I'm locked in now—if I fail to follow through, I'll have the most powerful shadow organization in Europe after me.

This is about revenge. Nothing more. And now it can be never more.

I reach for my phone, dialing her number. When her voice comes over the line, it's less shaky than before, but I can still tell she's unsettled. I feel that small flicker of emotion, and then I shut it down before it can flare into more.

"I can't see you tonight," I tell her flatly. "I'm busy this evening. Two nights from now, if you like."

Before she can respond, I hang up.

Natalia

"Are you alright?"

I hear Ruby's voice from behind me as I look down at the phone in my hand, confusion filling me. I nod quickly, squeezing the phone in my hand as I turn to look at her.

"I'm fine. I just—"

"Who was that?" She gestures at the phone, and I have the urge to lie to her, to tell her it was anyone else—but I'd only just been upset at her earlier this evening for not telling me everything she knew about Igor. I *can't* tell her everything, not without putting her in danger, but I can, at the very least, be honest with her about this.

"I called Mikhail." I'm still clenching the phone in my hand. "I thought—I don't know what I thought. I know he paid Igor something to make up for taking my time away from the club. I guess I thought—I thought he might be able to help or something—" I trail off. Saying the words aloud makes me feel stupid, as if I shouldn't have made the call at all.

"Was he angry?" Ruby frowns, leaning back against the wall. We're standing on the iron stairwell outside the club, effectually blocking the door for anyone else who wants to come out, but at this particular moment, I don't really care. I don't want anyone to overhear our conversation anyway.

"I didn't tell him what happened. Not yet. I just–I asked if I could see him tonight. I thought it might be better if I told him about it in person. And he–"

"He wasn't angry with *you*, was he?" Ruby looks outraged at the idea, and I laugh softly.

"No, not exactly. More just–cold. Different. He was curt, said he was busy, and that he'd see me two nights from now. I just–" I swallow hard, wrapping my arms around myself. "What if he's lost interest? Before what happened tonight with Igor, that might not have been so bad. But now Igor is taking half my earnings tonight, and he expects a huge chunk of what I have from Mikhail. He knows what I'm supposed to bring him. I was counting on making more from Mikhail to make up for it–"

And you were hoping to see him again. Don't lie to yourself.

I push the thought aside as I look down at Ruby, feeling panic wind its way through me. "I guess I just wait until the evening after next–"

Ruby purses her lips. "I don't know about that. You know where his place is now?"

I look at her in confusion. "Yeah, but–"

"He's playing a game." Ruby shrugs. "This whole thing is a game. You have to play it, too. He's paying for your time, and he's probably getting a little salty about it. Men get that way sometimes, they remember that you're doing this for money, and it makes them feel bad. He's going cold on you because he wants to feel wanted."

"I don't know if that's true." I chew on my lower lip, thinking about the conversations I've had with Mikhail and the way he's behaved in the past. I think about the possibility that he could be the one leaving me the threatening notes, and a cold pit settles in my stomach.

"Hey." Ruby bumps my elbow with hers, giving me a reassuring smile. "I've done this before, remember? I really think that's all it is."

"So what do you think I should do?" I feel my teeth sinking into my lip as I swallow hard, trying not to think about the rest of the night, giving Igor half of the meager amount I've earned tonight, coming back tomorrow night with even more for him out of what I've made so far. "I have to wait on what he wants—"

"No, you don't, and I don't think that's what you should do. I think you should go over there tonight. Make him think that you want him so much that you couldn't wait to see him. That the money doesn't matter. And then he'll feel good, and it'll make him even more generous the next time."

It feels wrong to me. I start to tell Ruby that she's wrong, that she doesn't know Mikhail, that he's not the type to want me to appear out of nowhere. But then I think back to our conversations, to him telling me that he paid me at the beginning of the date so he could spend the rest of it imagining that it's real, and I feel my certainty falter.

What if she's right? What if he just wants me to make a move, so that he doesn't feel that this is as one-sided as it's supposed to be? What if this is a part of the game, and I just don't understand it?

I know at least a part of me is letting my feelings talk me into this, that I really do want to see him, to tell him about Igor and come up with some kind of solution, that Mikhail might be able to fix it. I don't want to go home alone and lie in my bed in the darkness, dreading the next time I go back to the club.

If Ruby is right, and this is a part of this back-and-forth, the game of having this kind of client, then you can't fuck it up. You'll lose so much more if you do.

The conversation with Igor has left me feeling shaky and desperate. My goal of getting free of all of this is suddenly further off than I thought it had been. I can feel my freedom slipping out of my fingers, and it causes me to make a decision I might not have otherwise.

"Okay," I tell Ruby, feeling my pulse beating hard in my throat. "I'll do it."

She grins at me. "It'll make him so much happier the next time. I promise. He'll probably give you something else nice. He'll feel like you really do want him."

It's not long until the end of the night. I hand over Igor the half that he demanded, forcing myself to ignore the way he insists on counting *everything* I made tonight, suspicious that it's so little. I let his lecture about that go in one ear and out of the other, holding myself together by a thread until I can get back to the dressing room and change into the little black dress I brought with me, just in case Mikhail had shown up and asked me to do something after work. It's nothing as fancy as what he's sent me, just a thigh-length, tight black dress made of a silky material with a deep boned v-neckline and thin straps, but paired with the heels he gave me and the delicate earrings, I know I look good enough to show up on his doorstep.

I just hope Ruby is right.

Despite how much it hurts, I fork over the money for a cab. The penthouse is further from the club than I'm comfortable walking alone, let alone in heels. I lean my head back on the leather seat as the cab pulls into traffic, trying not to think about how much I've lost tonight.

There are no strange looks as I walk into the building. I know exactly what the concierge thinks I am as he sees me, a beautiful girl in a short dress in a place far beyond her means, and it sends a flush of shame through me to know that now he's right. Once upon a time, I could have had the penthouse for myself. Now I'm going begging to the front door, and it bolsters my resolve to see this through with Mikhail, to do what I need to in order to get out of this city and somewhere that I can be free.

I want to be able to walk where I please, without eyes judging me, without wondering which ones are following me and might know who I am.

My heart is pounding in my ears as I step out of the elevator and walk up to Mikhail's door. It occurs to me that he might not be home, that he'd said he was busy tonight—and then a worse thought, that he might be with another woman.

Fuck. I hadn't considered that, that I might not be the only one whose company he's paying for or even that he might have a girlfriend or a wife that might be here tonight. *Fuck, fuck, fuck.* Uncertainty fills me, and I start to turn around, but I think of tomorrow night and how much I owe Igor.

If there's even a chance that Mikhail can help me with this, I have to try.

I knock on the door, firmly, and then again after a few seconds. I don't hear anything at first, and my heart sinks, thinking he's not home. *What do I do? Do I just wait?*

And then I hear footsteps.

A moment later, the door swings open, and Mikhail is standing there. He's dressed more casually than I've ever seen him, in black joggers and a tight white t-shirt, and I feel a sharp flutter of desire at how handsome he looks. His hair is a little messy, his blue eyes widening with stunned surprise at the sight of me, and for a single moment, I forget that I'm here because I need something, everything I'd come here to say replaced with a wave of warm need.

And then his face hardens into anger, and I know I've made a mistake.

I should have trusted my gut over Ruby.

"What are you doing here?" he growls. "You showing up unexpectedly isn't part of the arrangement."

"I–" I hear my voice falter, all my confidence and resolve slipping away in the face of the anger shimmering in his eyes, hard as chips of ice. "I just–I needed to see you. Igor confronted me at the club tonight–"

The words rush out of me then, more frightened than I meant them to be, tumbling out one over another as I look up at Mikhail. "He threatened me, said whatever you paid him isn't enough for the loss of my time at the club, that he needs to be cut in on whatever you pay me. He demanded that I give him sixty percent of what you gave me so far since he had to coax it out of me and thirty from now on. He threatened to hurt me if I didn't, to–"

The anger on Mikhail's face grows steadily as I speak, and I have a moment's wild hope that he's furious with Igor, that his anger with me is replaced by what I've told him. His eyes narrow, and I look at him, feeling shaky and small.

"I didn't tell you that you could show up here unannounced," he growls, and my heart sinks all the way down to my toes.

"I'm sorry–if there's someone else here–" I start to turn away, a panicked, hopeless feeling spreading through me. *Ruby was wrong. I've made it all so much worse.*

I feel his hand close around my upper arm, just a little too tightly, squeezing. He pulls me backward sharply, spinning me around, both of his hands on my upper arms now.

He looks down at me, his face hard and tense, his jaw clenched. "There's no one else here. But that doesn't matter. I gave you instructions, and you disobeyed them. You've been a bad girl, Ekaterina. And bad girls need to be punished."

My mouth drops open, a bolt of fear piercing through me, but before I can say a word, he pulls me into the apartment, the door slamming shut behind me as he kicks it closed.

"This isn't part of the agreement!" I know how foolish the words sound as soon as they come out of my mouth in a strangled, fearful yelp, but I can't help it. I've never seen him this angry, never felt him touch me like this, so forcefully. He'd been forceful and demanding when I'd gone down on him, but it hadn't been like this. I hadn't felt this afraid, as if I might be in a situation with no way out. "I just thought you should know about Igor, that he's cheating you too—I didn't come here for this! This—whatever you're about to do, you haven't paid; this isn't part of it—"

"Neither was you showing up on my doorstep without permission," he snarls, his fingers pressing into my arms. He pulls me up against him, roughly. I can feel how hard he is, his cock grinding into me as he grins down at me coldly, seeing the recognition of what might be about to happen on my face. "Now I get to take something *I* want, without asking first."

I gasp, tensing to fight back, but he's too quick. He lets go of one of my arms, his hand fisting in my hair as he drags my head back, his eyes raking down the front of me. "You dressed so nicely for me, *devochka*. It would be a shame to let it go to waste."

He spins me around, as easily as if I were a doll. I felt like I was on our second "date," pushing me roughly face-first against the door. His hand in my hair holds me pinned there, my face pressed against the wood as his other hand finds the hem of my dress, yanking it up over my ass to my waist, leaving me bare to him except for the lacy thong I'm wearing.

"What are you doing?" I gasp as his hand curls around the thong, and I cry out as he yanks, tearing the material away from me and flinging it onto the floor. I squeeze my thighs together, horrified at the bolt of arousal that rushes through me at the violence of his hands on me, the way he has me pinned to the wall as he strips me bare. "You can't touch me like this! I didn't agree—"

"And I didn't agree to you showing up here and interrupting my night." His hand tightens in my hair as his other slides up my hip and over my bare ass, exploring me as if he has all the time in the world. "So now I get to punish you. Those are the rules here, Ekaterina. I thought I was very clear when you called that I could not see you tonight."

"You said you wouldn't push this further than I wanted it—"

"Are you telling me you don't want it?" His fingers slip lower, between my thighs, and I close my eyes with a shudder as he strokes the soft, bare folds of my pussy. "You're not so wet that you're leaking yet, *sladkiy*, but if I part this pretty pussy, I know what I'll find. Are you going to admit it, or will you make me prove it?"

Another shudder goes through me, and at that moment, the mingled fear and shock and desire are replaced with anger, with that resentment and fury that he's made me feel so often before.

"Fuck you," I hiss, forgetting that I need his money, that I came here because I thought it might make things better, not so much worse. "You can't make me do anything. You lied—"

His hand tightens in my hair, almost to the point of pain, pushing my face against the door. "I don't lie, *suka*," he hisses. "I told you that it would not go further than you wanted. I promise you, it is *your* lying mouth that speaks right now."

I feel him spread me open as he says it, his fingers pushing deeper, sliding between my sensitive folds. I clench my teeth against a moan of pleasure as I feel myself tighten, wanting his fingers inside of me. I knew what he'd find, that I'm already wet from the forceful way he's handled me, and I feel myself flush with shame as he chuckles behind me.

"Such a lying little brat," he purrs, his voice low and satisfied as he rubs his fingers against me, just shy of my clit. "You're already wet, just as I knew you would be. You want it. So you see? I'm not doing more than you want. *I'm* not lying, *devochka*. So now, for your punishment."

His fingers tease my entrance, and I bite my lip hard, refusing to make a noise, even as I can feel my body heating, softening, wanting.

"You can't make me do anything," I repeat, grinding out the words from between gritted teeth, and he laughs.

"I can make you do whatever I want. And I've decided what your punishment should be."

His hand loosens in my hair, his fingers still on the edge of slipping inside of me. "Don't move, Ekaterina, or it will be so much worse for you. If you try to run, I will catch you." He looks pointedly at the doorknob, so close to me. "I will catch you, and before the night is over, I will fill every single one of your holes full of my cum, and you will go home without that envelope of money that you've been so accustomed to. But if you stay still, the punishment will not be so bad."

"What–" I swallow hard, frozen in place as his hands slide down my body, and he drops down to his knees behind me. "Mikhail, no! You can't–"

"I can." His voice is low and hoarse, thickening with desire as his hands squeeze my bare hips, holding me in place. "And I will. I will make you beg to come before I'm finished, *sladkiy*, and that will be your punishment, to beg me for it while I shame you."

"I won't fucking beg you for anything," I hiss through clenched teeth, my hands fist against the door. The temptation to try to run is strong, to try to get free of his grasp and grab the doorknob, to make a run for it. But he's holding me tightly, and I know there's a good chance I wouldn't make it out of the door, let alone out of the building, before he caught me. And if he did–

Shame floods me all over again as I picture him throwing me onto his bed, forcing his cock into my mouth, my pussy, and my ass. Desire twists with fear, a flood of heat gathering between my thighs. "I hate you," I grind out as his hands smooth over my ass, squeezing as he lets out a low groan of anticipation, pressing my forehead against the door, and I hear him chuckle.

"You can hate me all you want, *kotenok*, but you *will* come for me."

I shudder as his fingers slip between my thighs, spreading my folds apart, as I feel the soft hum of his groan against my skin as his tongue slides over them. "So wet," he murmurs, his voice thick with lust, and I feel my thighs tremble as his tongue pushes through my swelling folds, seeking out my already aching clit.

I don't know how I'm going to stop myself from coming, only that I can't allow it. I can't give him the satisfaction. I clench my jaw so hard that it hurts, trying not to moan, not to make a single sound as he teases my sensitive flesh, making me tremble with the pleasure of it as his tongue flicks upwards, towards my clit.

I've never been eaten out from behind like this. I can feel his nose brushing against the curve of my ass, too close to the tight hole there for my comfort, and I feel my face heating at the thought of his nose pressed against the crease of my ass as he licks me. I know it's on purpose, to humiliate me in my pleasure. I close my eyes tightly, trying to ignore how good his tongue feels, how it slides over my clit slowly, teasingly, building to what I know from experience will be so much harder to fight.

"You taste so sweet, *kotenok*," he murmurs, his lips still brushing over me, his breath warm against my skin. "I wonder how much sweeter you will taste when I make you beg."

His tongue slides over me again, teasing, running over the outside of my pussy as I clench my fists, my nails digging into my palms. My clit is throbbing, teased by his tongue until it's hard and swollen, my body vibrating with the need for more, and I grit my teeth until they grind together, trying to hold back.

He pushes the tip of his tongue against my entrance, pressing, teasing. I feel it slide inside of me like a small cock, thrusting, curling, fucking me with soft pressure as I close my eyes and feel the pleasure flood over me. It feels so good, but not enough to make me come, and I tell myself that I can hold on, that I won't beg.

Even if I lose the battle with my orgasm, I won't beg.

He fucks me with his tongue for a long, slow minute, his lips sucking at me as he does, and I feel his nose pressing against my ass. He breathes in, long and deep, as his tongue slides out of me, and I feel tears of embarrassment coming to my eyes as he groans with pleasure.

"I will taste you here, too, before I'm finished, *malen'kiy*." His tongue flicks out, lapping up the arousal that's flowing freely from me now, soaking my thighs and his mouth.

"What?" The word slips out before I can stop it, sharp and gasping. "No—you can't—"

"I can do whatever I want." His tongue flicks over my clit, and I'm too startled to stop the moan that shudders out of me, my body tensing under the sudden burst of pleasure. "I will taste you wherever I please, and you *will* beg for me before I'm finished."

"Fuck you," I hiss, swallowing hard and closing my eyes tightly as he runs his tongue over me again, nipping lightly at my swollen pussy as he sucks my flesh into his mouth. "You can't make me—"

He chuckles, low and deep. "Oh, I can."

It feels so fucking good. I hate it, and I want it, and I hate myself for wanting it as I feel my body arching and softening under his onslaught despite myself. We've only done this once before, but it's as if he remembers every spot, every rhythm that makes pushes me to the very brink. I can feel him teasing me, pressing his mouth against me and licking firmly, sucking my clit into his mouth until I'm shuddering with pleasure. It's all I can do not to cry out, my nails biting into my palms, and then he backs off. He teases my pussy with slow, light licks, avoiding my clit, circling around it, until I can feel myself vibrating from the inside out with need and anger and shame, wanting so badly to come that it hurts.

"Beg me, *kotenok*," he murmurs, his lips pressing against the inside of my thigh. "Beg, and I'll make you come harder than you ever have in your life."

The worst part is that I know he could. I've hovered on the edge for so long now, so many minutes of torturous pleasure, that I know the orgasm would make me collapse, bring me to my knees. All I would have to do is ask, and he would make me come. It would feel so good.

All I have to do is give in.

I can't. I won't. "Fuck you." I try to spit out the words, but to my everlasting shame, it sounds like more of a whimper than anything else, my entire body clenching and shuddering on the edge of a climax that it's desperate for by now. "I came to you for help. I thought you cared—and you did this. Fuck you. You can twist the orgasm out of me if you want, but I won't fucking ask you for anything ever again—"

"Oh, yes, you will." He grips my ass, parting my cheeks, and I let out a yelp of mingled horror and shock as the tip of his tongue teases my tight hole. He circles it, his tongue hot and stiff as a small cock, and I feel the fingers of his right hand sliding through the folds of my pussy, gathering up all the slick arousal as he laps it up, spreading it until I'm wetter than I've ever been.

"No, no. I don't like that, I—" I let out a small cry as he pushes his tongue into my asshole, his fingers finding my clit as he does. The pleasure that bursts through me at the combined sensations is so strong and startling that my knees almost buckle, and I almost lose control. I'm so aroused, so sensitive, and his fingers find exactly the rhythm I like, circling my clit just the way I do as I touch myself. I hear myself moan, and I flush hot and red with humiliation.

No one has ever done this to me before. I've never had anything in my ass, not a finger or a cock and certainly not a tongue. As Mikhail eats me from behind, rubbing my clit in firm, quick motions, I know

I'm so close to slipping over the edge. I'm panting, breathless, unable to stop making noises of helpless need as he pleasures me in a way I never even fantasized about. I know all I have left is the power not to beg him to make me come.

I'm going to come one way or another, I'm sure of it. I can't hold out much longer, my entire body strung tight and hovering on the edge, but I can control what happens next.

Until he feels me, so close to unraveling, my clit throbbing under his fingertips—and he stops.

He pulls away, leaving me shaking, drenched, my body tormented with pleasure. "Beg," he murmurs, his voice low and mocking. "Beg me for pleasure, Ekaterina. Beg to come with my tongue in your ass. Beg, and I will let you have it."

"What if I don't?" My voice is shaking, cracking apart, and I'm sure I'm losing my mind. I've never felt anything like this, the need flooding through me, a desperation for pleasure that I hadn't known was possible. "What the fuck are you going to do?"

Mikhail laughs, his fingers digging into the side of my ass. There's no need to hold me in place, I couldn't run now if I tried, but I know he's enjoying it just for the sake of it. "I'll tie you to the bed and tease you until you cry. I'll leave you there as long as I please, unsatisfied. We have a date in two days, remember? There are forty-eight whole hours before you are supposed to be back at the club. That's a long time to stay like this, *malen'kiy*."

Something cracks inside of me at the threat. I know he'll do it. I feel on the verge of collapsing already, tortured with need, and I feel his hand slip between my thighs again, ever so gingerly brushing over the stiff, aching bud of my clit.

"Beg," he whispers, and that last word, combined with the fragile touch, breaks me. "Please," I sob, my hips jerking forward into his hand, so close that even that small friction almost makes me come. "Please let me come. Please, please—"

"That's not enough now." His finger presses down, not moving, just held against my throbbing clit. "Beg to come with my tongue in your ass. You have three seconds, *devochka*—"

"Yes!" I cry out, my hips rolling, grinding against his unmoving finger, my will shattered. "Please! I want your tongue in my ass. Just make me come, make me come while you do it, please—"

I hear him laugh, the wicked sound of it fraying my nerves and tingling across me like electricity as he presses his tongue against my ass again, flicking, circling, as his fingers move against my clit. I feel him push his tongue into my ass as he rubs me, quick and hard, shoving me over the edge.

I scream when I come. I can hear the high-pitched shriek, feel the way I come apart at the seams as the pleasure bursts over me, shattering me, and I hear his groan as my knees buckle and he catches me with his other arm. He holds me there, pinioned against the door, as I come in fracturing waves, his fingers and tongue never stopping until I'm limp and breathless, tears of relief running down my face as I shudder with the aftershocks of my climax.

I start to try to pull away from him, and he laughs.

"Oh no, *kotenok*. We're not done yet."

He stands up behind me, his hand hard between my shoulder blades as he pushes me against the door, my face turned to the side so that I can see what he does. He yanks down the front of his joggers with his other hand, his cock springing free, huge and thick and hard. I gasp, twisting under his hand, sure that he's going to shove it inside of me, and he laughs again, his eyes hard and filled with a wicked, victorious gleam.

"Oh, I'm not going to fuck you tonight," he growls. "Not yet. But it's my turn to come, *devochka*, and you're going to take it on your ass, like the filthy slut you are."

His hand wraps around his cock, and I close my eyes, tears still slipping down my face at the shame of how I feel, the flood of heat that goes through me at the sight of him stroking his thick cock. Even after that orgasm, I feel my pussy clench, aching to know what it would feel like to be filled up by it, fucked hard and rough, used.

I hate myself for it, and I hate him as he growls at me to open my eyes, to watch as he comes on my bare ass.

"You will watch me," he snarls, his hand jerking up and down the throbbing, veiny shaft, his hips jerking in a lewd mimicry of what I know he wants to be doing at this moment. "See how hard you make me, *kotenok*? What you do to me?"

"Stop calling me that. I'm not—"

His hand presses harder against my back, his mouth twisting in a cruel smirk as he steps closer, the swollen head of his cock nearly touching my skin. "I'll call you what I want. And you *will* watch, or I will change my mind about where else my cock might go tonight."

A shudder of fear goes through me, as I see his gaze flick to my ass, his cockhead so very close to the tight hole that's never felt a cock inside of it before. I force myself to watch, knowing with a flush of shame that deep down, I want to. I'm horribly aroused all over again, seeing the flex of his hard abdomen as he strokes, the bulge of the muscles in his arms, the straining flesh of his cock as he devours me with his eyes, just the sight and taste of me enough to drive him to such a furious and uncontrollable lust.

"It won't take long," he rasps. "You taste so fucking sweet when you come, especially when you beg, oh *fuck*, *bladya*—"

He curses in Russian, groaning as I see his cock harden and swell. "I've dreamed of seeing you covered in my cum, *shlyukha*—"

I feel the first hot burst of it, splattering against my skin as his fingers dig into my back, his entire body shuddering with the force of the orgasm that washes over him. His hand strokes frantically, a stream of curses and frantic groans spilling from his lips as his cum splashes against the bare skin of my ass, dripping down my flesh and over my thighs. He lurches forwards, pushing his cockhead between the cheeks of my ass, against my tight hole, and I feel the last spurt of his cum there, where no one has ever come before.

He rubs his cock against me, and I let out a cry as pleasure bursts over my skin, hot and prickling. "I would love to fuck you here," he rasps. "How much would that cost me, *suka?*"

I swallow hard, unable to speak. I feel his cock drop away from me, and for a brief moment, I think he's going to let me go, until I feel his hand on my ass, dragging his fingers through the cum there.

"I enjoyed the other night," he murmurs, leaning close. "Knowing my cum was inside of you while you rode my fingers. Should I let you come again, do you think?"

I cry out as he suddenly shoves two cum-covered fingers deep inside of me, holding me there against the door with his thumb against my asshole. He laughs as I tighten reflexively around him.

"Maybe I was wrong not to fuck you tonight. You seem to love my cum inside of you. I could get it so much deeper with my cock, fill you up so much more—"

"No!" I twist under his grasp, trying to get away, to get his fingers out of me. "Stop! This is too much. I shouldn't have let you do it the first time—"

"But you did. And it made you come." He pumps his fingers inside of me and then yanks them out, wiping his hand over my ass and thighs where he's drenched me in his cum. I feel his fingers push roughly between my legs again, smearing his cum over my clit, my pussy, pushing them inside of me again until there's not an inch between my thighs that isn't soaked in his cum.

And then, as I feel panicked, tears welling up again, he yanks my dress down, the fabric clinging wetly to my cum-drenched skin.

"Get the fuck *out!*" he snarls, his voice raising to a shout as he steps back. "Now, before I change my mind and fuck you the way I should have."

I don't wait a second longer. I don't even look at him. Humiliated, covered in cum, and still shaking from my own orgasm, I wrench the door open and rush into the hall, letting it slam behind me.

This time, I run. And I don't stop.

Mikhail

As she runs out of the penthouse, I'm shaking.

Somehow, I manage to get myself back into some semblance of order, tucking my cock back in and adjusting my clothing as the adrenaline pumps through me.

It's a heady thing, the thrill of humiliating the woman I want to use for my revenge. I can still taste her on my tongue, sharp and sweet, and I can feel myself throbbing with the satisfaction of what I did to her, the pleasure of it from beginning to end.

The feeling of the first victory.

She'd come to me, wanting help, and I taught her a lesson. Taught her that she can't just show up wherever she pleases, demanding things, disobeying. That there are rules in this world, even for former spoiled Bratva princesses.

What now, though?

As the thrill ebbs, something else replaces it. A reminder that I might have gone too far, too soon–and something else, too.

Something that makes me furiously angry all over again.

A flicker of guilt.

What the fuck is wrong with me?

It's unfamiliar to me, this possible feeling of regret for something I've done, for a punishment I've enacted. She deserved it for stepping out of line in that way, for assuming that I could be at her beck and call. She'd done such a good job up until now of pretending to be so unsure of our arrangement, so hesitant, but I knew the spoiled, entitled side of her would make itself known eventually.

And it had.

So why should *I* feel guilty?

Why the fuck should I feel anything but satisfaction.

Anger surges in me, at her and at myself–her for making me doubt, and myself for allowing her to get under my skin at all. I've been working towards this for so long, spending effort and money, and I *deserved* tonight's pleasure.

The first taste.

The last, if you don't do something about how she left.

"*Bladya!*" I curse aloud, spinning on my heel and stalking to the bedroom. The blood is roaring in my ears, my hands clenched into fists as I pace, trying to think it through, if I really had handled things poorly. *She deserved it, deserved it,* I think over and over, the words on a loop in my head, but even as I think it, I know that I might have sacrificed a sweeter ending.

I can take her captive anytime I want. It wouldn't be hard to snatch her. But I wanted to drop the bombshell when she was sweet and malleable, wanting me on her own, begging me for more without having to be forced. I wanted to break her apart in a different way than I had tonight, and I realize with an infuriating certainty that I jumped the gun.

Tonight should have happened later. *I could even have taken her tonight. Listened to her, gotten her into bed, and then snatched the rug out from under her.*

But Vladimir said to do it at the house I'll have the keys to. To wait.

I curse again through gritted teeth. I'm beholden to someone other than myself now, with other fingers on the strings I wanted to play on my own. My decisions are not entirely my own any longer, and that angers me even more, making me regret the choice to bring the Syndicate in on this.

But I can't go back now.

And my own weakness, my fury at her daring to subvert what I told her to do, might have robbed me of the moment I'd been waiting for.

I could apologize to her.

"Fuck that!" I snarl aloud, hating myself all over again for the small part of me that wants to do just that–and not entirely to manipulate her. There's a part of myself that feels truly guilty for treating her that way when she'd come to me for help, clearly frightened and distraught, and it makes me furious with a boiling rage.

She's not Mika. She's not here for you to fucking protect. She's part of the reason Mika is gone. Part of that whole fucking family. Don't feel anything for her. Anything but hate.

I need her trust back, or I won't have what I want. It won't be as good.

I rub my hands over my face, suppressing the urge to scream again. *I could apologize to her for that. To gain her trust. I don't have to mean it. I won't mean it.*

A brief sense of calm washes over me at that, slowing my pulse and bringing me to a standstill in the middle of the room. *That's it. I don't have to mean it. It's just to convince her to trust me. To still meet me the night after tomorrow. And then–*

By then, I'll have the keys to the house where I'll take her. If I can soften her enough to agree to come back on her own, I might even be able to enjoy her willingly, before I let her know the trap is sprung.

Fuck. I still have to meet Valeria, too. I calculate the hours I have, pulling out my phone to send her a message. If I leave now and arrive tomorrow, I'll make it back in time to meet Vladimir. I can arrange something to be sent to her as an apology, more gifts to soften her up, and with any luck, she'll be there.

And then—

Then I'll have everything I need.

By the time I'm back in Moscow the following evening, I'm exhausted. I've slept very little, only an hour or two at my own apartment, before Vladimir called me and told me to be at the compound within two hours. But as I down a cup of black coffee before heading out, I can't bring myself to care.

By now, Natalia will have my apology. And tomorrow night, unless she refuses, I'll have her in my grasp.

I hadn't forgotten what she told me about what Igor had said to her. I know that she'll be at the club tonight, and that he'd planned to extort the money out of her. I thought about it all the way to Novogrod and back, my fury rising with each kilometer there and back.

She's mine to threaten. Mine to hurt. Mine to punish. Mine to touch and fuck.

He'd threatened to violate her, she'd said, and that angered me most of all. That he would dare to touch what I've bought, the woman that I've decided to have for myself, that I've focused so much of my efforts on. *Igor*, a man no better than the mud on my shoe, a cheap imitation of the Bratva man I know he longs to be.

I paid him, too, just as Natalia had said. I'd given him a healthy sum to avoid just this, to have her time for myself without him giving her trouble over it and risking her backing out of the arrangement out of fear for her job.

Not only had he threatened what's mine, but he also lied to me.

I don't take being lied to well.

I had just enough time, between returning from Novogrod and catching a quick nap before meeting with Vladimir to handle the problem of Igor.

I have no doubt that the apology Natalia will find tonight will please her even more than the dress and jewelry that she'll find tomorrow. That it will make her see that the violence of last night was only because I want her so badly.

She'll believe me once she sees what I've done for her.

"*Smert elo milost.*" I give the password at the gate, and this time I'm let in quickly once I tell my name. I stop in the same place in front of the building, handing over my keys and weapons without having to be asked.

But this time, the guards escort me down a different hall.

"Am I not seeing Vladimir?" I demand, and one of the guards glances back at me.

"You think he handles giving money and keys to the help? You think the *Volk* does such things?" He laughs. "Someone else will give you what you need."

A burn of bitter resentment ignites in my gut, but I force myself to ignore it. *You're getting paid. Who fucking cares who it is that hands over the rubles? You're not Vladimir's left hand, as you once were to Viktor, and you're better for it. You don't want to be so close to a man like that.*

The building I'm taken to is dim, dank, the concrete walls bare and forbidding. I can smell the ripe stench of unwashed bodies coming from far away, hear faint screams from some room hallways away, and a cold shudder ripples down my spine.

I know what place I've been brought to and why.

It's no mistake, no accident, that I'm going to be handed my money and keys here. Vladimir did this on purpose, to remind me of what could happen if I don't hold up my end of the bargain. To remind me that if I cross him, it will be my unwashed body peeled of its flesh in some filthy room here.

As resentful as it makes me, I can't deny that it's a reminder I could use after last night.

Don't lose yourself in your revenge. Take it, and go, or else you'll find yourself in this hell with no way out. No pleasure is worth the pain you'd find here.

"Here." A stocky man approaches, shaking me out of my thoughts. "Kasilov?"

I nod, feeling my throat tighten with nerves. "That's me."

He hands me a thick envelope and a keyring. "The address is inside the envelope. It's tucked away, just outside of the city. No one will bother you. The money is half for now, half to be wired to an account of your choosing when Vladimir is satisfied that the girl is dead."

"That's all? Proof that she's dead?"

The man shrugs. "Information will please the Wolf. But he cares only for her life. The Obelensky line must not survive."

"Fair enough." I take it, shoving the envelope into my waistband and the keys into my pocket. "Anything else?"

The man smirks, an evil glint in his eye. "Don't take too long, Kasilov."

A scream punctuates the air as I turn to leave, faint and reedy in the distance, reminding me once again of the dangerous bargain I've made.

—

I tell myself that there's no need to see her tonight. That tomorrow will be enough. But as I drive back from the Syndicate compound, I feel fidgety and unsettled, the creeping need of my obsession with her crowding into my head. I haven't heard from her, and by now, she should have received my gifts and apology–*all* of it.

By now, she'll be on her way home.

I haven't watched her through her window again. I haven't needed to. But now, thinking of her standing in her bedroom, thinking of me, I feel my cock twitch and a shudder of need run through me, a craving to see her, even if only for a moment. To be reminded of my power over her, that she can't be free of my eyes, even for a night.

Before I can fully make the decision, I find myself driving in the direction of her neighborhood. I park a considerable distance away, not wanting to risk her spying the car if she's walking back from work, or to see me as I walk through the shadows, avoiding the pools of light left by the streetlamps.

I stop on the other side of the street from her building, waiting to see the lights go on in her bedroom. When they flick on, I feel a thrill of adrenaline, watching for her.

The moment she steps into the room, I feel my cock stiffen, and I crouch near the spot I'd hidden in before, waiting to see what she might do. The thought of seeing her touch herself again, lost in willing pleasure, makes me feel nearly feral with lust.

But what I see catches me off guard.

She stands there in the middle of the room, her arms wrapped tightly around herself, looking around with an expression that I recognize clearly. It's the same look she'd worn last night when she appeared on my doorstep, frightened and upset and confused, and I see her press one hand over her mouth, her shoulders hunching as if she's fighting back the tears.

Did she not see what I did for her? What I did to make up for hurting her so soon? Something knots in my gut, an uncertainty, and I feel something else, too, something not unlike the guilt I felt last night.

What if this isn't what I should be doing at all? What if she had nothing to do with—

I see her shoulders shake as if she's crying now, and I feel my heart twist in my chest. This woman, standing here broken and frightened, doesn't look like the Natalia Obelensky I've been chasing. She doesn't look like the spoiled daughter of a cruel Bratva *pakhan*, a woman capable of knowing that her father is torturing women and children while doing nothing about it, while continuing to enjoy her status and power. She looks like a broken woman herself—cowering in the face of men who want to hurt her, and I realize with a shuddering impact that I'm one of those men.

I hurt her. I did that. I'm part of why she's standing in her bedroom, sobbing.

My arousal fades, forgotten. For one brief moment, I feel my world spinning like a top, all of it threatening to topple. And then my rage comes back in a flooding, hot rush that nearly knocks me flat.

What the fuck are you thinking? Because she cries a few tears that she's not at fault? That she knew nothing? That she's not an Obelensky, the only way you have remaining to avenge what was taken from you?

"Don't be so fucking *weak*," I hiss in the darkness, aimed at myself and no one else.

I have half a mind to find my way into her apartment now, take her to the house Vladimir loaned me, and put an end to this. But as I picture the terror on her face as I slide the needle into her neck that will put her to sleep, the fear when she wakes again, I can't find the satisfaction in it.

Something is missing. I know what it is.

I want her to go home willingly with me, tomorrow night. I want the moment I've planned for.

I see her fumble for something, fingers moving just out of sight. And then, as I'm trying to make sense of what she's doing, I feel my phone vibrate in my pocket.

There, on the screen, is her name—or at least, the name she once gave me.

Ekaterina.

Natalia

By the next morning, after fleeing Mikhail's apartment, I'm still horrified with myself for how I reacted.

No one has ever handled me that way before, touched me so forcefully, demanded such shameful things. No man in my life before would ever have dared. They all knew who I was, the name I carried, and the risk they took by coming to my bed at all. If I told my father that any of them had hurt me, punished me against my will, or raised a single finger to me without my permission, he'd have cut them apart slowly so that they could see the insides of themselves as they died.

Of course, I would have been in trouble, too, if my father had ever found out about any of my dalliances. But none of them would have ever taken the risk that I'd put keeping the truth about my virginity over punishing anyone who dared hurt me.

I should have been turned off by it, frozen, unable to feel anything but fear. Instead, he played me skillfully, making me come apart under his hands and tongue–and I *enjoyed it*. I tried to fight him–but it felt good. I can't pretend that it didn't, and I'm horrified by that.

I never considered that I might have desires like this, that I might enjoy a man handling me in a way that completely discounted my feelings about what he was doing, that I might enjoy being *used*. I don't know what it says about me, and I'm too ashamed of what I did to ask Ruby.

I've never even let a man *touch* me there before, let alone use his tongue to—

I close my eyes, forcing back the flood of warmth that surges through me at the memory, tingling over my skin. I've never come with anyone the way I do with him, and even after how he treated me last night, a part of me wants to know what it would feel like to fuck him. To have him hold me down, use me roughly, take me in any way he pleases while I scream and plead and moan.

Natalia Obelensky could never have behaved like that. But I—I'm not her, not here, not with him. I could be anyone I wanted.

I could be the kind of woman who wanted that.

I know he wants it too, that if I offered, he'd take it gladly. Maybe *too* eagerly. And I know better than to offer something like that up without payment, especially after what Igor has done to extort me.

After what he did, I still have to decide if I even want to go out with him again tomorrow night. I hated him for it, in the moment. I still might. In the time that I've known him, my feelings towards him have vacillated wildly between irritation, desire, hatred, and back again. It's the most confusing dynamic I've ever been a part of—and yet, despite what he did, I'm not entirely sure I'm ready to get off this ride.

Today is an errand-running day, and I spend it making my way quickly through the stores I need to stop at, careful of everything I purchase. I'm very aware of how much of my savings I have to fork over to Igor tonight, and it makes me sick every time I think about it.

There were no threatening notes waiting for me this morning when I walked out into my kitchen, but wondering what I might find when I get back home leaves only deepens the pit of anxiety in my stomach. I'm so on edge that I jump when I see the box waiting by my door, even though it looks very much like the ones that Mikhail has left for me before—this time matte black, smaller than the others.

I pick it up, letting myself quickly into the apartment. I open it carefully, setting aside the lid, as I reach inside and pull out a soft, rose pink dress made of a bustier-style bodysuit and an attached skirt that falls in soft folds that would reach just above my knees. Something in my stomach twists as I look at it, a cold chill of foreboding creeping up my neck.

I felt something similar when he sent me the black dress. That one had had a ballet-styled feel to it, but I passed it off as just being something that was in fashion that he'd found aesthetically pleasing—or a personal shopper had. But this—

It looks like a ballerina's costume turned into a dress. I've never once mentioned ballet to Mikhail. It would skew far too close to my actual identity for comfort. I'd very nearly discounted any thought of him being the one who's been stalking me and leaving the threatening notes and strange gifts, but the dress makes me feel a rush of fear all over again, especially after last night.

I set it aside, reaching for the smaller box inside. I know it's going to be jewelry before I even open it, and I'm not surprised to find a pair of pink sapphire drop earrings inside. There's a note tucked under the box, and I pick it up, expecting some kind of instructions about wearing the gifts he sent. Instead, I read something very different.

I behaved abominably last night, Ekaterina. Please accept these as an apology. I would love for you to wear them on our date tomorrow night. I hope this can show you how very sorry I am.

Mikhail

I bite my lower lip, chewing on it as I look down at the gifts and the note, wondering what I'm supposed to do. The tangle of emotions feels like too much to navigate, facing what I am tonight with Igor. I desperately want to ask Ruby's advice. But then again–

She'd told me to go to Mikhail's apartment last night, and that had gone horribly wrong.

Fuck it. I fold up the dress, grabbing it, the earrings, and the note, and take them into the bedroom to stuff them into my bag that I take with me to the club. I'm not terribly fond of the idea of carrying clothes and jewelry worth so much through my neighborhood and the block that the *Cat's Meow* is on, but I want to show Ruby. Even if her advice isn't better than what she gave last night, it's still more than I can figure out right now.

Not to mention that the cash for Igor is already more than even the dress and jewelry are worth, so it hardly fucking matters at this point.

My heart is pounding when I leave the apartment for work. I cling to the bag over my shoulder, knowing I probably look more than a little suspicious, but terrified that someone will sneak up on me and snatch it. I walk as briskly as I can to the club, slipping in through the back door and setting the bag down as I look around for Ruby. There's no one in the dressing room, which is strange for this time of night.

"Ruby?" I call out her name, frowning as I walk towards the door that leads out to the club. It opens in less than an hour, and it makes no sense for there to be no one getting ready at all. "Taffy? Crystal?"

There's no answer, but as I push the door open, I hear the sound of gasps and low conversation coming from the hall that leads down to Igor's office and the storage rooms. I walk down the rough-carpeted steps, making a turn towards his office, painfully aware of the money waiting for him in my bag. *I should have just grabbed it and gotten it over with,* I think, and then I stop as I see every single girl on the schedule for tonight, all crowded around Igor's office door.

"What's going on?" I walk forward, looking for Ruby. "Did something happen?"

"You could say that." Taffy's voice is shaking as she turns to look at me. The group of girls parts, letting me see Ruby standing at the front of them, looking into Igor's office with an expression of pale shock. "Igor–"

"What's happened?" I push past them toward Ruby–and then freeze in place as I see exactly what it is that she's looking at.

Igor's body is sprawled on the bloody carpet, his throat sliced open, his fingers scattered on the carpet, and his palms slashed. His pants are pulled down around his hips, and I have to look away before I can see the rest, bile rising in my throat.

Ruby lifts a hand, pointing shakily toward the wall behind his desk. There, scrawled in blood, is a message.

Vory umirayut medlenno.

Thieves die slow.

"Do you know who might have done this?" Ruby looks at me in stunned horror, and I shake my head, backing up, feeling the sting of acid still in my mouth.

"Why would I–" I trail off, realizing in a flash of clarity exactly why she would think that. Igor threatened me, extorted me, just last night. And I told her about it. "No, of course not! I would never–I don't know anything about–"

I swallow hard, feeling the other girls looking at me. A blind panic fills me as the possibilities of what could happen now occur to me.

A body means cops. Cops mean questions, and my story can't hold up against that kind of questioning.

I need to get out of here.

I spin on my heel, rushing back toward the dressing room, and I hear footsteps behind me. I know it's Ruby before she even calls after me. Still, I keep going, all the way back into the warm safety of the familiar room, as I wrap my arms around myself, trying not to go from melt down into a full panic.

"Athena." Ruby's voice is calm as she steps into the room, shutting the door behind her. "I wasn't saying I thought you had anything to do with this. Just that—you might know who did."

"No—of course I don't!" I turn towards her, wiping tears away from my eyes before they can fall. "I can't believe—"

"You don't think Mikhail had anything to do with this?" Ruby raises an eyebrow. "After you went to his house last night? You didn't say anything to him?"

"I did, but—" I bite my lip, trying to think past the swirling panic. "He didn't care. He was *furious* with me for showing up. He was so angry—he pinned me up against the door, and he—"

Ruby's eyes go round with horror. "He didn't—"

I shake my head. "No. But he did other things. I barely said anything about Igor—he didn't want to hear it. He was too caught up in being pissed about me showing up out of nowhere. I don't think—"

That's not the truth.

But I can't tell Ruby the truth, that I think there's a very real possibility that Mikhail, in the aftermath of his furious lust, remembered what I said and decided to finish off Igor for his greed. That his possessiveness, his jealousy, found a new outlet when he was finished taking it out on me.

I told him that Igor threatened to violate me. That he was going to take my money.

Thieves die slow.

I've behaved abominably—

I shake my head, determined to stick to my story. I can't let Ruby think that Mikhail had anything to do with this or that there's any reason to suspect me. I've trusted her, and I believe she's my friend—but I'm not so stupid or naive as to know that there are boundaries to friendship. I don't know for sure what hers are—or if this crosses it.

"This isn't Mikhail," I tell her firmly. "Look, I brought this with me. He sent it to my house as an apology. He wouldn't have done this—"

I reach for my bag, opening it, and show her the gifts and the note. "He had these sent over today. *This* is his way of apologizing. Not—"

"Quite an apology." Ruby scans the note. "You have a date with him tomorrow?"

I nod, swallowing hard as I wipe away the last of the tears. "I don't know if I should go or not."

"Honestly—after that, I don't either. I'm sorry I told you to go over there, only for that to happen. But—" Ruby shrugs. "Men who know they've done a bad thing are easily manipulated. He might want to make it up to you. You can use that. Hell, look at it as getting him back for what he did, if you want to. If he's still being fucking weird, don't see him again. Pawn the shit he's given you and move on to the next guy."

I nod, feeling my throat tighten. "What are we going to do about—"

Ruby's lips thin. "There's not a girl here who wants the police involved. We'll find a way to get rid of the body, make it look like he just ran off. After that—I don't know what's going to happen to the club. That's why the girls are all so upset—not because they gave a shit about Igor, but because there's no telling who might take over, or if it'll just get shut down, and we'll all be looking for new jobs."

Fuck. I don't want to go to a different club, deal with worse managers, bosses who will grope me and try to push my limits, try to sell me to men who want to pay for more than my time. I don't want to start all over again, and if anything, that makes me want to tell Mikhail that, yes, I'll go on the date tomorrow. I'll wear his clothes, and maybe I'll even fuck him, and then—

Then, it'll be time to make my escape. There's no Igor to take my money now, no one to stop me. It's not as much as I hoped, but it should be enough to get someone to make me a fake passport if Mikhail gives me more on this date, and I'll figure out the rest as I go.

It's time to leave. I know that for sure.

Or, you could just go.

"You should go." Ruby's voice cuts through my thoughts, and I look up at her, startled. "It's probably better if the girls don't see you here tonight. They'll forget about any suspicions quickly enough, but you should go home. You're in no shape to dance tonight anyway. Come back in a couple of nights, when you're not seeing Mikhail, and I'll fill you in on what's going on. Or just come by my place, if the club is closed up. You can show up at *mine* anytime."

She wiggles her eyebrows teasingly at me, clearly trying to lighten the mood, and I let out a choked laugh, forcing a smile. "Alright. I could probably use the break anyway." I pick up my bag, hesitating. "You're sure you'll be alright, handling this on your own?"

Ruby nods firmly. "I've got this. Just go home, and stay safe."

I take a cab back to my apartment. I can't fathom making that walk again with so much in my bag that could be stolen, and my knees feel like water, as if they might go out from under me at any moment.

Safely back in my apartment, I drop the bag on my bedroom floor, wrapping my arms around me as I try to think. I'd been certain after talking to Ruby that going on the date was the right thing to do, one last windfall of money before I leave this place for good. Now in the quiet silence of my apartment, I'm no longer so sure.

If he killed Igor–

What if I'm not safe with him?

I can feel myself starting to shake as tears well up in my eyes, and I try to breathe through the fear. It feels as if every worry and moment of paranoia and fear are crashing over me all at once, making me wonder if Mikhail has been behind all of this, if I'm setting myself up for something terrible by spending another night with him.

I don't know who to trust. I never really have. And now—

Even if he killed Igor, is it really so bad? Now your money isn't gone. Now you have a way out still.

But that makes him a murderer. And after what he did to me, too—

What you have is enough. You'll figure it out. You have so far.

The fear is too much to handle. I don't know how I'd even get through a date, feeling as shaky and panicked as I do. I reach for my phone in my pocket, fumbling it out and finding Mikhail's contact. *Better to just cut it off now. Get the passport as quickly as you can, and you'll be out of here before you know it.*

Quickly, I type out the text, my hands shaking as I do.

I'm sorry. I can't meet you tomorrow night. I appreciate the apology, but I don't think I can do this anymore.

I sit down on the edge of the bed, clutching the phone in my hand. I expect to have to wait for a reply, but in a matter of seconds, it buzzes in my hand.

I look down at the screen and see the name there.

Mikhail.

Natalia

I click on the text with shaking hands, glancing over my shoulder as I do, towards the wide windows that look out onto the street. I have that strange feeling again that there are eyes on me. I've never wished so much for window coverings, not even on the nights when anyone could have walked past and seen me touching myself. Exhibitionism is one thing, but the feeling that I'm being watched, hunted, *stalked–*

You're just on edge. It's fine.

I swallow hard as I open the text, my heart pounding, hoping it won't be another outburst of anger. I'm not sure I can take it just now.

I understand. I meant to wire you the allowance you'd receive this week. But if you're turning down our evening together, then that will be the end of it. I wish you the best. Of course, if you want to reconsider–

"Fuck." I whisper it aloud to the empty air of my bedroom, closing my eyes. Sending a wire likely means more money than he'd want to hand me in person. *How can I turn that down?* Even if I'm not sure I feel safe–trying to leave the country with a fake passport isn't safe either. I'm willing to do that for my freedom. Is this so much worse?

One more night. You can do it. No matter what he does, you can get through it. Even if he killed Igor. Even if he takes more than you think you want to give. One night.

I feel that flicker of heat again, thinking of what he did, tempting me with the possibility of a night where I could let myself do and say and want anything I could think of, anything I feel, and then leave it all behind. I'd never see him again.

Just do it. The worst that could happen is that you end up a little roughed up and humiliated again. And then you can leave this all behind forever.

I give it a few minutes before I text back. I don't want him to think it's instantly the money that changed my mind–I have a feeling that might make him angry.

Can I let you know in the morning? I want to sleep on it.

A few minutes pass before I get a response, and I feel that cold pit of anxiety again, wondering if I've lost my chance. And then my phone buzzes.

Of course. You know what answer I'm hoping for. And again–I'm sorry for my behavior.

I let out a sigh, setting the phone on my side table as I flop back into the bed. I'll reply in the morning, but I already know what I'm going to say.

—

My compromise is that I take a cab to the restaurant he's picked for our date, with the agreement that he can drop me off later, if the date goes well. The speed with which he agreed reassured me a little, even if I know it likely has something to do with the fact that he's hoping I'll be spending the night with him.

A small part of me hopes so, too.

He picked a more intimate setting for our date this time, a small French bistro I've heard of but have never been to. I worried that eventually, he might end up taking me to a place I frequented before, as Natalia, and that I'd have to be concerned with running into someone who knew me. But so far, it's been restaurants that I've never gone to.

The dress fit me perfectly, as I expected it would, and I'd done my best to shrug off my uncertainty about how ballet-adjacent the style is. I felt a pang of nostalgia, looking at myself in the mirror with the rose-pink fabric against my skin, clinging to me like a leotard, the skirt falling in folds that mimicked the tulle pleats of a tutu, just without the puffiness.

It's just a coincidence, I told myself as I did my makeup, putting my hair up in a twist to show off the beautiful earrings. *You are still a dancer, after all, even if it's a different kind. That's probably why he's chosen these styles for you.*

He's already waiting for me at the restaurant with a table, and I see a satisfied smile spread over his face as he stands when the hostess shows me to it. "Ekaterina—" He takes my hands in his, pulling me in to kiss me lightly on the lips. It's so different from the roughness of the last night I saw him that it startles me at first, making me freeze in place.

"I'm so glad you came. You look stunning." He pulls my chair out for me, letting me sit down before sliding it to the table and returning to his seat. "I ordered wine for us already, and there's cheese and escargot coming to the table as well."

"I've never tried that." I watch as he pours me a glass of wine, feeling the nerves bubble up in my stomach. It's a lie, of course.

"Cheese?" He grins at his own joke, nudging the glass closer to me. "It's delightful."

"Of course, I've had cheese." I shake my head at him, feeling myself relax the tiniest bit despite myself. "I meant the escargot."

"Oh, well—that is an acquired taste. But we'll see how you like it. After all—remember, you should try anything at least once."

His gaze heats as he says it, landing squarely on mine. I can feel myself flushing red at the memory of the last thing I tried for the first time with him—against my will, but I enjoyed it nonetheless.

"You seemed upset last night when you texted me." He swirls the wine in his glass, looking at me curiously. "Did something happen?"

I feel my stomach clench. "No," I tell him quickly. "No—just unsure if I should have come tonight, after—"

His eyes narrow. "Are you sure that's all it is?" He reaches out, his fingers brushing against the back of mine as he looks at me intently. "I'd like for you to feel that you can tell me anything, Ekaterina."

For a moment, I'm inclined to lie again. But then, as I look at him, I realize it's an opportunity to get some clarity. If I tell him about Igor, I'll be able to see his response. I might get some idea of if he really did have anything to do with it or not.

"You remember, I told you—" my voice falters slightly, and I nudge my wine glass back and forth, trying to find the right words. I don't have to pretend that it's difficult to talk about. "I told you about what Igor did—"

Mikhail's face hardens. "That he threatened you, yes. A cowardly way to handle the situation. What I paid him for your time should have been more than enough. I hope you haven't paid him the sixty percent yet. I intend to have a firm conversation with him—"

A laugh bubbles up in my throat. I can't help it. "You won't be able to do that," I tell him shakily. "He's dead."

There's a look of such absolute astonishment on Mikhail's face that my doubts start to fade in an instant. "Dead? When?"

"Last night." I take a sip of my wine, giving myself a moment. "He was—it wasn't a clean death. And someone wrote a message on the wall—*thieves die slow*. In Russian."

Mikhail raises his eyebrows, sitting back in his chair. "It sounds like you weren't the only one Igor was extorting."

He doesn't seem to give the slightest hint that he thinks I might have been involved, and a relief I hadn't expected to feel washes over me.

"No wonder you were so on edge last night. I can't blame you." He pauses for a moment, as if considering something, and his eyes widen. "You didn't think that I–"

"I–" My voice breaks off. I meant to lie, to say of course not, but I don't seem to be able to make the words come out. "I didn't–"

"I was in Novogrod yesterday." He says it smoothly as if he's not in the least bit offended that I might have thought he had something to do with Igor's death. "I can show you receipts from things I purchased there if you like–but after having spent so much time together, it would make me feel so much better if you were willing to trust me. I know there was a breach of that–and my only excuse, Ekaterina, is that I'm not accustomed to being disobeyed. That, combined with how much I want you–"

A light shudder runs over him, and he gives me a faint smile. "I can see why you would think I might have killed him. He insulted me, by attempting to extort and harm you. Truthfully, I wish I had. But it wasn't me, Ekaterina. I promise you that."

I hadn't known if he'd try to deny it or not. I hadn't been sure if I believed him if he did. But now, watching him as he speaks, I don't know how I can *not* believe him. He seems so earnest, and as he explains his alibi, I can feel myself starting to trust that he's telling the truth.

To my surprise, I'm almost disappointed. I hadn't realized until exactly this moment that a small part of me had been hoping that Mikhail *had* swooped down, like some kind of avenging angel and taken care of the problem of Igor for me.

Someone had, though. Someone dangerous. The fact that it doesn't seem to have been Mikhail makes me all the more certain that I need to make my escape after tonight. It feels clear to me now that Mikhail isn't the one who's been stalking me, but *someone* has. It could be the same person.

I wasn't safe here before, and I'm much less so now. Looking across the table at Mikhail, I make a decision.

If he wants me to go home with him tonight, I will. I'll enjoy one night where I give into anything I might desire. And then tomorrow, I'll go to someone who can make me a fake passport, fake cards, and an ID, and I'll leave Russia for good.

―

With the question of Igor out of the way, I find myself enjoying the dinner. We finish the bottle of wine and open another, the courses of the meal coming and going. I know what the end to this night will be before Mikhail even looks at me as he pays the check, his gaze heating as it sweeps over me.

"I have a house outside of town that I'd very much like to show you, Ekaterina. I think you might find it even more charming than my penthouse. But it's a little bit of a drive—you'd have to stay the night. Would you be willing to do that?"

I know what he's insinuating. I have a moment's hesitation at the idea of going out of the city with him, to a strange location, but I remind myself that all my paranoia so far has been unfounded, with the exception of one bad night that he's apologized for, multiple times now.

One night. And then you leave.

"I would love that." I smile at him, forcing my nerves away. "I don't know if *charming* is the word I'd use for the penthouse, but I'd love to see what kind of home you have that warrants that description."

"And I'd love to show you." He offers me his arm as we both stand up. "After you, *kotenok*."

That word sparks something in me as we walk to the car, a mingled desire and fear that I have a feeling will remain for the rest of the night. I remember his voice murmuring that word all too well, low and rough as he'd punished me.

But tonight, I'm willing to admit that I want it. That I crave the feeling of giving in, submitting, giving over control just once to a man that I know can take that power and turn it into a night of explosive pleasure for us both, a night that I won't ever forget.

A night that I might even be willing to enjoy for free, even if Ruby would have my head for thinking it.

I'll decide that later. For now, I want to enjoy this.

Just this once.

Mikhail

I can't believe my good fortune.

I hadn't known if she'd buy it. Especially once I realized that, while she suspected me of being the one who killed Igor, she wasn't as happy about it as I expected.

I had two reactions prepared—one for if she was upset and one for if she'd been glad to have the problem taken care of. It irritates me that she hadn't seemed happy, after the lengths I'd gone to in order to make sure he was taken care of. It's not as if I hadn't taken pleasure in it—killing him gruesomely had been more than enjoyable, after his insult to me and his threats to the woman I consider *mine*.

I hadn't known if she'd buy my alibi. But she had. I'd seen it in her face as she'd started to believe me, the relief when she'd decided that I wasn't the culprit. I know now why she'd been so upset last night, when I watched her in her room.

I wondered if I'd be able to get her back to the house after that. Good sense would have dictated that she wouldn't agree to go out of the city with me and stay in a strange place, especially overnight. But incredibly, she had.

Which means every last piece has fallen into place.

The knowledge that she's decided to trust me, to go home with me without even negotiating the price beforehand, that she chose to believe me, is more satisfying than anything else that has happened so far, even that first night in my penthouse. I can feel the rising flood of adrenaline as I take her back to the car, knowing how the rest of the night will go. I'm going to fuck Natalia Obelensky within an inch of her life, make her scream my name and come for me, make her *beg* for more, and then—

There's not an ounce of resistance as she gets into my car. Not a word about money. I wired her the "allowance" we'd agreed on, and I'd given her a little extra, just to help sweeten the deal. It seems to have worked, because it seems to be the last thing on her mind. As I drive out of the city, I feel her reach over, her slender fingertips tracing the back of my hand.

"What made you decide to get a place outside of the city?" she asks curiously. "Did you just want the quiet?"

I wanted a place where no one would be able to hear you scream. Fortunately, the most dangerous assassin in Moscow offered me the keys to hang onto for a little while.

"Exactly." I glance over at her, smiling wryly. "The city gets to be too much, sometimes. It's nice to have a place to go where there's no noise other than my own thoughts. I like the peace—a garden to read in, to write. Solitude. It's harder to come by these days."

She gives me a soft, surprised smile. "I wouldn't have thought you would be the 'reading in the garden' type."

"Well, now you know."

"Who knows what else I'll find out tonight." There's a hint of soft seduction in her voice that surprises me. I expected that she'd hold out until we'd negotiated for *something* before she started to flirt. It sends a thrill through me to think that she might be starting to feel something of the same relentless desire that's been coursing through me for weeks now.

She leans forward slightly as we drive up the long gravel driveway that leads to the house. She'd grown progressively quieter as we'd left the city, and I suspected that her nerves were starting to get the better of her, but now she seems intrigued again. The house is tucked back behind several stands of trees, well away from any other homes, and I have a feeling that Vladimir likely bought up a good deal of the land around it, to keep it secluded.

"It really is charming!" Natalia exclaims as we get closer, and the two-story stone house comes into view. It's larger than what I personally would call *charming*, just shy of being the size of an estate house, but I'm not about to argue. If she's pleased, it will make what I have planned that much easier.

"Do you want a drink or a tour first?" I ask as we walk inside. "I do have to warn you, the tour is likely to end up in my bedroom."

"We'll start with a drink, then," she says with a teasing grin, walking past me towards the living room. "Can you make me the same thing you made me that first night at your other place? The old-fashioned?"

"Coming right up." I feel a burn of irritation at what feels like something just shy of an order from her, but it's quickly salved with the thought of her on her knees, her hair wrapped around my fist as I give her something else to fill her mouth with. *Soon. Just a little longer.* I'd been hoping she'd opt for the tour, but I can wait.

I've been patient this long.

She's sitting on the long grey couch when I bring the drinks, and she accepts hers with a smile, waiting for me to sit down next to her. "How long have you had this place?" she asks, looking around at the art on the walls and the tasteful decorations. "Did you hire someone? It's beautifully done."

"I did. Someone with better taste than me." I grin wryly at her. "They did a wonderful job, and now all I have to do is keep it up—well, the housekeeper who comes once a week and me."

"Oh?" She raises an eyebrow. "She's not going to walk in on us, is she?"

A bolt of lust shoots down my spine at the clear innuendo, stiffening my cock instantly. "Why?" I ask silkily. "What would we be doing?"

Natalia leans closer, a faint smile on her lips. "Well, I think it will depend on how I'm feeling when we get to the end of that tour."

Her mouth is very close to mine, and I have a burning urge to grab her chin and drag her the rest of the way, crushing her lips against my mouth, forcing my tongue inside to taste the sharp tang of whiskey there.

"Shouldn't you tell me what I'll have to pay first?" I almost want to bite back the words as I say them, but I want to hear her say that she wants me. I want her to tell me that money isn't necessary. I want her to give me everything.

Her eyes flick up to mine, her face tilting that much closer. "We can talk about it later," she says softly. "I'm sure you won't come up-short."

"You know that already." I can hear the rough note of lust in my voice, and my hands itch to grab her. "You're so very tempting, Ekaterina. I'd rather have the taste of you on my lips than this drink."

"Well, we already did this on a couch once." She grins at me. "So you'll have to wait until you take me upstairs. I like novelty."

I stand up, reaching for her hand. "We'll take the tour as we drink, then, or I won't be able to wait long enough to give you what you want."

I half expect her to argue, but she stands up, too, tucking her hand in my elbow as we walk. I feel as if I'm vibrating with need, adrenaline flooding me at the idea of having her under my power completely, but I force myself to slow down, to show her around the house—the gardens out back, the kitchen, formal dining room, and the study, before taking her upstairs to the second floor. "I could show you all of the guest bedrooms," I tell her, low and dark, as I lean closer to her, pinning her against the side of the banister. "But I think I'd rather show you mine, first."

"I like that idea," she breathes, and I see that the glass in her hand is empty.

I pluck it out of her fingers smoothly, leading her to the master suite. I open the double doors, letting her walk in first. The click of them shutting behind us is the most satisfying thing I've heard since the sound of her begging me to let her come with my tongue in her ass.

She won't be leaving this room again, not until I allow it.

She turns to face me, her hand lifting to take her hair down, but I shake my head. "Let me," I tell her firmly, setting both of our glasses aside as I step towards her. I stop just shy of our bodies touching, letting her feel the heat in the space between us as I reach up, brushing my fingers over the knot of her hair at the back of her head.

I hear her soft intake of breath as I pluck the pins out of it, letting it fall in heavy black waves around her shoulders. Her lips part as she looks up at me, and I can feel my cock straining behind my fly, already so hard and aching that I can hardly bear it.

My hand slides into her hair, tightening, fingers knotting in the soft fall of it. I can feel that obsession that I've been barely holding back churning in my mind, pushing at the walls I've tried to put up around it, to keep myself in check. To keep a clear head.

I have her here at last. Natalia Obelensky, under *my* power. Far away from anyone who could help her—as if anyone would, if they knew who she was. *I* know. I've never been so grateful for anything as the day that Yuri slipped that photo to me, telling me that a dancer at a shitty strip club I would have never gone to on my own was the last chance I had to get revenge on the family that took everything from me.

It's almost enough to make me feel bad for what I did to him.

I hear her gasp as my hand tightens in her hair, tugging her head back. The urge to hurt her, to punish her, to *devour* her is almost too strong. It clambers in my head, desperate to get out, my muscles tightening and my cock rigid as the anticipation of everything I've planned washes over me in a hot, burning wave.

"You're *mine*," I growl before I can stop myself. It's almost too low for her to hear, and for a moment, I think she hasn't–but then her eyes widen in fear.

"Mikhail–"

I can see the moment she starts to change her mind, the moment that she decides this might have been a mistake. "You said yes." My voice is low and rough, filling the space between us. "There are no safe words here, Ekaterina. You walked into this room. Now I get to do what I like with you."

"I–" Her voice catches in her throat as I push her down to her knees with my fist in her hair, yanking her head back. "Mikhail, stop! I didn't say–"

"You won't say anything at all with my cock in your mouth. Now open your pretty lips and put that tongue out for me like a good girl–"

She rears back, twisting in my grip. "You fucking–"

I laugh. I can't help it. "You can stop pretending, Ekaterina. I know you like this. Remember, I've seen *exactly* how wet you can get when I put my hands on you in the way you're so *desperate* to pretend like you don't enjoy. You can fight me if you like, but you'll come for me in the end, and you'll love every second of it."

"I could bite your fucking cock," she hisses. "If I don't want it down my throat."

"You could, but you'd pay for it," I smirk at her, still holding her head back. "Now, are you going to obey me, or—"

"What if *I* tried to tell *you* what to do?" she snaps. "You wouldn't like that very much, would you? If I grabbed your hair and forced you down between my legs? Sat on your face while I forced you to make me come? How would you like that, *svoloch'*?"

I've never heard her curse at me in Russian before, and it sends a bolt of lust through me so forceful and heady that I feel for a moment as if I'm going to lose control. "You could try," I tell her. "But you'd have to get the upper hand on me, first."

"Just wait," she hisses as I drag down my zipper. "We'll see how this night goes."

"We certainly will."

It only takes a second for me to palm my hard cock out of my trousers. The swollen head smacks against Natalia's lips as it slides free, smearing pre-cum over her mouth, and her tongue darts out despite herself, licking it off as I watch.

I laugh, my hand still wrapped in her hair. "Oh, you don't want it? You don't want my cock in your mouth? It doesn't look that way to me."

She glares at me, a stubborn light in her eyes, and tries to twist her head away as I push my cockhead against her lips. She can't move very far, my grip is too tight, and as she tries to keep me from forcing myself into her mouth, I reach down and squeeze the side of her cheeks, making her open up.

Her squeal of protest is immediately muffled as I shove myself into her mouth, hard and fast, without giving her a moment to accommodate. My cock slides all the way to the back of her throat as I groan, the hot, wet tightness of it sending shudders of pleasure through me, and I pull her down farther, the look on her face turning me on that much more.

"That's right," I groan, forcing myself deeper into her throat, feeling her muscles convulse around the thick, hard invasion. "Deep-throat my cock, *kotenok*. Take it all. Good girl, *god*, that's so fucking good–"

Natalia twists in my grasp, moaning and choking around me, but I can feel her resistance lessening. I can tell that she likes it, that it's arousing her, and that drives my own lust even higher, until I can barely control myself.

My balls tighten, throbbing warningly as her nose brushes against my abs, the tight choking sensation threatening to push me over the edge. I have every intention of coming more than once tonight–but not so soon.

I yank my cock out of her mouth as she chokes and coughs, still holding on to her hair as she looks up at me with teary eyes. "You fucking–"

"What a way to talk to the man who's about to make you come," I chasten her, dragging her to her feet with my hand in her hair and the other on her arm, backing her towards the bed. "Take your panties off, *malen'kiy*. I want to see just how much you want me to eat that sweet pussy."

I let go of her abruptly, and she stumbles back towards the bed. *Now is when I see if she really wants to stay or not.* I'm prepared for her to change her mind, to make a break for it, but I'm hoping for a different outcome. It will make the end of the night that much better.

There's a moment when I see her consider it. Her eyes flick between me and the door, and then she glares at me, her hands sliding up beneath her skirt. "I hate you," she hisses, and I laugh.

"Oh, I know, *kotenok*. But that spice makes the night all that much sweeter, doesn't it?" I step towards her, swiftly undoing the buttons of my shirt. "Haven't you ever fucked someone you hated before?"

"No." She eyes me defiantly as she pushes the lace panties she's wearing down her legs, stepping out of them and kicking them aside along with her heels. "Is this one of the things I should try once?"

"I hope it'll be more than once." I shrug off the shirt, letting it fall to the floor, my hands going to my belt. "I'll make you come so hard you'll be begging for me to fuck your face, your ass, to take you as roughly as I want so long as I give you what you *need*."

I shove my trousers down my hips, my cock springing free once again as I advance toward her, entirely nude. There's a rush of power that floods through me as I loom over her still-clothed body, my hands going to her waist as she looks up at me with an expression of mingled fear and hate that makes me feel as if I'm going mad with arousal.

I pick her up as if she weighs nothing at all, tossing her back onto the bed as I follow her onto the mattress, crawling towards her like a predator stalking its prey. She shrinks back into the pillows, but there's nowhere for her to escape me now.

Just the thought is almost enough to make me come, my cock slapping against my abs as it lurches, hard and straining.

My hands close around her ankles, and she gasps as I yank them open, my hands smoothing up her calves, the insides of her knees, higher still. I fist them in the skirt of her dress, feeling the smooth silk bunch against my palms, and as she stares down at me, her hands braced against the mattress, I rip it apart.

"Mikhail!" She cries out, startled, and I laugh, tearing the fabric to either side.

"I'll buy you a new one," I lie to her, ripping it until I can see the bare apex of her thighs between the shredded silk, her soft pink pussy already damp. My fingertips press into the soft flesh of her inner thighs, pushing her open, wider, and then wider still, watching her folds open for me so that I can see every soft, soaked inch of her.

"You're so fucking wet, *malen'kiy*," My voice is softly mocking as I slide my hands higher, my thumbs spreading her open entirely. I slide them upwards, framing her stiff pink clit, and I see the flush of embarrassment rising up her chest and neck to her pretty cheeks at being so lewdly exposed. "Such a pretty pussy. It tells me the truth even when you try to lie. You might not deserve to come, Ekaterina, for lying to me—but this pussy deserves my tongue. And I'm going to fucking devour it until you scream for me."

I can feel her shaking under my hands as I lean forward, flicking my tongue over her tight entrance, sliding the very tip up the soft flesh of her inner folds. Her head falls back, her mouth opening on a soft cry.

Her helpless moan as I slide my tongue over her clit, the sound of her surrender, is the sweetest fucking thing I've ever heard in my life.

Natalia

I *fucking hate him.*

It's hard to hold onto the feeling, though, when his tongue is fluttering against my clit, sending waves of pleasure through me that threaten to topple me into an orgasm within seconds.

It feels so fucking good. I want to slap him, claw at him, bite his fucking dick for the way he shoved it down my throat–*but in a few minutes, when he's done with this.* His tongue is exquisite, flicking and circling around my clit, curling over it as he holds me open wide with his hands on my inner thighs. I feel as if I'm going insane with pleasure.

His mouth presses against me, tighter, his lips fastening around my clit as he sucks, and I know in one blinding moment that he's not going to tease me this time. I'd been expecting a slow build, a long path to the climax I already desperately need, but the suction on my clit has me crying out, my hands tangling in his hair as I arch upwards, grinding against his mouth as he shoves me over the edge of the cliff and into shattering bliss.

"Fuck! Fuck—Mikhail—" I scream his name without meaning to as he presses his tongue against my clit, rubbing, sucking, pushing me through the orgasm, and I forget everything except how good it feels, how hard he's making me come. Somewhere in the middle of it, I feel one of his hands slide just below his mouth, two fingers pushing into me as my pussy clenches tightly around them. I feel him start to fuck me hard and fast with those fingers, curling them as he keeps licking my over-sensitive clit, sending me from one orgasm directly into a second.

I feel as if I'm coming apart at the seams. My voice is one long cry of pleasure, my hand pressing his mouth down against my pussy, soaking his lips and chin with my release as I come hard. At that moment, it makes me forget about everything—how angry I am with him, how much I hate his arrogance and entitlement, how much he scares me sometimes, how he humiliated me in his penthouse with his tongue on my ass. I want to know what it feels like to have his cock inside of me, filling me, fucking me hard, and from the way he laughs as he comes up from between my legs, I know I said it out loud.

"Turn over, *printsessa*," he growls, his voice low and dark as his damp fingers slide up my hips. "Put that pretty ass in the air for me."

"I don't want—"

He chuckles. "Oh, don't worry, *kotenok*, I won't put it in your ass just yet. I want that sweet pussy wrapped around my cock first. We can negotiate the rest later."

Something about the way he says *negotiate* makes me think that there won't be any of that, that he'll fuck my ass if he wants it, and how I feel about it one way or another won't be considered. The worst part of it is that, even though I've never been fucked in the ass before, I have no doubt he could make me come that way if he wanted. He seems to know how to play my traitorous body like an instrument, making me sing for him every time.

His hands turn me over, getting me onto my hands and knees as he leans over me, his hands sliding over the curves of my ass and hips. He slides his fingers through the wet folds of my pussy, groaning as he feels how slick and hot I am, and I hear the sound of flesh on flesh as his hand wraps around his cock, stroking as he angles himself behind me.

"Are you ready to take my cock, *malen'kiy*?" he asks, the words almost a threat, but it sends a ripple of need down my spine as I arch my back helplessly, wanting to be filled, fucked, *destroyed* by his huge cock.

"*Yes*," I whisper, my resolve fracturing and dissolving in the aftermath of the shattering orgasm he'd given me. I feel hollow, aching to be filled up, and I let out a low moan as I feel his swollen cockhead press against my entrance. Even as wet as I am, he's too big for me, and I have to spread my legs wider to have a chance of being able to take him inside.

"Fuck, you're going to feel so fucking tight—" Mikhail's hands squeeze my hips, holding me still as he struggles to push the tip of his cock into me. "Fuck, what a perfect fucking pussy—"

I moan again as the filthy words wash over me, sending a flood of arousal gushing between my thighs, the pressure of his cock pushing inside of me drawing a low keen of pained pleasure from my lips. He's too big, but in the best way, and I start to open my mouth to ask him to go slowly, but it's too late.

"Fuck—I need—*fuck*!" He curses aloud, and I feel his hips jerk as he loses the battle of wills between his effort to enter me slowly and his need to be inside of the wet, tight heat waiting for him. His hips snap forward, shoving him into me, huge and thick and too much. I let out a scream of pain that turns into pleasure as he sinks into me to the hilt, filling me beyond anything I've ever felt before.

"Fucking take it—" he hisses between clenched teeth as his hand wraps in my hair again, pulling my head back as his hips rock against me. Tears well in my eyes, the burn of his cock warring with the satisfaction of being so well-filled, and I let out a low, sobbing moan.

His hand slips beneath me, his fingertips finding my slick, sensitive clit, and I gasp as he starts to rub me there, more gently than I expected. "That's right," he murmurs as my hips twitch, leaning back into him. "Take it, ah–*fuck*–that's a good girl. Take all of my big fucking cock. *Fuck*–"

I can feel another orgasm building. His fingers roll over my clit, slow and steady, in the perfect rhythm as he starts to thrust. Slow and shallow at first, rocking his hips into me as he pushes himself as deeply as he can go again and again, and then he pulls out to the tip, keeping me stretched with his swollen cockhead as he rubs my clit faster, stroking the first inch of his cock in and out of me.

"Are you ready, *kotenok*?" he murmurs, his fingers leaving my clit as he reaches for my hand, replacing his fingers with my own. "I'm going to fuck you hard now, and I want you to come when I do. Touch yourself for me, good girl–"

I start to stroke my clit, lost in a fog of pleasure that feels like almost too much, his dirty talk only serving to intensify all of it. I never in my life thought I'd like any of this, that it would turn me on almost beyond what I can take. Still, I feel as if I'm floating in a sea of sensation, everything swirling around me until I feel raw and aroused beyond description, on the verge of a climax that I know he expects me to hold back until he comes.

I should ask him to put on a condom. It occurs to me a second too late as he slams his cock into me, driving me forward into the pillows, and I can't speak.

He thrusts into me relentlessly, driving into me again and again, his groans of pleasure filling the air as I rub my clit frantically, my hand wedged between my thighs as he pins me to the bed with only my ass up in the air, a vessel for his pistoning cock. I feel helpless, used, my body nothing but a means for his pleasure, a place for him to come, and something about that feeling of utter helplessness in the face of his need and mine makes me feel unable to do anything except lose myself in it.

"I'm going to come—" he groans, his fingers sinking into the flesh of my hips, holding me in place as he plunges his cock into me again, his hips grinding against my ass. "Fuck, it's too good. I can't—"

I *feel* the moment he comes, the hard swelling of his cock, the hot rush of his cum as I let myself go too, my body spasming and clenching rhythmically around his as he pushes my face down into the pillow, his hand in my hair as he holds me down to empty his cum inside of me.

"Fuck, that's so fucking good—I can feel you coming, *fuck*—" Mikhail's hips slam into my ass again, driving his cock deeper. I can feel the heat of his cum on my thighs, dripping out of me as he shudders with the last spasms of his climax. "Oh *fuck*—"

I can't move. My hand is still wedged between my thighs, my body shuddering with pleasure, and I feel more of his cum spill out of me as he pulls out, his cock sliding half-hard against my thigh as he rolls to one side. I don't think I could get up if my life depended on it, and I let out a low, shuddering sigh as I feel his hand stroking the small of my back.

"You should stay," he says, his voice low and drowsy. "I said it already—but it's late. And besides, who knows what we'll get up to in the morning? I'll make you breakfast."

"I don't think I can walk anyway," I say softly, laughing as I finally find the strength to roll onto my side, facing him. He looks even more gorgeously handsome like this, his sandy blond hair falling into his face, clinging a little to his forehead with sweat, his hard, muscled body entirely on display for me. Even softened, his cock is impressive, lying against his thigh as he looks at me, his hand still stroking my hip. His body is utter perfection, lean and chiseled, and I reach out despite myself, running the tips of my fingers over the ridges of his abs. I feel him shudder beneath my touch, and I feel myself forgetting how angry I was with him, how much I hate him sometimes.

It would be nice to sleep next to someone for a change. I have no idea when it might happen again.

"I'll stay," I say softly.

I don't expect us to cuddle as we sleep, and we don't, but his hand stays on my hip, my fingers brushing against his stomach. I vaguely feel him pulling a blanket over us both, but my eyes are heavy and my body exhausted, and I slip into sleep before I'm even really aware that's what's happening.

When I feel his hands on me again, I think I'm dreaming. I feel pleasure tingling over my skin, strong fingers massaging my clit, and I hear the low groan of a man lost in his own lust. I feel a thick cock pressing against my sore entrance; my body protests as it starts to fill me again.

"Mikhail?" I ask sleepily, my eyes opening to see him above me, pinning me onto my back as he thrusts into me, his body a straining shape in the darkness.

"Shh," he murmurs, his hips jerking as he slides deeper. "So fucking good–I woke up so fucking hard. I had to fuck you again. You take my cock so fucking well–I want to feel you come on it again–"

I'm sore beyond belief from the rough sex earlier. However, I can feel my body responding to him already, still wet from before and aroused all over again. He slides against me, hard and muscular, his cock sinking into me as deeply as he can go as he reaches for my hands, pinning them over my head.

I gasp, moaning as his pelvic bone grinds against my clit, pressing down as he rocks against me, deep and hard, making my entire body shudder. "Oh god, you're going to make me–"

"That's right, come for me," he croons, his hands tightening around my wrists as he starts to thrust harder, faster, making my entire body tense as pleasure bursts through me. I'm so close, hovering on the edge, and every stroke of his thick cock pushes me closer, the friction against my clit making it that much easier to reach the release I suddenly need so desperately again.

"Come for me," he whispers against my ear, his body pinning me to the bed, holding my hands against the headboard, and I feel myself starting to shudder, the first waves of my climax uncoiling inside of me—

And then I feel something else.

It feels like cold metal around my wrists, like *cuffs*, and I jerk under him, my entire body tensing as I try to pull away. He thrusts, hard, holding me down with his weight, impaling me on his cock, and a flood of fear washes over me as I hear the *click* of handcuffs closing around my wrists in the same instant that I start to come.

I twist underneath him, pleasure and terror tangled up with one another as I try to jerk away and realize that I *can't*. My hands are held in place, and the thought has trouble taking shape as I convulse and shudder through the orgasm that's still tearing through me, driven by the thrust of his cock into me, his fingers that are now rubbing my clit as I moan helplessly, caught by him in more ways than one.

As the fog of pleasure starts to clear, I jerk at the cuffs again, the cold terror of what he's doing beginning to wash everything else away. "What are you doing?" I ask angrily, yanking hard. "I don't like this, Mikhail! This is too far. I didn't agree to this—let me go!" I jerk at them again, twisting, trying to dislodge him from where he's still leaning on my hips, his hard cock still inside of me. "Let me fucking go!"

He laughs, his blue eyes bright in the darkness.

"I don't think so." He slides off of me, *out* of me, and I can see the shape of him kneeling between my thighs, his hard cock still jutting out in front of him. He wraps his hand around it, his expression dimly visible in the moonlight coming through the window as he starts to stroke himself, looking down at me with a satisfaction that terrifies me.

"I don't understand." I yank at the cuffs again, ineffectually, trying to speak as calmly as I can. "This isn't a turn-on, Mikhail—"

He grins. "It's not meant to be. I have you right where I want you—and I have no intention of letting you go, *Ekaterina*."

At the tone of his voice, I feel a deathlike cold start to spread through me, dread filling me down to the bone. "What the fuck are you talking about?" I ask, my voice shaking, and his hand stills on his cock as he leans forward, switching on the lamp next to the bed. In the flood of light, I can clearly see the cruel smile on his face, and I know in that instant that I've made a horrible mistake.

"I know your name isn't the one you gave me," he says, his expression triumphant and wicked all at once.

"You don't know anything—"

He laughs. "I know you're Natalia Obelensky. And now?"

Mikhail leans forward, cupping my chin in his hand, holding it so I can't look away as his ice-blue eyes bore deeply into mine.

"Now, you're mine to do with as I please."

Can't get enough of this enemies to lovers, stalker romance? Click here to check out the next book in the Wicked Trilogy… Wicked Beauty.

Want more of Natalia and Mikhail's sexy, love story? Click here for a hot bonus scene from Mikhail's POV.

Printed in Great Britain
by Amazon